W9-BNO-205

On Borrowed Crime

Also available by Kate Young

Marygene Brown
Southern Sass and a Crispy Corpse
Southern Sass and Killer Cravings

On Borrowed Crime

A JANE DOE BOOK CLUB MYSTERY

Kate Young

CROOKED
LANE

NEW YORK

Copyright © 2020 by Kate Young

Published in the United States by Crooked Lane Books, an imprint of The Quick Brown Fox & Company LLC.

Crooked Lane Books and its logo are trademarks of The Quick Brown Fox & Company LLC.

Library of Congress Catalog-in-Publication data available upon request.

ISBN (hardcover): 978-1-64385-462-5
ISBN (ebook): 978-1-64385-463-2

Cover illustration by Mary Ann Lasher

Printed in the United States.

www.crookedlanebooks.com

Crooked Lane Books
34 West 27th St., 10th Floor
New York, NY 10001

First Edition: October 2020

10 9 8 7 6 5 4 3 2 1

For my family, with love.

With special gratitude to Kendall, who
eagerly reads everything I write.
You have been a blessing from
the beginning.

Chapter One

The white wrap-around dress would have me in hot water if my mother heard I'd committed the heinous crime of wearing white after Labor Day. In the Moody household, September marked the arrival of fall fashions, and my mother always said that here, in the deep South, everyone who was anyone heeded that rule. Nevertheless, my uncle Calvin instructed me on the phone last night to wear something professional to work this morning, and it was the only dress left in my closet, since my best friend and next-door neighbor had borrowed half my wardrobe for her cruise. There were more important things than adhering to society's whims, like being on time for work.

Stuck three cars behind the train track as the locomotive moved at the speed of poured molasses, I feared I'd be late. Cousins Investigative Services was a new venture for me. My uncle had needed a receptionist/secretary after Harriet Wiseman took maternity leave to have baby number three. I'd leaped at the opportunity. Much to the chagrin of Mother and Daddy, who always envisioned me married and raising a couple of children by now. I liked men. I liked men *a lot*. I just hadn't found one I wanted to keep forever. And if not married, and despite the fact I'd studied psychology, Mother would rather see me behind the makeup counter at Belk or helping out with one of her many charities. She thought working around her brother, who'd been a detective for sixteen years before retiring to open his own private investigation firm, would only further enhance my fascination with murder and true crime. Mother believed the Jane Does, my mystery book club, to be abhorrent and a complete waste of my time.

Here in Sweet Mountain, forty-five minutes north of Atlanta, old Southern families resided. Our tea was sweet, our accents were sweeter, and our ladies were expected to be the same. Murder didn't quite fit in.

The railroad crossing gate lifted, and I thanked my lucky stars. I pressed down on the accelerator of my late-model cherry-red Maxima. Bessie shimmied forward a couple of yards, then made a little clunking sound, followed by a groan, and hissed to a stop in finale.

"Not now, *please*." I attempted to start the engine again. The car made a tick tick tick sound, and then smoke billowed from under the hood. Those rude folks behind me laid on their horns. After I turned on my flashers, I rolled down my window and waved for them to go around. As if it were necessary. Anyone with eyes could see the vehicle wasn't going anywhere. When the lane cleared, I got out, slung my bag over my shoulder, and tiptoed in my sling-back pumps off the tracks, crossing the street to the gas station. My cell buzzed inside my carryall. It was Uncle Calvin.

I blurted without preamble, "I'm so sorry. My car broke down on Old Mill Road. Don't fire me." I wasn't sure why I'd added the last bit, but I'd felt remiss not to.

"Calm down, Lyla. I'm calling to tell you the meeting's been moved to the Lee, Martin, and Harvey law offices. You wouldn't make it to Atlanta with the morning traffic being what it is." I heard his blinker. "It's not a problem, and now I know you're having car trouble, I'll forward the office's calls to your cell."

"Oh." I walked up under the Fast Trip's awning and stood beside the door. "Okay then."

"Do you want me to call roadside assistance for ya?"

The wind whipped around, and I held my dress against my bare legs with my spare hand. "No. That's okay. This is an important meeting. I've got it. Break a leg."

He chuckled at my comment and disconnected the call. This account would be a real win if we could get them to sign on. My uncle was a utilitarian sort of man. He was plain speaking, without an ounce of finesse, which suited his profession. And he was excellent at his job. But I hoped that, with my attention to detail, analytical brain, added sparkle, and penchant for charm, I could help land more clients. After all, I firmly believed in taking advantage of what the good Lord gave you. And he gave me an ample portion of the gift of gab and a curious mentality, along with a great head of copper-colored hair and porcelain skin that I took excellent care of. Mother taught me well.

After I phoned Triple A, I went inside to get myself a fountain drink and maybe a doughnut. A doughnut should be out of the question since I needed to lose a few pounds before the holidays, where I historically put on anywhere from five to eight, but, after seeing Bessie, my cherry-red beauty, bite the dust, I needed some therapy. Sugar was my crutch.

With powdered sugar on my fingertips and carrying my large drink, I walked outside to check on whether help had arrived. A car whizzed around the corner and slammed on the brakes, a few inches from me. My drink slipped from my fingers and splashed on the hood of the black BMW sedan, splattering all over my dress. An unladylike word left my lips at the sight of my ruined garment. Covered in bright blue splotches, I looked like I'd been in a paint gun war. When I lifted my gaze to meet the culprit's behind the wheel, ready to give them a piece of my mind, my jaw dropped. In the driver's seat, blubbering her eyes out, sat Carol Timms, a member of the Jane Doe Book Club. And in the passenger seat I spied an unrecognizable individual with a camo baseball cap pulled down over their eyes. Before I could say a howdy-do and inquire to her state, Carol backed up and sped off from the gas station.

* * *

After I thanked the Triple A driver, I hopped out of the front seat of the tow truck and walked up the bricked driveway of Mother and Daddy's grandiose home. I grew up on a street of pre–Civil War, plantation-style houses. The structures were designed to handle Georgia's hot, humid weather, with large, deep front porches that boasted comfortable rocking chairs and whirling ceiling fans. Front porch sittin' fostered a sense of community. Having a glass of iced tea and chatting with a neighbor made a hot, humid evening more bearable. But if you asked my daddy, he called the monstrosity a money pit and a heating and cooling nightmare. Daddy liked to complain. Especially when Mother was around to hear him.

Mother came waltzing out the front door and stood next to one of the white pillars that framed the grand front oak doors. "Lyla Jane Moody! Land sakes alive, what happened to you, child?"

"Bessie broke down. Your house is the closest." I mounted the bricked steps.

Mother's face held both shock and horror at the sight of me. "Are you wearing white?"

I fought an eye roll. Mother wouldn't abide such a gesture, finding it highly unbecoming.

She clucked her tongue as Gran joined us on the front porch.

"My, my, looks like you had quite a mornin'." Gran was smiling. "Something interesting always happens when my little Lyla is around." Gran had moved in with us when I was thirteen, after my grandfather suffered a heart attack. She'd been a coconspirator in all my endeavors and remained one of my best friends. These days she was slipping a little. Symptomatic of aging, Daddy said.

"Daisy, don't encourage her." My mother fiddled with her pearls, a nervous habit of hers.

Gran winked at me. Where Mother always dressed in what most folks referred to as their Sunday best, Gran preferred to be comfortable and casual. Daddy had inherited her laid-back personality and charming wit.

"Young lady, you and I need to have a serious conversation." Mother's stern face, with an undertone of pity in her eyes, gave me no desire to hear anything she had to say.

My ego had already taken a major blow, and hearing how disappointed she was in me wasn't going to improve my mood.

"Come on inside, sugar, and we'll get you a change of clothes. I ordered you the new Sue Grafton mystery."

Y Is for Yesterday? I gave Gran a little smile as she nodded. I'd been dying to buy a copy and suggest it to the book club.

"I got same-day delivery too. You've got to love this online shopping." Gran had managed to figure out how to use her new smartphone Daddy bought her.

"My soul, she doesn't need to read that sort of novel. You know how impressionable she is. She'll never stop going to the dead club." Mother rubbed her index finger between her creased brows.

"The Jane Does," I corrected Mother, which she didn't seem to appreciate. She opened her mouth, I assumed to lecture me on my manners, when Gran jumped in.

"Better get this girl out of these wet clothes. And aren't you going to be late for the hospital fundraising meeting?" Gran shook her head at Mother in a chastising sort of way.

It wasn't that I enjoyed distressing my mother. It was simply that being true to who I was and perusing my interests conflicted with what she found suitable.

"My stars." Mother glanced at her watch. "Young lady, our discussion will have to wait."

Gran looped her arm through mine and directed me into the house.

The first floor of my parents' house had high ceilings, an enormous foyer, a sweeping open stairway, a grand dining room, and a formal living room we never used. The chef's dream of a kitchen was located at the back of the house, where wonderful meals were made by caterers. Adjacent to the kitchen was the place everyone gathered, the great room. The floor-to-ceiling windows brought in abundant light. Off to the left of the great room, Daddy had converted the library into his home office. The second floor held six bedrooms, each with an en suite. The house, furnished in custom-designed furniture to mirror something out of *Southern Living* magazine, pleased my mother.

There wasn't a speck of dust in Mother's house, unlike my townhome. She had a cleaning service come in three times a week. *"Cleanliness is next to godliness"* I'd heard all my life.

Gran and I were in my old bedroom, where Mother still kept the clothes she continued to buy for me. Mother loved to shop. I'd given my grandmother the lowdown on the events of my morning while I'd changed into a pair of tan slacks and a baby-blue tunic that matched my eyes, and slipped my feet into a pair of flat gray Mary Janes.

Gran had an odd expression as she stood behind me. In the reflection of the full-length mirror, her wrinkled lips puckered. I'd inherited my looks from her. Mother's side of the family were dark-haired. Mother's hair had been highlighted to a caramel color, and her piercing emerald-green eyes stood out on her pale face. In her youth, Mother had won the Miss Georgia beauty pageant.

"What is it?"

Secrets and Gran were an oxymoron. I loved that about her.

"Well,"—Gran got really close and lowered her tone—"you didn't hear this from me, but that Carol Timms has had several appointments with your daddy. Like several months of appointments. Bless her heart, she's been experiencing some, um, emotional problems." Gran's pleased-as-punch expression to be able to share a piece of juicy gossip almost made me smile.

Unbeknownst to my sweet, nosy Gran, seeing a psychiatrist did not fall into gossip territory. We all had issues, and these days folks weren't ashamed to seek help. Progress, I'd say. Still, I wondered how Gran came to be privy to Carol's doctor visits. "Did this come from a reliable source? Not Sally Anne at your beauty parlor?"

"Came straight from the horse's mouth." Gran folded her bony arms across her chest.

"If by 'the horse' you mean Daddy, I don't think so." Daddy never discussed his patients. It wouldn't matter if God himself had scheduled an appointment. Doctor–patient confidentiality was serious business.

"James left his office unlocked, and I might have had a peek at the file on his desk." Gran had the decency to blush a little.

Daddy would be livid if he found out. No one was allowed to go into his office without permission. He kept an extra set of files on his patients at home in case an emergency arose. While his practice had gone digital years ago, my old-fashioned daddy kept hard copies as well. If Gran found a folder on Carol out of the cabinet, it could only mean she was a new patient or she had more problems than Gran let on.

My phone rang. I held up my finger, and Gran nodded. "Cousins Investigative Services."

"I need to speak to Calvin," a gruff voice demanded.

"He's offsite at the moment. Can I take a message?" I rummaged through my bag for my tablet and stylus.

"Have him call Judge David Timms. My wife is missing."

My eyes went wide as I met my grandmother's curious, cool blue gaze.

I put the stylus down on the ruffle-covered mattress of my old canopy bed. "Judge Timms, this is Lyla Moody. I just saw Carol at the Fast Trip about an hour ago."

"Are you sure? I haven't seen or heard from my wife in four days. Her purse, cell phone, keys, and car are here, along with all her clothes. She would never go anywhere without her purse."

I swallowed hard. He was right. There wasn't a Southern woman anywhere that would leave her bag full of essentials behind.

The judge did sound distraught and completely truthful. But I *was* positive it had been Carol who nearly ran me over.

"Yes, sir. She was driving a black BMW, and there was someone else in the car with her. She seemed upset."

The line went dead silent.

"Judge Timms, are you there?"

Gran kept mouthing, "What's going on?"

"I'm here. I'm going to need you to tell the police what you saw. I want everyone on this, including your uncle. Someone has abducted my wife."

Chapter Two

The Jane Does, the members of the Jane Doe Book Club, rotated through all the members' homes, going to a different one each time for our monthly meeting. A time or two we met at the local library when our numbers were higher and we had a special guest, usually a mystery author. Once, we hosted a retired special investigator from Atlanta, who discussed the ins and outs of investigations in reference to John and Jane Does, a special interest to our group. True crime stories always intrigued the club.

Tonight, Valerie Heinz, a founding member, hosted us at her new Craftsman-style house in Love Creek. The latest development in Sweet Mountain offered its residents a whole host of amenities. We were all sitting around in her living room, the night air circulating through the open French doors that led out to her backyard. The group totaled four tonight, as Melanie was on vacation and the Lord only knew what was going on with Carol.

"Did David say anything else?" Val was going around refilling wineglasses.

When she made it around to me, I held mine up. "Nothing more than what I told you. He sounded shaken and deeply concerned. I left a message for the officer in charge of the investigation, like he asked me to." I took a sip of Merlot, allowing the subtle black cherry and plum flavors to dance on my tongue before swallowing. "I also gathered from his phone call that, for some reason, the police weren't doing enough. He wanted to enlist Calvin as well."

"Well, the police must have good reasons for not going all out. Like she obviously isn't missing." Patsy raised her manicured index finger as she sat down next to Amelia on the leather reclining sofa, after powdering her nose. She'd given birth to a set of twins three months ago and was constantly telling us how hard it was to lose her baby weight. I thought she looked beautiful. Motherhood suited her.

"Okay," Patsy clasped her copy of *And Then There Were None*, by Agatha Christie, between her hands, "I'm so happy we decided to start adding in classics every other month. Because, y'all—wow!"

"Wait a sec, Pats. But who was the guy in the car with Carol?" Amelia took a block of cheese from the tray on the coffee table.

Amelia Klein and her lovely husband were transplants. Born and raised in Maryland, Amelia had been thrilled to find our little group last year after her husband's job brought them to the metro area. She told us the second she and her husband laid eyes on our sleepy little town, it stole their hearts. They loved the historic downtown district, breathtaking mountain scenery, and our award-winning wineries, and felt his commute to Atlanta would be worth it. I explained that, in fact, Sweet Mountain had now been deemed part of the heart of the North Georgia wine country. Amelia and I immediately connected, finding commonality in our nonconforming ways. She had tight, curly silver hair she'd decided to never color, big chocolate-brown eyes, and a flawless copper-colored complexion.

"I have no idea. And it might've been a woman." I placed my wineglass on the end table next to me, slipped off my Mary Janes, and rocked back in the recliner. "Y'all should have seen her mascara-streaked face." My heart ached every time I thought of her distress.

"Carol has always been prone to dramatics." Val ate a Kalamata olive off a toothpick and placed her book on her lap.

"That's true." Patsy sat forward. "Remember when her stylist moved away? She bawled her eyes out for three days. I mean, I understand how important it is to find someone you're comfortable with, but the way she carried on was ridiculous."

"Still." I shook my head. "Now I'm aware her husband hasn't seen her for four days, I feel sort of responsible for not throwing myself on the hood of the car and rescuing her. What if I witnessed her abduction, and all I was worried about was my dress?"

"Don't be so hard on yourself." Val leaned over and patted my knee. "She's probably sowing some wild oats or something. It's no secret her marriage isn't the best." Val let out a little sigh. "I love Carol—y'all know I do—but she adores attention of any kind. Like the time we had Melanie's birthday party and she threw a hissy fit because of the lack of vegetarian options."

"Carol's a vegetarian?" Amelia refilled her glass. "She never said anything to me. I had her and the judge over last week, and she ate meatloaf with us without saying a single word."

"She isn't." Val rolled her eyes. "She went on a fad diet, hoping to lose fifteen pounds in a week. It lasted three days, if I recall correctly."

"Well, I'm concerned, y'all. It isn't like Carol to run off. And even if she's having an affair, like Val suggests, she wouldn't miss tonight's meeting. She loves our book club," I said.

"I agree with Lyla." Amelia nodded. "And I bet if Melanie were here, she would too."

Melanie would. Amelia was right.

"I'm sure she'll turn up." Patsy shifted in her seat, looking uncomfortable. "Speaking of Melanie, when does she get back?"

"Tonight, I think. She's having a great time. She read our club pick on a sandy white beach. She said it really added to the experience."

"I bet it did." Patsy's head bobbed up and down.

"She said it was a perfect trip with the exception that the airline lost her luggage during a connecting flight."

Everyone appeared horrified. That was a traveler's worst nightmare. I hoped they'd recovered it because that suitcase contained *my* belongings. Money wasn't flowing for me at the moment, and with my car in the shop, I couldn't afford new clothes. I hated to ask Mother and Daddy for another loan. I'd already had to raid my old closet.

"I think I saw something about that on Facebook. But on a positive note, she'll have an excuse to buy a whole new wardrobe." Patsy grinned, and I could tell she really wanted to lighten the mood and move on to our club's pick.

I didn't want to upset my friends further, but something needed to be done. "Back to Carol. I'm unable to shake this bad feeling. She didn't seem—I don't know—*right* to me."

"Well, I, for one, think she's fine." Patsy crossed her legs. "And since Lyla insists on discussing this as if it were a real case, allow me to reference all the cases we've studied where the person was reported missing only for it to be discovered they were never really missing in the first place. They simply didn't want to be found."

I let Patsy's reference sink in for a moment. Carol and I were friends, but I supposed that'd only been a recent development—the closeness anyway. Since she'd joined the Jane Does. If she needed to get away, wouldn't she have felt comfortable confiding in me? I didn't know.

"But remember the docuseries we watched last month? The one where foul play was involved on murder mountain and the police didn't have the manpower or the cooperation of the civilians? It took a few of the neighbors to speak up for them to get anywhere," Amelia pointed out.

"Yeah, I'm with Amelia. I can't shake the uneasiness about the situation. And if y'all had seen her, you'd understand.

"To be on the safe side, I'll call her and get to the bottom of things." Val twisted her long black hair up in a bun.

Unusual silence filled the space. The tension in the room was palpable. I didn't want to point out, for the second time, that Carol had left her phone behind.

Do y'all want to put a pin in this month's discussion? To wait on Carol, Val offered.

Patsy made a pouty face. "How about we just postpone it till next week. We could still vote on the next read. I'm eager to dig into a new story, even if this one left me with a little bit of a book hangover."

"Sounds good to me." I stretched my neck. Patsy was right about the book hangover. Mysteries didn't get any better than the ones penned from the queen of mystery herself.

Amelia chewed on her bottom lip. "Um, you guys don't think this has something to do with the e-mail Carol sent?"

"What e-mail?" Glances were exchanged around the room.

"You mean, none of you guys have read it yet? I thought it would be part of this meeting's discussion. That Carol herself would lead it. She mentioned to me that she'd be e-mailing me and asked me to print it for the group. She, um, didn't want the judge to see it."

Everyone began digging through their bags for their phone.

"I've kind of had my hands full with the twins, so I haven't."

Amelia pulled a folder from her bag, and I sat forward. "Now I'm concerned. At first I thought she didn't want to involve her husband because he made fun of our club and didn't care for her interest in crime." She let out a loud sigh. "In hindsight," Amelia gripped the papers, "she wasn't quite herself. She'd had several glasses of wine—more than usual—and to Val's point regarding their marriage, she and the judge didn't seem to be on the best terms. He kept making snide remarks during dinner."

"Like what?" Patsy scooted closer to Amelia.

"I shouldn't be gossiping." Amelia covered her face with her hands.

"You're not. We're all friends. Carol would tell us herself if she were here," Patsy encouraged, and it was the truth. "And now I feel bad. I want to help her too."

Carol shared everything, even things we would rather she didn't.

Amelia dropped her hands. "Okay, but I'm only confiding in the group because I agree with you—she'd tell you guys herself. I mean, she cc'd all of us on this e-mail."

Everyone nodded as if to say, "Go on." I scanned the terse e-mail that read, *I think I know who this Jane Doe is.* There were links to a Facebook page and attachments.

"A lot happened at my house. She was already in a bad mood because the judge scolded her during dinner, saying she was a poor example of what a Southern lady ought to be. And he used finger quotes when he said 'lady.'"

We each sucked in a breath.

Poor Carol.

"Appalling is what it was, though I think he was joking. I mean, he laughed and all."

"How on this earth can Carol stand him? I understand he's accustomed to everyone bowing to his whims in his courtroom, but rudeness like that is inexcusable." Patsy shook her head with wide eyes. "What else did he say?"

"He peppered in his digs throughout the meal. Called her 'the mouth of the South' and said that'd she'd make a whore blush with her language. Things like that. We were so uncomfortable."

We all nodded sympathetically. Maybe Carol just needed some time. Especially having to deal with that jerk day in and day out.

"David's all talk. Carol knows that. Not that I'm happy about him defaming her character in such a manner." Val sipped from her glass, looking irritated. "He thinks he's a big shot. And he's merely a small-time court judge in our little ole town. Carol gives it right back. She does have a mouth on her, not to mention she's stubborn when she gets something in her head." Val sounded as if she more than approved of Carol's ability to hold her own.

Carol did get a little loose-lipped when she'd had a few. Still, that gave him no right to berate her in such a fashion. And I had to agree with Val on one point: the man did seem to think too much of himself.

"Oddly, now that I think about it, I might've been more upset about it than she was. Carol rolled her eyes at him but didn't seem all that bothered. I asked her if she was okay later, when we were alone, and she said he was an idiot. Nothing he said mattered to her anymore. But why I'm really worried is what's in this e-mail." She took a breath. "Here—the copies will make it easier to read."

With her dark brows furrowed, she handed out stapled printouts entitled "Do You Know This Jane Doe?" Everyone sat up straighter after digesting the material.

The article was compelling, describing a woman with long, spiraled black hair swept away from her dark face, and it gave a figurative account of her last day. The writer did a splendid job of humanizing the Jane Doe, whose identity had been stripped away by years of exposure to nature's elements. There were three other similar articles, and by the end, I was both intrigued and shaken.

"All these bodies were located up I-85." I was aghast as I thumbed through the papers.

Amelia nodded. "And there are about thirty Jane Doe cases to date that have gone cold. They call the area that runs along the interstate, mostly near the northern tip of the state, the dumping grounds. Carol said she recognized something linked to this one." She pointed to the case that described the woman with spiraled hair.

"We should definitely look into this," I said. "If Carol knew the Jane, maybe we all do. Or those of us who grew up here."

"I don't like this one bit." Patsy flipped through the pages. Her face paled.

Val's wide-eyed gaze roamed the room. "It's one thing when we're reading a mystery or watching those docuseries about cold cases. It's a whole other thing when it's right here in our backyard."

We all nodded.

"True, but maybe we could help. You know, do some good with what we've learned. No matter what's going on with Carol, she planned on introducing this in tonight's meeting." I fiddled with the printouts on my lap. "We can wait on her before really digging in, though."

I continued to scan the pages. "Wow. It makes sense. There are so many rural areas with vegetation off I-85. And if no one reports the victims as missing, the bodies could only be found by happenstance." As I flipped to the last page, I picked up my wineglass. So many cold cases. I wondered if Uncle Calvin would be interested in delving into any of these. But, with the requirement of being pro bono, I highly doubted it.

"I Googled and found an old news broadcast where the investigator in charge of these cast-offs"—Amelia showed us her palms—"their words, not mine, pleaded with the public for help."

"That's probably the reason they've taken to social media. How better to reach large masses of people? I mean, it's what I'd do."

"What is Carol thinking? My God, that's nuts." Patsy cast a shocked glance my way. "I'm sorry, but it is. I understand why you would be interested, Lyla. Since you started working for your uncle and all." She redirected her attention toward Amelia. "You, of all people, can't seriously be suggesting you agree with Carol and want us to actually investigate these crimes?" Patsy appeared appalled. "Like Val said, it's one thing having a bit of fun guessing whodunit with these well-known cases and fiction." She continued to shake her head as if it would shake the notion right out of the room.

"We understand, Patsy. No one will force you to take part in anything you're uncomfortable with." Val sounded sympathetic to our friend's plight.

Amelia sighed and sat back against the overstuffed sofa, her lips thinned to a flat line.

"Does anyone mind if we move on?" Patsy asked sweetly.

We all agreed to take a step back and wait until we found out more. It was highly possible that, with our heads filled with all those murders and mysteries, we might be overreacting.

When no one added more, Val said, "It's either Patsy or Lyla's turn to suggest our next read."

Patsy looked relieved, and I felt bad. The twins kept her up late, and her hormones were still in overdrive. It wasn't fair to stress her out when she came out for a little girl talk and book discussion. Amelia seemed to be on the same page as me when she sat back and put her folder back into her bag.

"You go ahead, Patsy." I forced a smile.

We voted and *Turn Of The Key*, by Ruth Ware, became our next read, ending our meeting. I drove home in Mother's Cadillac, which had plush leather seats that felt like a hug, with a sense of foreboding. Preoccupied, I hadn't minded not suggesting the last book in The Kinsey Millhone series to my club. I hoped Carol would return home. The situation was disconcerting, to say the least. Our club started out with more than a dozen members. Then life got in the way, and the group dwindled to half that. The intimate crowd gave us a sense of closeness.

I pulled up to the gated complex, punched in the code, and pulled through, waving at the security guard as I drove by. I swayed to Beethoven's "Für Elise" as I pulled into the small space in front of my house. Each of the townhouses had a designated parking space. I cast a glance at Melanie's vacant space.

To my left sat a moving van. The movers were unloading into a neighboring townhouse. The building catty-cornered to Mel's and mine.

I had a smile pasted on my face to greet my new neighbors. Moodys prided ourselves on common politeness. I'd have to get a welcome basket together and take it over. I'd probably wait until Mel got back and we could go over together.

A man with wavy dark-brown hair came out of the town-house to hold the door open for the movers. My advance slowed as I got closer and recognition hit. He saw me at the exact same time and smiled. *Smiled!*

"'Evening, neighbor."

I nearly choked. "Kevin, what on earth are you doing here? You can't possibly be moving in near me."

Before Kevin and I broke up six months ago, he and I been an item for about a year. Most of the time we fought like cats and dogs. But when it was good, it was *mind-blowing*.

"It's a free country. Besides, Ellen and I needed a fresh start. Her lease was up at her apartment, and she fell in love with it here, with the swimming pools, tennis courts, and gym."

My gorgeous dark-haired, hour-glass-shaped, thrice-divorced cousin walked out of the house and snuggled up next to Kevin. "Hi, Lyla. Do you want to come in and see the lovely house-warming gift Val gave us?"

I couldn't believe what I was hearing. Val should have fore-warned me about this invasion. I was just with her, for heaven's sake.

"A little birdie told me you had an embarrassing encounter at the Fast Trip this morning," Ellen grated on, "and you were wearing white and everything." She smirked in the same annoy-ing, "whatcha-gonna-do-about-it" way she had as a child. The one I always lost my temper over and smacked her for. Ellen was one of those people who always managed to push my buttons and draw out the rebellious child who, I believed, lay dormant within each of us.

"I have no idea what you're referring to." My face blistered. "We . . . welcome to the community." Before I did something to disparage my character, I walked up the driveway, keeping my stroll even and confident as I moved onto my slabbed front stoop.

"Why thank you, cuz. Stop by anytime," Ellen called across the parking lot.

There wasn't anything to obstruct their view of me, and I wouldn't make a scene. A piece of luggage leaned against my front door as I rammed the key into the lock and twisted. The airline must have delivered Mel's bag to my house by mistake. I grabbed the handle and gave it a tug, shocked with the weight of the thing. It took effort to roll the bag inside, and I closed the door on my humiliation.

How could they do this to me?

Kevin had an apartment. They could have lived there. Why move to be near me? And Mother must know about this. The devil's spawn was her sister's child, after all. Like myself, Ellen had been an only child, except her mother spoiled her rotten. Mine insisted I apologize for everything under the sun. Aunt Elizabeth believed her child could do no wrong. No wonder Ellen grew into a monstrous creature.

Well, I certainly wasn't moving. My fifteen-hundred-square-foot, two-story, cookie-cutter, white-washed brick townhouse had an open floorplan, a living room, a kitchen, and a dining room, with a powder room on the first floor and two bedrooms and a full bath on the second floor. It wasn't my dream home or anything, but the house represented my independence. I'd made it my own with tasteful pieces I'd picked up here and there. My favorite acquisition stood next to the flat screen. The antique bookshelf displayed all my irreplaceable beauties. Just seeing the full mahogany shelves with true crime novels, mysteries, and thrillers usually brought me joy. Sadly, it didn't have the same effect tonight. After I placed the *Y is for Yesterday* on the shelf, organized in alphabetical order, I moved into the living room and slunk down into my cream-tufted group sofa. I pulled my cell phone out of my bag and scrolled through my favorites until the appropriate icon appeared.

"Lyla Jane." Mother always answered my calls that way.

"Mother. Guess who I ran into?"

"Ellen and Kevin."

She did know! "Why didn't you tell me?"

"Lyla, my ears." I could envision Mother massaging her ear as if I'd ruptured her eardrum.

I rubbed my forehead. "Sorry." I lowered my tone. "But you can't even imagine how blindsided I was when I came home tonight. They were unloading a moving van in the building near mine."

"I made an attempt to discuss it with you this morning." So that's what she'd wanted to tell me. "However, I had no idea they'd be moving in that close to you. That is uncouth." Mother started whispering something to Daddy. "Your father says they called him from the mechanic shop, and the value of your car isn't worth investing in the repairs."

I'd specifically told them at our family mechanic shop to stop calling Daddy when I brought Bessie in.

"He'll drive you over to the Chevrolet dealership to pick out a new one next week."

Daddy only bought American-made cars and would insist I do the same.

"Tell him I appreciate it, but I can manage." I loved my daddy to bits and knew he would give me the moon without a blink. But I needed to be my own person and stand on my own two feet.

"How are you going to manage on what Calvin pays you? You'll never be able to make payments on anything decent." Mother meant well.

"I can manage. And please don't start in on my working for Uncle Calvin again. You've known for ages I'd work in the field in some capacity."

"I'd hoped it was a phase." Mother sighed.

"Well, it isn't. I enjoy it and I'm good at it. If I could just borrow your car for a few more days, that'd be great." I got up and walked to the refrigerator, opening the door. There was half a gallon of skim milk, an old Chinese takeout carton, some leftovers I'd brought home from Mother's last week, and a couple containers of Greek yogurt. Something had most definitely spoiled. I retrieved a wild berry fruit on the bottom and checked the date. I had two days.

"I'm not going to harp." Tonight, she meant. "You could do something more with your life is all I'm saying. And if living near your cousin and ex is too much, you can always come home. Go back to school and find another path. You might even meet a nice young man while you're at it." There it was. Mother always wanted me to move back home until I found a husband.

"I'm thirty-one. I can't live at home. I love y'all, but I need my independence." I stirred the yogurt.

Mother, Daddy, and Gran would be having coffee cake or pastry in the great room by now. Well, Mother wouldn't touch hers, but Daddy and Gran would be enjoying theirs immensely. I frowned and glanced at my watery, fat-free concoction. It was worth the sacrifice, but I'd surely be stopping off at Hugs with Mugs, my favorite coffee shop to purchase a yeasty, sugar-covered treat ASAP. Everyone needed a splurge day. Mother's stocked pantry was one of the things I missed most about living at home. I sure could use a hunk of chocolate cake right about now.

Mother sighed again. "I'm proud of your strong will and determination, honey. I just worry about you."

"No need to worry. I'm fine," I said, to convince myself as much as her.

"Hold on a second." Another huff. "Your grandmother would like to speak to you. Where your persistence comes from isn't a mystery. I'll speak to you later, darlin'."

Gran ranted for a solid twenty minutes on the audacity of Ellen and her disgusting behavior. I could always count on Gran to be on my side, no matter what. Once we put the world to rights, I let her go with a promise I'd keep her apprised on what I found out about Carol. She'd heard from one of Carol's in-laws, a great-aunt or something, while at the senior center, that Carol had been spotted coming out of that cheap motel on the outskirts of town and driving a new car.

Chapter Three

Morning brought cloudy skies, rumbling thunder, and Melanie Smart. She woke me up pounding on my front door at an ungodly hour. I tied my robe and swung open the door to see my best friend sunburned to the color of a lobster. Her blonde hair was pulled into a bun on the top of her head, and she wore a pink floral shirt with a giant teddy bear on it.

I met her bloodshot chocolate-brown gaze. "Wow."

She rushed past me and tossed her duffle bag onto the floor in front of the kitchen bar. "Don't say a word. I'd hug you, but I stink, and I've had the worst night. My plane had mechanical difficulties. We were stuck in Newark for four hours. When we were finally called to board, I sat next to a woman with a screaming child, with an ear infection, who threw up all over me and inside my Chanel bag."

Both my hands went to my mouth.

"I know—it's the only good thing I got out of my marriage. I could have cried." She shook her head, despair written all over her face. "Then I had to change in the tiny airplane bathroom into the only thing I had in my carry-on. This was meant to be a joke present for you." She pulled at the hem of the ghastly floral shirt tied in little knots.

Then she threw herself down on my sofa. "Do you have my spare key? I don't want to wade through vomit to find mine."

"You poor thing," I fussed. "Your hair looks damp. Is it raining?"

Her hand went to her hair. "Oh, yeah, um, a little."

"Maybe we can clean your bag."

She pointed to the once-gorgeous little bag, now covered in dried red and yellow chunks.

"I'm so sorry," I breathed.

Melanie hung her head.

"I'll go get your key. You want me to brew some coffee? I'd offer you breakfast, except I have nothing in the house."

She waved off my offer, and I went upstairs to retrieve her spare key. When I came back down, she had dozed off. I wasn't sure whether to wake her or not. The keys rattled and she startled awake with a snort.

"Sorry. Here you go."

She yawned and took the keys from me. "Thanks. Don't worry about waking me. I've got to get back on my work schedule anyway. I have to be back at the shop tomorrow."

Melanie owned a specialty cookie store called Smart Cookie. She and her cousin opened it five years ago, and it had done very well. Everyone who worked there was either a Smart or related to a Smart. It was a real family business.

"Did I see Kevin's car outside parked across from your mom's car?"

I nodded. "I'm borrowing Mother's car because mine bit the dust. For good this time."

"Poor Bessie. She was a good car."

I nodded, and we both gave her a moment of silence.

"And Kevin moved in practically next door to us."

She bolted upright. *"What?"*

I ran my fingers through my tangled hair. "He and *Ellen* moved in last night."

"Ellen, as in your cousin, the Wicked Witch of the West, Ellen?"

I started for the Keurig. "The same. I still don't know how I'm going to react to this. It isn't that I want Kevin back or anything. I just don't want him with *her*. Or living so close to *me*."

"Of course not." After her divorce to the world's biggest poser, Melanie prided herself on being able to spot a loser a mile away. "He has to be doing this to get your attention." She joined me in the kitchen. My news seemed to energize her. "Ellen doesn't hold a candle to you, and his desire to throw the relationship in your face is proof he isn't over you. Living in a small town it's hard enough to avoid exes, but this, well, this just takes the cake."

"There's a country song in there somewhere." I closed the lid on the pod and opened the refrigerator to retrieve the almond milk creamer.

"What's that smell? It isn't me, is it?" Horrified, Melanie began sniffing herself.

"No. I need to clean the refrigerator out. Some leftovers are way past their prime." I slid a mug in front of her and repeated the process for myself.

"Other than Kevin and Ellen lowering the standard of our community, what's been going on? How did the club meeting go last night? Did y'all talk about the e-mail Carol sent? That was some creepy stuff." She fingered the printouts of the dumping grounds Amelia gave me and the map I'd printed out after I'd hung up with Gran last night. Dismayed, I'd needed something to take my mind off Kevin. It'd done the trick. I'd highlighted the interstate where the bodies had been discovered, and I wondered how many others had yet to be found.

We sipped our coffees while I filled her in on everything. Like myself, Melanie was both intrigued and uneasy.

"Do you think Calvin can help with these?" Melanie finished off her coffee.

My shoulders rose and fell. "His time needs to be invested on revenue-generating cases. I plan to ask, but I'm not holding out much hope."

"We could do it. You have access to everything you need."

I shook my head. "I don't know, Mel. He's funny about his encrypted software."

"Doesn't hurt to ask."

We moved on and discussed Carol at length, and Melanie agreed with Patsy that our friend was probably after attention. A half hour passed like a blink. It always did when Mel and I were together, and I needed to get ready for work.

"Want to go have Mexican food this evening? I'm dying for a margarita and chimichanga with extra guacamole." Melanie hopped off the bar stool. "And don't even say a word about calories. I'm declaring today an all-out splurge day. We both deserve it."

"Sounds good." I rinsed our mugs and put them in the dishwasher.

"That doesn't smell like spoiled food to me." Melanie picked up her duffle bag and paused close to the door. "It's coming from this suitcase."

"Really? Maybe something spilled on it in transit from the airport."

Melanie glanced over at me. "I'm lost."

"This is your luggage, isn't it?" I pointed to the large, soft-sided navy spinner suitcase. "They delivered it to my house by mistake."

She shook her head. "It looks like mine. But older. I bet the stupid airline sent the wrong bag, and by the smell of it, the owners smuggled in some rancid cheese or something."

Melanie leaned forward and lifted the tag on the top of the bag, pinching her nose. How in the world had I not realized this bag reeked last night? She dropped the tag as if burned. "It says Carol Timms!" She bumped the bag as she leaped backward, and the suitcase toppled over with a loud thump. Two fingers popped out where the zipper hadn't been closed tight.

"Oh my God!" I fell back into a squeaking Melanie.

Melanie went pale as a ghost. Her eyes grew wide, and one of her mental-patient giggles escaped her lips. "Call someone!"

"What if the person is alive? What if it's Carol?" The room began to spin a little, and I fought to gain my balance. "We have to help her."

With trembling fingers, I stooped down and unzipped the bag, hoping and praying that whoever was inside was still alive, knowing it wasn't possible. The smell of what could only be described as death overwhelmed me, and I covered my face with my arm. Never in a million years would I forget the scent or the way the woman lay crumpled inside. Rigor mortis froze her in a position no living person could manage. Carol Timms was undeniably dead.

Melanie giggled again, then fainted, falling forward into me.

I rolled Mel off me and scrambled away from the body. Somehow, I managed to keep my thoughts coherent enough to locate my phone and dial 911. I hardly recognized my voice as I pleaded for the operator to send help. And I vaguely remembered calling Uncle Calvin after Mel came to.

Law enforcement in Sweet Mountain wasn't a large force, and I was familiar with most of them. Even more familiar with the chief of police, who hadn't shown up. Men in blue and medical personnel filled my living spaces as Melanie and I sat at the dining room table, trying not to glance back at the covered body on the floor. Mel and I had already given our statements.

"I can't believe this," Melanie whispered. "I'm sorry I passed out. I've never seen anything like that before. I'm usually so good in a crisis. You know—the solid one."

I reached over and hugged her. "Of course you are." She wasn't, but I let her have her fantasies. "It's like a nightmare. It still hasn't sunk in."

"I keep seeing her fingers sticking out . . ." She let out one of her disconcerting high-pitched giggles, then slapped both hands over her mouth.

Officer Taylor narrowed his eyes in our direction.

"She isn't being disrespectful. She giggles when she's frightened." I'd hardly spoken to the man since our school days, and I didn't want him to get the wrong idea about my friend.

"I think I recall something about your nervous laugh from high school." Officer Taylor's gaze zeroed in on Mel, and she nodded.

"It's an affliction, really." Mel cleared her throat.

I patted her shoulder, and Taylor's attention seemed to linger on her face.

After the body had been taken away, Melanie gave her account and was allowed to go to her apartment and shower and change. Calvin, Officer Taylor, and yours truly were left at my dining room table. Calvin sat back with his arms folded across his chest. His weathered face showed no emotion, but his green eyes were intense, full of warning.

The officer began questioning me about earlier, when Carol had been alive. I couldn't stop the tears as I gave the account in detail.

The heavyset man jotted everything down on his little pad. He scratched the thinning hair on top of his round head with the back of the pen. "So, you didn't actually speak to Mrs. Timms?"

"No, sir. I didn't get a chance. She peeled out of the parking lot." I wiped my cheeks. "It was her, though. No doubt about it." I crossed my legs and laced my fingers together over my knee to keep my leg from shaking.

"Other than the camo hat, did the other person have any distinguishing marks? Hair peeking out from under the cap? Small or large person? Man or woman?"

I shook my head. "I think they were slumped down a little. Might have been tall, trying to appear short. That's clearly speculation, of course. I didn't see any hair, but I was covered in cold blue raspberry slushy and didn't pay all that much attention until they were driving away. I couldn't see their face—" Suddenly, I recalled the person adjusting the cap lower. I uncrossed my leg and scooted to the edge of my seat, placing my hands on the table. "They were light skinned. I remember the hand pulling the bill of the ballcap down. The fingers were thin and white-ish. Now that I think about it"—I bit the inside of my cheek as I considered— "they were unnaturally white, like they were wearing gloves."

"Where did you go after that?"

A little taken off guard by the question, I stuttered. "I-I called a tow truck and they dropped me off at my mother's house." I shouldn't have been nervous. I'd studied enough homicide cases to know that in the beginning everyone was a suspect. Especially the one who found the body. The authorities wouldn't be doing their job properly if they didn't investigate everyone.

"And then you spoke to Judge Timms?" The officer wiped his forehead. He had the look of a man sweating out a night of heavy drinking.

"Yes. Calvin had a meeting off-site, so the calls were forwarded to my cell. He expressed an interest in hiring us to locate his wife. He had apprehensions regarding the police taking the matter seriously. That's when I told him about seeing Carol, and he asked me to report it to the police. I left a message with someone at the station."

"Why would you accept delivery of an unknown piece of luggage?" The officer sounded suspicious.

"Well, first of all, I was startled by my ex-boyfriend moving in practically next door to me. I'll admit I wasn't in my normal headspace. And it wasn't as if a delivery man handed it over. It was waiting on my front stoop. Melanie had told me her luggage had been lost by the airline. Naturally, I assumed they'd gotten her address mixed up with mine. It happens all the time—the address mix-up, I mean. I'm six one six, and she's six one eight. She gets my packages, and I get hers."

"I see." He scribbled a few things down. "But you didn't open it last night? Didn't notice the odor?"

I fiddled with my hands under the table. Uncle Calvin reached under and gave my hand a quick reassuring squeeze. "I'm ashamed to admit I don't always clean out my refrigerator in a timely manner. I figured something had spoiled. I planned to take care of it after work today. Then you know the rest. Melanie came in and we discovered Ca . . ." I couldn't finish.

Poor Carol. Who could do such a horrible thing to her? Why? And what was an even more terrifying question: Why would they deliver her to me?

He got up and retrieved a bag marked "Evidence" and placed it on the table in front of me. Inside were the copies Carol had printed out and the map I'd marked last night. He didn't say anything as he walked over to my bookshelf and took notice of the titles I stocked. Calvin gave me a pointed glare that told me to keep my mouth shut until a question was asked. I obeyed and sat quiet as a mouse until the officer rejoined us at the table.

"Can you explain why you have these maps and images of skeletal remains?"

"I belong to a club called the Jane Doe Book Club. We read murder mysteries and watch films about them while trying to discover the culprit before the book or movie ends. We read both fiction and true crime novels. Carol e-mailed the members with these docs."

"Melanie belong to the club as well?"

I nodded.

"An odd fascination with crime and death for such a pretty young woman like Miss Smart." His eyes narrowed. "And for you."

"Is there a question in there somewhere, Taylor?" Calvin asked in his laid-back sort of way that said, *"I don't need to raise my voice to mean business."*

"Cousins, I've allowed you to remain here out of professional courtesy. You interject again, and my courtesy won't remain."

"If your questions don't end soon, I'll have a lawyer here, and your courtesy won't be required." The two men faced off in a silent staring contest.

Several long seconds passed.

Officer Taylor broke eye contact first. "You said Melanie Smart's luggage went missing."

I nodded.

"This her bag?"

"She told you it wasn't. She has one like it, but it's newer."

"Uh-huh. I'm going to need contact information of everyone in your club."

I looked over at Calvin, never feeling more thankful for him in my life. His guidance was invaluable. He nodded and I pulled up my contacts list on my phone, jotted down the info on the officer's pad, and slid it back over to him.

"Do you have somewhere else you can stay?"

I nodded.

"I'll need the address of where you'll be and the keys to your townhouse."

"Okay." I'd taken a firm stand on not moving. Now, after seeing poor Carol deceased and in my personal space, Mother was going to get her wish.

Chapter Four

The front porch light shone like a beacon as I pulled Mother's Cadillac into the driveway. I wouldn't even attempt to park it in the garage. My daddy, who was very particular, would pull it out and repark it anyway. He had a garage system.

Uncle Calvin pulled in behind me. I turned the ignition off and took a couple of little breaths, holding each one for a few seconds. I checked my reflection in the rearview mirror. My hair was up in a messy bun. A few strands had escaped and looked planned, so I left them. In Sweet Mountain, you learned from an early age that beauty does matter—to be gorgeously groomed before leaving the house. It became an impulse always to look my best. Now it seemed ludicrous to be concerned about such matters.

I stared into my bloodshot blue eyes. *Who are you?*

I blinked the tears away and got out of the car. Uncle Calvin went to retrieve the rolling bag containing the minimum number of essentials such as makeup, skin care, and a few articles of clothing from the trunk. I hadn't even bothered packing much in the wardrobe department. Mother would have my dresser, chest of drawers, and closet fully stocked.

Every fiber of my being hated bringing my troubles to my parents' front porch. Mother *needed* peace. I stared at the house; the red and yellow mums were placed on either side of the front door and lined the staircase. The rocking chair cushions matched the mums—ideal for the season.

"You ready?"

I nodded, squared my shoulders, and held my head high.

He gave me a little pat on the back. "It'll be alright."

I should feel comforted. *Why the dread?*

When trouble brewed, the Moody household held an undertone of something I couldn't precisely identify. Sometimes it felt like a heaviness that threatened to pull everything crashing down around us. Mother fought hard to make everything perfect, as if her life depended on it. She managed to orchestrate our lives to appear drama-free. She wouldn't be happy about this.

The front door swung open before we made it onto the porch. Mother must have ESP, sensing the scandalous disturbance in the air. In the South, behind closed doors, every family had their secrets, and no one was interested in airing their dirty laundry to the world.

She didn't even look at me. Her round eyes narrowed and zeroed in on her brother. And my sturdy, six-foot, two-hundred-plus-pound uncle slightly withered.

Mother had that effect on people. "Calvin, what have you involved my daughter in?"

Uncle Calvin scratched his salt-and-pepper-goateed chin. I was guessing he needed a minute to dredge up enough courage to face his older sister.

"Now, Frances, don't get riled up. The girl's been through an ordeal."

"If she has, I place the blame entirely on you." Mother's tone was low and controlled. "The phone hasn't stopped ringing with wagging tongues eager to discuss my daughter's involvement in something ghastly."

"Please stop talking about me like I'm not even here." Relegated in a matter of moments from an independent woman to an indignant sixteen-year-old child.

"Stop being melodramatic and calm down, young lady." Mother shook her head.

"Melodramatic? My friend Carol was dead and in a suitcase!" I immediately lowered my tone. "In a suitcase in *my* house, Mother."

Mother flinched. Whatever she'd heard about what transpired at my place left out that detail. She grabbed me by the arm and pulled me inside and pushed on the door.

Calvin's boot forced it open as he cleared his throat. "May I come inside too?" He'd be allowed inside now without too much afront from Mother. She had no desire to continue this discussion on the front porch.

Mother turned around as if seeing Uncle Calvin for the first time. "Yes, of course. I . . . um, I apologize, Calvin." Mother stepped aside as Gran came hurrying down the hallway.

She was swinging her arms, her pointy elbows rising high as she puffed. "This isn't some joke, is it?" She panted as if she'd taken the stairs.

I shook my head; my eyes were wide and unblinking.

"Oh my word! Is it true?" There was a twinkle in Gran's eyes. "Selma Townsends's granddaughter lives in your complex. She said there were cops everywhere, and they had your townhouse under surveillance with drug-sniffin' dogs and everything! Oh, this is exciting."

Seeing her reaction made the butterflies calm a little.

Mother glanced heavenward as if to say, *"Why me, sweet Jesus?"* before closing the door. She fiddled with her pearls rapidly.

"Gran." I embraced her, being careful to avoid her sharp edges. "Your sources didn't quite get their facts straight."

"But it was a crime scene? And someone died?"

"Yes, ma'am." I released her, and she searched my face.

Her smile faded. "You're okay, right? You weren't in any imminent danger, were you, child?"

"No, ma'am. Shaken up, but fine."

"Tough little cookie. You get that from me. We spit in the eye of danger." She pinched my nose and winked. "You'll have another dynamite story to tell for years to come."

"I'm not sure I want to tell this story, Gran. It was awful." I swallowed and fought to keep my lip from quivering.

"Calvin, explain." Mother reached out and took my hand, clutching it to her chest.

Gran gave her daughter-in-law a pitying expression.

"Don't you want James to hear this? It might be easier to tell everyone at once. The police might also come by here to speak with her again." Calvin had fallen back into his usual demeanor. All business.

He glanced around as if expecting Daddy to appear. Truthfully, I had too.

"He's at the hospital. I'll relay the information." Mother wrapped her other hand around mine.

Calvin explained the events in the detached way of his, facts only. I watched the faces of the two most important women in my family. Mother and Gran's faces held two utterly different expressions. Mother looked horrified, and Gran appeared to be wrestling with warring emotions.

Gran took my other hand, and I was pulled in two directions. "Now tell us from your perspective. Was it awful? Scary? Gruesome?"

"Yes, yes, and yes."

"That sounds dreadful. Maybe I should move in with you, Lyla. I'm a dead-eye with my Smith and Wesson. I'll protect you." Her eyes glinted hopefully.

A nervous half laugh escaped my lips.

"Daisy, please," Mother said demurely.

My flustered mother met my gaze. "It could have been you instead of that poor woman. Working in this dangerous field and reading about murders with that dead club. This isn't the life for a respectable young lady. You can only push your luck so far. You're done working for your uncle, Lyla Jane Moody. Do you understand me?"

"I love you, Mother, but this isn't your decision."

Gran bit her lip, and Mother's face turned an unhealthy shade of puce.

"Calm down, Franny," Calvin placated.

Mother sent him her worst glare. "Thank you for seeing her home, but I must insist you respect my wishes for a change. My child is *my* business. You aren't the boss here. We aren't children any longer." My ears perked at the reference to their being children. The topic had historically been taboo in our home.

"Franny, let's not do this now." Uncle Calvin rubbed the nape of his neck.

"May I speak to you for a moment alone, please?" Mother said through clenched teeth, and my mouth fell open.

"Yeah, sure, Franny. Sure." No one ever called her Franny except Uncle Calvin, and usually she corrected him. This time she hadn't batted an eye. My mother and uncle had an unusual relationship. Something tragic had happened during their child-hood, and neither felt comfortable discussing it with me. It'd uniquely bonded them.

Mother kissed my cheek before releasing my hand. She was not the most affectionate woman in the world, and her behavior alarmed me. She'd been a doting parent and provided me with the best of everything. She'd not approved effusive behavior of the other parents in our circle. She'd insisted they made their children weak. Me she wanted unbreakable.

"I bet you need some cake. Frances bought a great big choc-olate one." Gran wrapped an arm around my waist; the top of her head rested against my shoulder.

Mother and Uncle Calvin excused themselves. The door to the living room closed.

The kitchen smelled homey, like buttery pastry and sugary comfort. My kitchen never had such aromas unless I ordered in or Melanie brought cookies over from her shop. Now, it smelled like decomposition. A chill ran up my spine.

"Unburden yourself, darlin'. It's not healthy to keep it bot-tled up." She patted a stool.

"I can honestly say it was the worst moment of my life." I took a seat on one of the six antique, white, Provencal Grapes swivel barstools as Gran picked up the cake plate and placed it on the island.

"Was the cake bought for a special occasion?" I asked.

Gran shrugged and took the dome off the shiny chocolate cake. She took out two dessert plates and sliced giant hunks, then handed me a fork.

"Your mother was going to take this to some ladies' club. But desperate times . . ." She dug into her massive piece, taking a huge bite.

"Mother's not going to like this." The guilt for distressing my mother caused me to hold back as Gran encouraged me to dig in.

"Frances won't be going to the ladies' club after all this." She waved her hand around, and a little icing fell from her fork. "Whoops."

She began to rise, and I put a hand on her shoulder. "Let me." I got a napkin and cleaned up after her.

"I heard this all happened after you found out about Kevin too?"

I dropped the napkin in the trash, sat back down on the stool, and sliced into the delicate crumb, loading my fork. My lips closed around the smooth, creamy chocolate with a delicious raspberry filling, and for a second it was bliss. I swallowed. "Yeah. It's been the worst twenty-four hours of my life. Not only did I find out that Ellen"—my lip curled and Gran turned up her nose—"is canoodling with my ex, which on any other day would be a nightmare, but it's also no way comparable to finding your friend's body stuffed inside a suitcase. Melanie and I were petrified. And the smell, Gran." I put my fork on the island. I tried hard not to see her distorted body.

"I wonder who did it?" Gran tore her piece of cake apart like a small child as she hunted for more raspberry filling.

Goose bumps traveled up my flesh as I wondered along with her.

Gran's features scrunched up in thought. "Could be some sordid love affair gone wrong. Like maybe the lover turned out to be some horrible psycho killer." Gran shoveled a giant bite into her mouth. "What about that guy you saw her with the other day?"

I met her curious gaze. "I just don't know." A flash of the passenger with his cap pulled down over his eyes came to me. I grasped at the memory, hoping to recall more. To remember something—anything—that would help. I put my hand over my stomach, now jumpy with nerves. Carol's red face was clear in my mind.

"What if she didn't know the man?" If I'd only coaxed my friend from the car at the Fast Trip, she might be alive today.

"Hmm. Maybe," Gran said around a mouthful. "We should sneak into the office and have another gander at her file." Chocolate frosting peeked from the corner of her mouth.

I motioned to her, and she wiped it away with her fingers.

In all the commotion, I'd completely forgotten about Gran's revelation about Carol's treatment with Daddy. I'd not mentioned it to Calvin or Officer Taylor.

"Maybe we should just let Daddy speak with the police." I picked my fork back up and forced another bite before deciding the cake and the nerves weren't getting along.

Mother came into the kitchen without saying a word about us indulging in the cake. She handed Gran and me each a proper napkin. As I unfolded the embroidered cloth and placed it in my lap, my mother poured herself a glass of wine and sipped. I spied a slight tremor in her hand holding the glass as she tilted her head back and focused on the recessed lighting. A large lump of trepidation developed in the back of my throat.

"I'm sorry I spoke so harshly to you earlier," I whispered, not wanting to be at odds with her. Life was too short.

Mother's gaze flittered to me, and she blinked a few times, almost as if she were struggling to focus. She stood in front of me, cupped my face in her hand, and the most peculiar expression spread across her face.

"She's okay, Frances, dear." Gran rubbed my back. "She's tough as nails."

Mother kept staring as she stroked my jawline with her thumb. She opened her mouth a few times to speak, yet nothing emerged.

She's opening up to me.

"You look pale, dear. A little lipstick could help."

I blinked up at her, stunned. "What?"

Her hand dropped, and she took a step back. "A woman's secret weapon is her lip color. You know that."

"Really, Mother? That's what you want to discuss now? Makeup?"

She sipped again and then sighed.

"Doesn't something like this make you take stock of your life? All the petty things, like hair, cosmetics, and fashion, are trivial in retrospect. My friend died. *Died!* Why aren't we discussing that?"

Mother looked genuinely stunned. "Well, forgive me for raising you to care about yourself."

"That's not what she meant, Frances. She wants to talk to you about her pain." Gran's gaze was soft and full of understanding.

Mother turned her head away, wrapping an arm across her rib cage, and propped her elbow on her wrist as she sipped more wine. The little wrinkle deepened between her brows.

I reached out and touched her arm. "Please sit down. I'm not a child any longer. We can discuss your stresses. I hate that this triggered a reaction. I know how important peace is for you."

She unfolded her arms as her eyes flashed hot. "I won't make you relive the ordeal and exhaust you further by having you describe the events again. Sometimes I think therapy is nonsense. Nothing good comes from reliving traumatic events."

I wouldn't argue with her; she was well aware of how my father and I heartily disagreed.

"And nothing was triggered, child. All this proves is you have poor judgment."

"Poor judgment? That has nothing to do with what happened. I found Carol deceased. You're deflecting." I swallowed as I recalled the body.

"You're too obsessed with death." Her tone matched her eyes, hot and challenging. "I blame your father for always indulging you when you were a child. I should have never listened to him when he insisted this fascination would pass. You're a bright beautiful girl with everything going for you. Why tempt fate?"

"Tempt fate? What does that mean?" *Am I in the* Twilight Zone? *Why am I here?* "I should've stayed with Melanie."

"Hush that talk," Gran said. "You're always welcome here at home. Right, Frances?"

"That goes without saying," Mother huffed, and stared into her glass. "You should probably get some rest now." She let out a long sigh as she left the room.

"Why won't she ever open up to me? Why must she always be so guarded?" I propped my elbows on the counter and buried my face in my hands.

"Frances comes from an era when you just lived with the thorn in your side. You find a way to plod along and not focus on the trouble. She does the best she can. Let's have some wine, sugar."

"Wine sounds delicious." I rubbed my finger across the smooth, cold surface of the granite. "I can understand the differences between the generations. At least it's some form of an explanation."

My grandmother struggled with the corkscrew. I opened my hands, and she passed the bottle over. Gran placed two crystal glasses in front of me. I twisted until it made a little pop sound, and then poured.

Mm, we always had the best wine in this house—a consolation.

Chapter Five

Hushed whispers woke me. I flung myself upright, gripping the damp sheets in my fists. My heart pounded as I scanned the room in the darkness. The creaking of footsteps against the floor sent me racing from the bed. Carol's bloated face burned in my brain.

"Quiet, James." Mother's voice brought me back to the present.

I relaxed a minuscule amount. I squinted at the clock on the bedside table—nearly two. Gran and I had stayed up till midnight, waiting on him. If my grandmother's memory could be trusted, she'd learned from my friends' file that Carol suffered from paranoia and a deep, overwhelming fear of dying and her flesh rotting away.

More whispers brought me from my reverie. I crept to the closed door, pressing my ear against the wood.

"She's asleep? In her room?"

"Honestly, James, where else would she be in the middle of the night." From the sound of it, Mother's annoyance had increased instead of abating.

"How did she seem?" Daddy didn't sound bothered by Mother's aggravated tone, and I mused on how he never did.

"Oh, you know Lyla. She doesn't react as a normal young woman would."

What does that mean?

"I think she needs a new group of friends," my mother continued. "I've never liked her association with the book club. She was doing so much better before she took up with them. Maybe we should . . ." Their voices became lost behind their bedroom door, which closed with a clunk.

Maybe they should what? What could they possibly do? Part of me wanted to confront them tonight. The other part decided nothing productive would come from such behavior. I crawled back into bed, my thoughts in a tumult. Their whispered concerns reminded me of days gone by.

I've always had a fascination with murder and crime, unsolved crimes in particular. And yes, Jane Doe cases were a point of major interest to me. My "obsession," as Mother referred to it, had landed me in therapy—Daddy's idea—as a late teen, and it continued into my early twenties. Despite my insistence that many of the world shared my enthusiasm, and my calling Mother's attention to the multitude of programs centered around crime detection, she hadn't relented. My compliance to evaluate my interest through therapeutic sessions did nothing to alter her perception. She claimed—and I quote—"Lyla's fixation with such ghoulish things is tantamount to thanatophobia." Nothing could have been further from the truth.

But Mother had succeeded in planting a seed of doubt. I traveled down the path of thinking maybe something was wrong with me. The notion fueled my desire to study psychology. My need to understand the human mind was derivative of needing to understand myself.

Quinn Daniels, our chief of police, and I were close at the time. If anyone could understand my need to find answers regarding the criminal psyche, I believed he would. Wrong. It got ugly; our breakup really messed with my head, and I neglected my studies.

I began working in retail and reading a lot. Books became my escape—my saving grace. Our book club started shortly after, and the idea that I was the town freak no longer dominated my thoughts.

Goose bumps erupted on my skin, and I succumbed to a full-body shiver as I thought of Carol. What kind of monster had done that to her? Had she cried out and hoped for rescue? Had she suffered? Too painful to focus on, so I shoved it from my mind and concentrated on why she ended up at my house. Perhaps the police had some leads. I should call Quinn. I had a reason to now. We'd given each other a wide berth around town—nothing official or unfriendly. But I still expected Chief Quinn Daniels to have shown up when he heard the address of the crime scene. His absence stung a little.

The clock read nearly three AM now. I put my earbuds in and turned on "Weightless," by Marconi Union, from my music app, with the hope that it would fulfill its promise to lower my heart rate and help me drift off to a peaceful slumber. But that didn't happen.

Chapter Six

That morning at seven, I snuck down the back steps. I smoothed out my high, sleek ponytail. I'd taken my time applying my makeup and fixing my hair. Despite what I'd said to Mother last night about the foolishness of worrying about superficial things, the ritual gave me a sense of normalcy—something I desperately needed. Not only because of the loss of my friend, but because I'd begun to believe, before sleep claimed me, I might've actually seen the killer.

I took one of Daddy's travel mugs from the cabinet and made myself a giant cup of black coffee to combat the exhaustion that had settled deep in my bones. Then took the dome off the beautiful platter of pastries mother bought and popped a couple of chocolate croissants into a brown paper bag. A sugar rush wouldn't hurt.

When I caught a glimpse of myself in the glass of the cabinet, I frowned and used my fingers to pat under my eyes. I'd tried my best to cover my dark circles. I applied a little extra highlighter for good measure.

"Lyla," Mother called over the intercom, "are you down there?"

"No!" I called up the stairs, and with a smirk, I opened the back door and escaped.

The sun dominated the bright blue sky and shone through the canopy of limbs overhead as I drove up the scenic road toward historic downtown. In a few weeks, the view would be breathtaking. Gorgeous hues—reds, golds, and burnt orange—would cover the landscape. Sweet Mountain would be gearing up for our annual fall festival. Venders and food trucks would line the square. The scent of hot chocolate, popcorn, and caramel-covered apples would permeate the air. Life would go on. It always had and always would. The notion that the world continued to turn despite our troubles insulted yet comforted. The dichotomy gave one perspective.

I rounded the vacant square that housed a mixture of brick and concrete storefronts that came alive around ten. The businesses here had signs alerting tourists, as well as residents of Sweet Mountain, they weren't open for business until late morning. Quite literally, the signs read "Open around 10ish." We didn't have a single chain establishment in our downtown district, and the city council planned to keep it that way. To quote Daddy, it was one of the things that kept our town Mayberry-esque.

When our sleepy town woke, there were dozens of delightful shops to discover and delicious restaurants, ranging from Mexican to fine Southern dining, to enjoy. We also had a couple of fun bars, coffee shops, the Smart family cookie shop, wine and spice shops, and a theater where local talent performed musicals, and concerts. Sweet Mountain embodied the sense of small-town living, and everyone here valued our community. Homicides were something we read about in our papers—the reason most folks chose to stay put and not venture into the city of Atlanta except for business or to catch a game.

The Mayberry essence of Sweet Mountain also made it so difficult to wrap my head around what had happened to Carol. That someone among us could do something so wholly heinous baffled me. In our community, children rode their bikes in their neighborhoods without worry. Some walked to school, and most folks didn't lock their doors. The winds of change blew.

I parallel parked Mother's Cadillac in front of the small brick office Cousins Investigative Services rented, located between Smart Cookie and the William Miles Salon, where my fabulous hairstylist and good friend rented a chair. The building, built in 1920, retained its old-world charm, even with the modern renovations from five years prior. The sweet smell of baked goods wafting over from my friend's cookie shop made me grateful for the breakfast I had as I unlocked the glass door and flipped on the lights.

The office was a fifteen-hundred-square-foot functional space. We had exposed brick walls with tan painted columns. The ceiling had been painted black to hide the exposed ductwork and beams. The floors were original hardwood, and I'd hung up some abstract art and added a couple of large floor plants to improve the feel of the space.

After I restocked the coffee station, I sat down at my small, industrial, carruca office desk, opened the laptop, and put my cell on charge beside me.

I'd received messages from each of the Jane Does. I didn't know what to say yet, so I wouldn't return any of the calls.

I pulled up my news feed and searched "Carol Timms."

"Local Woman Found Dead at the Home of a Resident of Mountain View Commons Townhome Community." I clicked the link.

The police are searching for answers to how a local woman, Carol Timms, ended up dead in a resident's townhome early Tuesday morning. Mrs. Timms had been reported missing several days ago, and her 2019 BMW 750i was found in the Atlanta Hartsfield-Jackson International Airport parking lot. Judge David Timms is pressing the authorities for answers. Local law enforcement did not comment except to remind the community the investigation is ongoing.

Meticulously scanning the article, I found no mention of the suitcase or Mel's or my name. The door swung open, and as if summoned, in she breezed, wearing her pink apron tied at the waist, with her beautiful honey-blonde hair with those amazing highlights expertly blended throughout her curls. She'd bound them up in a high ponytail, and her mane trailed down to the middle of her back. The gods had gifted Mel with a perfectly proportioned frame and with a metabolism I'd dreamed of having.

She adjusted the top of her apron strap, situating the giant cookie in the middle, embroidered in white with "Smart Cookie," at the top of the apron. "You see the article on your feed this morning?"

"I just Googled it."

"I'm still in shock." She flung herself in one of the three chairs against the wall and crossed her legs. "I couldn't sleep last night." She scrubbed her face with her fingers. "I kept seeing her."

"Same."

She dropped her hands to her lap. "Who could've done that to her? It freaks me out the effort it'd take to crumple her up to fit in a suitcase. Does your uncle know anything?"

"No, he doesn't. And I have no idea about the significance of the suitcase. According to the article, her car was found at the airport. The BMW I saw her in belonged to her. She obviously bought a new car, one her husband didn't know about."

Mel's eye's widened.

I leaned forward. "I also know Daddy was treating her because Gran snooped in her file."

She sat up straighter, and her mouth gaped.

"Don't ask." I shook my head. "From what I gathered, and bearing in mind this is completely reliant on Gran's memory, Carol was experiencing bouts of paranoia and fear of dying. To add to the drama, Gran heard from her friend at the senior center, a man closely related to the Timms, that Carol was having an affair. Someone spotted her coming out of the cheap motel right at the I-85 entrance."

"Rumors, huh." Mel glanced off, looking thoughtful.

"Rumors notwithstanding, it must hold some validity. Rumors usually do."

Mel nodded, chewing on her bottom lip. "I agree. "People do crazy things sometimes. And don't forget about her research regarding the dumping grounds. Those bodies found up I-85. That guy in the car could have something to do with that."

Mel and I were so in sync it was spooky.

"True." I swallowed. "I think Carol would be dismayed if we didn't at least point out the potential connection. And her fears could've easily stemmed from getting involved in all that." My fingers got moving over the keyboard. I searched the keywords "dumping grounds."

The door swung open, and Melanie's cousin popped her head inside. "Mel, you about done?"

Melanie leaped to her feet and checked her watch. "Sorry. I just meant to sit for a second. I'm coming now."

"Hey, Lyla. You okay? Awful about poor Carol."

I glanced up at the shorter woman, about ten years older than Melanie and myself. She had dishwater-brown hair and a round face with rosy cheeks. "Hey, Teresa. It's kinda hit me hard, you know?"

Teresa furrowed her brows, "I bet. It's crazy how you and Melanie found her."

"Terrifying, actually." Mel readjusted her apron.

"You're telling me. With some nutcase on the loose, I'm not letting my kids play in the backyard by themselves until they catch this guy. And I bet you my next two paychecks that when they catch the guy, he's one of those released from Fulton County Corrections because of overcrowding." Her brows furrowed even more tightly. "It just makes me sick. I'm even thinking about investing in one of those trained watchdogs and having Tommy keep his shotguns loaded."

"Oh." I didn't know what else to say.

She shivered and tapped her wrist where a watch would be. "I've gotta run."

Mel took the hint. "Two secs."

"Okay. Take care, Lyla."

The door closed.

"She doesn't know about the suitcase or any of the specifics. I found myself choking over the words and couldn't share it." Melanie moved to the door. "I guess we better decide if we're going to let the others in on the gritty details. Maybe we should call an emergency meeting of the Jane Does."

"Yeah, maybe. But I'm not sure the police would want us to share everything. The journalist kept the specifics out of the paper."

"I hadn't thought of that. They should've said something. Besides, if the club keeps it quiet, it shouldn't pose a problem to the investigation."

"Have you spoken to anyone in the group?"

She shook her head. "See ya. Let me know what else you find."

Chapter Seven

I'd just hit "Save" when Uncle Calvin came in. I'd collated all the documents Carol had shared, plus a few more detailed reports, and compiled them into one file. It surprised me, the amount of information the authorities were releasing to the public, complete with images and old police reports. The call for help from the Georgia Bureau of Investigation, asking the general public to identify the victims of the dumping grounds, told me resources were scarce. No wonder since some of the cases spanned years. The victims were found a short drive from Sweet Mountain. A plea was on a local news Facebook page entitled, "Do You Know This Jane Doe?" And I applauded the GBI's efforts to seek help in the identification process. Using the public could prove advantageous.

I set my tablet on the desk as my uncle made himself a cup of coffee.

"How was it after I left?"

I shrugged. "It was fine. Hopefully, I won't be at home for long." I gently shook the paper bag. "The perks are pretty great. I have two chocolate croissants. Want one?"

He waved off my offer; his mannerisms were remarkably similar to Mother's. He and Mother favored each other considerably. He had the same-shaped emerald eyes that shone like gemstones, big round orbs that reminded me of those paintings of big-eyed dolls. I'd never known my maternal side of the family other than my much-younger aunt Elizabeth, born when Mother and Calvin were teenagers, my grandmother's only child with her second husband. I'd only seen my grandmother on major holidays. It'd been obvious she hadn't cared much for children. The only thing I had from my late grandmother was a custom necklace she'd had made for me. She'd had one made for Ellen as well, and had given them to us one Christmas when we were very young, about a year before she passed away.

"You never told me how the meeting went in Atlanta."

"We got the job. It'll mean some travel, but it's well worth it."

"That's terrific." I tried to sound upbeat. Great news for the company was always welcome.

Calvin nodded. "Sit down for a minute, Lyla." He stirred the creamer into his coffee, and I began to get butterflies when he wouldn't meet my gaze. "I've been in touch with Chief Daniels already this morning."

Chief Daniels sounds so formal, I thought.

"They're planning to perform an autopsy on the victim."

The victim. A lump formed in my throat.

"Don't worry. There wasn't any evidence recovered from your house other than the body. There are a lot of prints on the suitcase. They're running what they can through the database." He shrugged as if the process was futile. "Your alibi and timeline check out."

"My alibi?" I mumbled numbly. Of course, they'd need to check my alibi. Being completely caught up in the tragedy of the event, I'd neglected to see how it all appeared to the police. I willed my brain to catch up.

"It's standard procedure."

I nodded. "Yes, I understand. It just sounds strange to hear it out loud in regard to me."

"Understandable." He cleared his throat.

My pulse quickened. "What?"

"You will be questioned again about Melanie."

I squinted at him, struggling to process what he was explaining.

"There's some discrepancy with her timeline." He shook his head. "I don't have all the details, and mind you the chief only gave me a heads-up out of professional curtesy. To protect you, I believe."

"Hold on." I waved my hands in a warding-off motion. "What are you telling me?"

"Don't withhold information. Not even for your friend. I'm not saying I believe Melanie had anything to do with Carol's death. I'm just saying—"

"Whoa! Mel was out of town when the bag was delivered."

"Her plane got in the morning before."

"That can't be! She took a cab from the airport to my house." *Didn't she?*

"I'm afraid not. Not all her movements are accounted for, but on this we're certain. There was no mix-up. Her departure from the plane is recorded.

I raised my eyebrows. "How?" Hartsfield was ginormous, and I had a hard time believing they could track Melanie in the masses.

Calvin nodded as the corner of his mouth turned up. "She's on tape arguing with the flight attendant for ten minutes, and it's time stamped."

I could imagine that clearly. When Mel got worked up, she tended to gesticulate wildly. Her explosive personality lent itself to making a scene. "Okay." I racked my brain to try to unravel the mystery as to why Mel would withhold that information from me and where she'd gone after leaving the airport.

"They're searching footage to see if they were able to make a positive ID on Mrs. Timms and see if she may have crossed paths with Melanie. Anyone could've dropped her car off at the parking lot."

And by "anyone," I took that to mean the killer. "They'll talk to Mel again. Maybe she was just thrown by discovering Carol, and left something out." *But why would she neglect to confide in me?* "Did you speak with the judge?"

Calvin shook his head. "Are you sure Melanie didn't tell you more? You aren't keeping anything from me out of loyalty, right?'

I swallowed. "No. I'm telling you there is some mix-up. Mel will straighten it out. I'm sure there's a reasonable explanation."

"Let's hope so. What worries me is why someone left her outside your door. Have you thought any more about her passenger and perhaps recalled more?"

"I've thought of little else." I rubbed between my neck and shoulder. "But no, nothing more has come to mind concerning the identity of the person. And that person certainly wasn't Melanie."

"I'm not saying it was. I've known Melanie all her life. I don't believe she's involved. All I'm cautioning is for neither one of you to hide anything. I'm sure the judge will put pressure on the police force to work speedily." He sipped from his mug. "He obviously believes someone abducted her."

I nodded. "Did Quinn mention anything else?"

"They're running a multitude of leads at this point. One of special interest was an inheritance Carol was to receive. Money is a powerful motivator for murder."

"An inheritance? From?"

Calvin shook his head. "I don't know."

"So," I said, studying him, "the abduction could have something to do with money? Was there a ransom call?"

"I don't have the answers to those questions. I highly doubt there was a ransom call. The police would've been prepared for the discovery then."

I fiddled with my hands in my lap as I digested this new information.

"When you arrived home, are you sure you didn't see anything out of the ordinary before you went inside?"

"Other than Kevin and Ellen, you mean?" I wrinkled my nose in distaste. "I certainly didn't spot anyone skulking around my house when I got home, but I'll admit, after being blindsided by those two, I was preoccupied. I would've checked the luggage tag if I hadn't been."

Calvin scratched his chin. "Anything else? Anything at all that could be helpful."

I considered. "Oh—wait!" I had missed something. "Val." I sat forward. "She came by and dropped off a housewarming gift for them. I was furious with her for not giving me a heads-up. She had ample time while I was at her house for our meeting. Then, when Kevin approached me, I forgot all about it. Maybe she saw something."

"This would be the girl adopted by the Heinz family?"

I nodded. "Valerie Heinz."

Val had been almost ten when she joined the Heinz family. The circumstances surrounding her adoption had been kept sealed. All we knew was that she'd lost her parents in some tragic accident, and the Heinzes, a couple up in age and without children of their own, had adopted her. It'd taken her a while to settle in here. Once she did, she'd become Miss Popularity.

"Make sure to mention that to Officer Taylor when he follows up with you."

"Okay. Did Quinn ask about me?"

Calvin raised his brows. "Have you begun seeing each other again?"

"No. Forget it." I lifted my hand, closed my eyes, and shook my head. "Quinn doesn't owe me anything. Never mind. I'll be sure to mention Val to Taylor." I pasted on a smile.

He scratched his chin. "If you want to take some time off, it's okay with me. I could call the temp agency and have them send someone over."

"You're not trying to get rid of me, are you?" I couldn't hide the concern in my tone. "I'm fine, truly. Plus, I'd hoped that once I proved myself, you might consider making me a more vital part of the business." I didn't say "partner," but had dreamed it. "I could even go back to school. I've been thinking about it," I said, pleading my case.

"No, I'm not getting rid of you. I've loved having you here, and you do a fantastic job. It's just that Frances worries."

At the mention of Mother, I relaxed.

"Before, I could reason with her. Now, with the gruesomeness of this case and your proximity to it—well, it's a lot."

"But it has nothing to do with my job here. Our cases aren't anything of the sort." I spoke the truth.

We handled missing persons, divorce investigations, child support, and background checks, plus corporate fraud investigations and workers comp. Sure, I'd imagined that once I learned the ropes, we'd expand to cases like the dumping grounds.

"I know you're right. And I'm not telling you what to do or how to live your life. I'm just saying you have options. You're young, and you could choose another line of work—something that doesn't stress you out as much." Ah, stress—my mother's favorite word when speaking to me about my choices.

"May I speak?" I'd prepared for this moment, my carefully rehearsed diatribe at the ready.

"Of course."

"Thank you. You know my feelings and Mother's differ. She's concerned about me not being able to handle this line of work, mainly because she finds it revolting. But honestly, whether I work here or not isn't going to change my goals."

I allowed a moment of silence to stretch between us. He needed to give my words some consideration for them to carry weight.

"I respect your decency in wanting to honor your sister's wishes and that you care about me. But these cases"—I tapped the open tablet with my index finger—"are what gets my blood pumping. I need to understand things—to find the answers to riddles laid out here. These people deserve to have their identity restored."

"Honey, I'm your advocate. I told Franny that despite your air of frivolity, you're an intelligent young woman with a promising career ahead of her." He perched on the edge of my desk. "I understand the need for answers—to close cases. Believe me. And maybe one day, we'll have extra resources to offer pro bono services or even manage to get on the payroll with the state."

Music to my ears, and my face must have shown my feeling, because he pointed his finger at me and made direct eye contact. He softened his tone and nodded toward the tablet.

"Digging into these types of cases shines a great big spotlight on the one holding the shovel. Those responsible won't like it."

I swallowed hard and looked him square in the face. "It's a scary world. I get what you're saying. I'm fully aware of the risks. I'll be careful. Now, allow me to be frank. If you decide to let me go, that won't halt my desire to work in this field."

He shook his head and defensively lifted his hands as he stood. "Okay, okay. You're right. The world is full of horrors. How does the quote go? *'Hell is empty, and all the devils are here'*?"

I nodded.

"I suppose I held out hope that in Sweet Mountain we'd effectively kept the demons at bay. It's your life and your decision, and I won't get in your way." He stretched. "You're a grown woman and should be allowed to make your own decisions. But promise me you'll be extra cautious and on alert at all times. Vigilance is the key until the perp is apprehended."

"That I can promise." I held out my hand, and he took it. "And I'll also promise to keep the frills to a minimum. No pink poufs or lacy tutus will grace the interior of this office. Ever."

He let out a deep belly laugh that coaxed a grin from me as he shook my hand. "You are more like your mother than you know, kid."

Ouch.

Chapter Eight

When the police car pulled up in front of the building, I ignorantly assumed they were coming to talk to me. My heart hammered against my chest when I saw Mel coming out of Smart Cookie with Officer Taylor. My chair flew backward as I leaped to my feet and raced out the door. "What's going on?"

"Miss Moody, please take a step back."

Melanie had a bewildered expression on her face, and I searched her eyes. "This is all a stupid misunderstanding. Don't worry. I'm just going down to the station to straighten this mess out."

"Mess? What mess?" *God, I knew what mess.* The discrepancy with her alibi.

Mel's eyes were wide as she shook her head. "It's stupid. I'm an idiot. And Lyla, I don't know how," she whispered, "but he said the bag *is* mine."

Her words literally knocked the wind out of me.

The crowd around the Smart Cookie grew. Teresa had her hands on her hips. "This is outrageous. Don't say a word, Melanie, until I call you a lawyer."

Melanie's face reddened as gasps went up from the crowd.

Officer Taylor opened the back door, and Melanie willingly slid onto the seat. "Now I need everyone to just back up!" he said as he moved around the car.

"I'm coming with her. Does she need a lawyer?" I asked.

"Not if she tells us the truth, and I would advise you"—he pointed at me—"to stay put. I'll be in touch when we want to speak to you again."

Uncle Calvin stood behind me and encouraged me to heed the officer's advice. Trusting him and not wanting to make matters worse for Mel, I agreed. But I glared furiously as he climbed into the front seat, hit the siren a couple of short times, and people cleared out of his way.

* * *

As I washed my hands, I stared at myself in the mirror of the small powder room and frowned at my appearance. I could hear my mother's voice: *"Lyla, honey, you look pale. A little lipstick will help."* I liberally applied rose-colored lipstick, and, like magic, my eyes looked brighter and my face appeared more refreshed. There was no denying it. Mother was absolutely correct. A pop of color could be a girl's best friend.

"Lyla!" Daddy's commanding baritone voice made me jump. Daddy was standing in front of my desk, next to Calvin, when I emerged from the powder room. My father stood an inch or two taller than Calvin but weighed less. Daddy was fairer than me, but not nearly as fair-skinned as Gran. He wore brown slacks that matched the shade of what hair he had left, and a button-down green shirt—his usual attire for work.

Now I prided myself on my resolve and my ability to face controversy with my head held high. I was an independent woman. But the second I saw my daddy, my eyes welled up with tears. I'd not mourned my friend Carol appropriately yet, and now Mel had been taken in for questioning. He opened his arms to me, and I went in for a hug. Being enveloped in my father's arms caused the dam to break, and I sobbed openly.

"I'll give you two a minute. Holler if you need me. I'll be in my office," Uncle Calvin said, and a moment later, we heard his office door click shut.

"My little Lylabug. You've experienced a great shock." Daddy patted my back, and I rested my head on his chest, taking a couple of deep, shuddering breaths. He smelled of Irish Spring soap and faintly of aftershave. "I'm here. I'm sorry I didn't get home before you went to bed last night. Your mother neglected to call me until late, and I should have checked one of your grandmother's three voicemails."

I sniffed and turned to pull a couple of tissues from the box of Puffs on my desk. I dabbed the tissues under my eyes. "I'm okay." I would be okay. "Mel—"

"Calvin told me. Don't worry. I'm perturbed with him, and you should have waited until I called William before you spoke with the police." Daddy shook his head as if concerned for my ability to make a sound judgment call. "It never hurts to have representation when the police are involved. Especially when the body was found in your townhouse."

"Calvin knows what he's doing. There was really no need for an attorney. I've not been accused of anything. They're still in the process of building a case, which is why my cooperation is so important. And you're right. Surely this thing with Mel is nothing."

Daddy put his hand on my shoulder and leaned down. His nearly gray eyes fixed on my face. "Your mother said the woman was folded up inside a suitcase. You can't be emotionally sound after witnessing your friend in such a condition."

I had a flashback, Carol's limbs were crumpled up inside that bag. I blinked to hold back more tears.

"We should sit down together. I can call and have Dr. Peters cover my patients."

I wiped my nose. "That won't be necessary."

He tilted his head and glanced down his nose at me disapprovingly. "That isn't a wise decision. And we understand how important our decision making is."

"Yes, Daddy. I haven't forgotten."

He sure knew how to ignite a flame of irritation in me.

I folded my arms.

"Good. We also need to have a serious conversation about what comes next."

I cleared my throat. "Meaning?"

Daddy's phone chirped. He frowned when he read the text, and then pocketed the phone. "Meaning, this isn't going to go away so easily. It's going to make headlines. The press will be involved. I'll call Quinn and see what he's doing to get a handle on rumors and protecting your identity. I'll inquire about Melanie as well." Daddy appeared confident he would be able to control the narrative and drive the investigation. Being a man accustomed to others following him drove this thought process. He'd never been a part of a criminal investigation before, and I hated to tell him he had no pull when it came to the law or the press.

"Later, when the perpetrator is apprehended, you'll be subjected to a trial. Testifying in open court unless a deal is made." He made a valid point. I hadn't even thought that far. "It's going to be difficult, and it'll put your mother through hell."

My tears dried up as anger began to build. "Well, it doesn't matter what I'll be subjected to or how Mother feels. I'll do what

I have to. Carol is the victim here, Daddy, not me—and certainly not Mother."

"There isn't anything we can do for that poor girl now, and it might be best for everyone if this case goes away quietly."

I took a step backward and sucked in a breath.

Daddy softened his tone, "Lylabug."

"Are you that self-absorbed? Mother's fear that this will somehow create a scandal around the Moody name is what concerns you the most? God, Daddy, how shallow."

The phone rang, saving me from more interaction that was swiftly speeding downhill. I cleared my throat as I walked around the desk, moving my tablet aside. "Thank you for coming by and checking on me, but you don't have to worry about me."

I answered the phone. "Cousins Investigative Services. Hold, please."

Daddy spied the dumping ground pdf. My tablet must've opened via facial recognition when I'd moved it. I immediately flipped it over.

"Lyla." The man wasn't the least bit bothered by my rant. "It isn't about a scandal. Obsessive tendencies don't just disappear. They're a constant struggle."

Sometimes having a shrink for a father got old. "If you don't mind, I'm working."

Daddy raised his brows and pierced me with his stern gaze.

The phone rang again. "Cousins Investigative Services," I said cheerily.

"I need to speak to Calvin." I recognized that voice.

"Will you hold, please?"

"No, I won't. Put the man on now!" Judge Timms bellowed.

"One moment." I put him on hold, pressed the intercom button, and asked Calvin if he'd take the call, before I transferred it back to his office. I was glad to have something to do.

"Can we talk about this later?" I fisted the tissue and squared my shoulders, willing my steadfastness into place.

"Yes. Tonight. I'll be home before nine. I strongly insist we talk about all of this. Will you commit to a conversation then?" Daddy would stand there all day if I didn't.

"Yes, sir."

Chapter Nine

The Jane Does all sat in my parents' family room. The timing had worked out because Mother and Gran were at their monthly Magnolia Ladies Society meeting. I had laid out a few reheated tapas. No one was particularly hungry, and most of the food went untouched except for the white-chocolate cookies Mel brought.

When she'd showed up, I'd squeezed her until she gave a squeak of protest. I knew she wasn't being detained; I'd pestered the front desk hourly until I received word Mel had concluded her interview. But I worried she wouldn't feel like attending our meeting after her ordeal. Not that I blamed her. The others began arriving before she could get into what had transpired at the police department.

Patsy, now on her third cookie, wiped the crumbs from her mouth. "I'm going to stop wearing gloss. Everything I eat sticks to my lips." She glanced around. "Sorry. I didn't mean to interrupt you, Melanie. I'm a stress eater. Please, continue."

"It's okay." Mel finished giving everyone the lowdown on what the papers had left out. Everyone wanted to hear from her, since she'd just been taken in for questioning. Mel was handling it like a champ.

"Let me get this straight." Val resituated herself on the sofa to my left. "Someone murdered our Carol and stuffed her in a suitcase, then left her on Lyla's front stoop?"

Melanie and I both nodded.

Val's deep-blue eyes were wide. "And you thought it wasn't yours, Mel, but it is."

"Yes." Melanie chewed on her bottom lip. "Someone put a sticker over the luggage tag and wrote Carol's name. And the bag had been pretty beat up, so I didn't recognize it."

"Okay." Patsy said slowly. "How is that possible if your luggage was lost."

Melanie lifted her shoulders. "I have no idea. The police said it was delivered the day before Lyla found it. But my alibi and security footage prove I wasn't there when it was delivered."

All eyes turned to me. "I have no idea how to explain the delivery discrepancy because I can positively say that it was not delivered to me until the day I found it."

"It's completely unfathomable." Amelia kept shaking her head.

"We know." Mel and I said in unison.

"Airlines make mistakes all the time," I added.

"They do. But what about the delivery scan from the airline? Was there a note? A plane ticket? Any evidence to either where she was going or where she'd been? Or whom she'd been with?" Val shot rapid-fire questions in my direction.

"The scan is wrong. It has to be. And as to the note, not that I found." I folded my legs underneath me.

"That makes no sense at all." Val kept shaking her head as if trying to make her brain find a pattern. "None." She focused on Mel. "And the police took you in for additional questioning because of the bag?"

"Surely they can't truly believe you were responsible." Amelia sounded deeply concerned.

"That and…" Mel rubbed her forehead. "Listen, y'all. I made a colossal mistake. I . . . I actually got in the day before I showed up to pick up my keys from Lyla. The day the say the suitcase was delivered."

I held my breath as Melanie stared me straight in the face. "I feel like a total fool. I ran into Tim."

"Tim as in—"

She nodded and blew out a breath. "As in the SOB who cheated on me. The man I divorced for ruining my life." Mel hung her head. "He was coming down the terminal when I was beside myself in tears. I could blame it on lack of sleep, but I won't. I went back to his place. I snuck out the next morning, reeking of alcohol. I couldn't tell you." She covered her flushed face with her hands. "I'm so embarrassed."

I raced across the room and went to my knees in front of my friend, hugging her tight. "We all make mistakes."

"I . . . I didn't think. And then Carol was there and—"

I rubbed her back. "It's okay. I'm sure now that the police know where you were, it'll be fine."

She nodded, sat up, and wiped her face. "They said they'd talk to Tim to corroborate my account."

Amelia handed her a tissue from the box on the end table beside her. "Sure, honey. What you did wasn't a crime."

Nods went around in unison.

"Thanks, y'all."

A thought occurred to me as I retook my seat. "Val, did Carol mention anything to you about an inheritance?"

Val stared at the ceiling for a moment, and then her eyes narrowed as she faced me. "Yes. It slipped my mind with everything. Um, a distant grandparent, I think, passed away. I think it was quite a lot."

"She had bought a car without her husband's knowledge. I mean, surely she knew he'd find out."

Val nodded. "Maybe the money was how she planned on starting over somewhere, and she just didn't care."

"That's what I was thinking too. It explains why her car was found at the airport parking lot." I let out a long sigh. "The rest of it doesn't make any sense, though."

"When has any murder made logical sense?" Amelia crossed her legs and shifted in her seat.

"I suppose that's the cruel genius of such a crime. Until the police figure out the subtle clues, we'll never have answers." Val rubbed her forehead.

"Someone must've left clues," Melanie said from Dad's favorite leather Crate and Barrel armchair by the fireplace; she wrapped her arms around herself. "Ergo, they wanted recognition. The suitcase could be a clue."

Patsy took a sip of coffee. "It's too awful to be real. Never in a million years would I believe this could happen here. Sweet Mountain has the lowest crime rate in the state! It's why I never moved away and wanted to raise my family here."

Amelia's dark gaze grew fierce, and she dropped the cookie she held into her napkin. "The police better be doing their jobs. I have every intention to force their hand, if necessary. My brother said they should have a profiler on staff. It's standard in weird cases like these. This case isn't a hit-and-run or another form of manslaughter. Time is precious. Heaven help us if we have a serial killer among us." She turned toward me. "I know it's terrifying, but we need to know why they chose your house. Out of all the places they could have left her, why your place?"

I held my hands out. "I wish I knew. The only thing I can presume is they believe I'm the only witness—" Chills ran up my spine. "What if the killer was watching me when I brought the suitcase inside?"

Mel and I shared a frightful glance as Mel said, "At least we know the police are being thorough. I hate the humiliation I endured today, but for Carol, I'd do it again."

"Can we please just stop! Please." Patsy's bottom lip quivered.

We all settled into silence for a few long moments. The crackles in the fireplace seemed to increase in volume over Patsy's sniffles. The flicker of the firelight danced on the sandstone-colored Persian rug. The warmth coming from the fire did nothing to break the chill in the room. Losing our fellow Jane Doe member the way we had left not only Melanie and me but also the others with a sense of instability. My guests starred at the flames—the spirit of foreboding palpable in the room. You never realize how fragile life is until your perfect little safety bubble is pierced.

"I can't believe she's gone. I kept picking up the phone today to call her, and had to stop myself." Val looked at her hands clasped in her lap. "She's always been there. Always. From the day I started middle school here. I could always count on Carol. Why her?" She swiped a hand across her cheek.

I reached out and took her hand. "I know you loved her." My throat felt thick as I swallowed.

"The police are still investigating. It's early." Patsy's voice quivered. "I'm not skeptical about the prowess of our police department like Amelia is. No offense, Amelia, but you haven't been here long enough to understand that although our law enforcement may move at a different pace or operate differently from what you're accustomed to, they've kept our town safe all these years. They'll restore order. I'm sure of it."

"I didn't mean to offend. I just care," Amelia said softly.

"We all know where your heart is. And you have every right to voice both your opinions and concerns and expect to be heard. That's the reason we're all here." I smiled at my friend.

"I didn't mean to be hateful, Amelia. Lyla's right. It's why we're here. I never dreamed of such a thing or believed we'd be discussing this. I knew Carol died, but not about the suitcase. God." Patsy's brown eyes were full of water as she pulled her blue cardigan tighter around herself. Her tight black curls bounced around her head as she shook it.

Amelia wrapped her arm around Patsy's shoulders. "You have nothing to apologize for. I'm angry because I spent maybe ten minutes with the officer when he came to my house. He didn't seem all that interested in what I had to say once I couldn't give him dates, times, and whereabouts. I debated heavily about telling him how the judge treated her at dinner."

"Did you?" Melanie leaned forward.

Amelia nodded. "I felt I had to in the interest of full disclosure. I wouldn't want anything to hinder the investigation. What about the man you saw her with, Lyla? Do the police know who he is or if he had anything to do with any of this?" She sounded pleased to get back on topic. Amelia was like me in that she despised unsolved cases.

"Not that they told me."

"What about Quinn? Has he spoken with you?" Val crossed her legs as I shook my head. "That surprises me. I can't believe he hasn't sat down with you. If for nothing but to check on how you're dealing with all of this."

"Well, he hasn't."

"Hmm. Lyla and our chief of police go way back." Val explained to Amelia.

"It sounds like everyone in this town goes way back." Amelia folded her arms.

"He has more important things he's working on, Val. He's an excellent chief of police. Our town is lucky he replaced that old windbag Marshall when he did. We can trust him to do his job." Patsy pulled a pillow into her lap and hugged it.

"I'm sure Patsy is right. Calvin believes the police can handle this case." I folded my arms.

Amelia looked skeptical but didn't comment.

"Well, I'll have a word with Quinn tomorrow. I'm going down to the station in the morning," Val announced. "Since I was in the vicinity, I'm required to make a statement. Y'all can't even begin to understand how horrible I feel. I could've talked some sense into Carol or done something to prevent this if I'd gotten to her earlier. Carol needed me, and I just went about my life. If only I'd been in touch with her a few days ago, who knows how differently this could have turned out?"

I reached out and squeezed her hand.

"Kevin's torn up too," Val whispered huskily.

"Why is Kevin so torn up?" Amelia wanted to know.

"He's Carol's stepbrother—or was when his dad was married to her mom. They grew up together." Explaining the connection to Amelia gave me a horrible sinking feeling in my stomach, and I felt bad I hadn't offered my condolences to him.

"Ellen's a wreck about it too, and not just for Kev." Val shifted on the sofa.

"Sure she is," Melanie grumbled.

Val dropped my hand, and her tone grew stronger. "I've known Ellen as long as I have the rest of you. Except for Amelia, that is. And just because you and Lyla don't get along with her doesn't mean she and I can't be friends, Melanie."

I waved my hand. "Of course not. It's fine. At this point, I couldn't care less about Ellen and Kevin."

"Under the circumstances, it would be puerile if you did."

I agreed with Val.

"Ellen told me this morning she and Kevin are going to the police department around the same time as me."

The silence stretched out another long minute.

Amelia leaned forward. "Has anyone else wondered if this has something to do with the dumping grounds?"

"Let's be careful." Val sat up straighter. "If we're wrong, and what happened to Carol hasn't anything to do with that, it might stall the investigation by forcing the limited resources this tiny town has down a wild goose chase."

Melanie sat forward. "We won't make a fuss until we have something solid. Carol began digging into the deaths of I-85, and now she's gone. What if she found out something? What if they killed her for discovering the identity of the Jane she mentioned to Amelia? Lyla has access to resources. She'll be able to help, right, Lyla?"

Amelia nodded eagerly. "That could be good."

I sat forward and nodded. "Yeah. As long as I don't interfere with the investigation, I could do some digging. That e-mail is the last any of us heard from her. Clearly, she was struggling with what she found, to the point she reached out for help." My gaze panned the room. "This is personal," I swallowed, "not just because she was our friend and some abhorrent creature took her from us but also because whoever is responsible had the audacity to deliver our precious friend to my front stoop."

"And in *my* bag."

"Right, and they somehow managed to get their hands on Mel's suitcase. They must've known hers was missing and that Melanie was on vacation. I can't explain how they got their hands on it or why'd they be attempting to frame her, but I plan on finding out. I propose we use our club meetings to discuss my findings and see what we can do to help with the investigation."

Mel and Amelia both nodded eagerly.

Patsy appeared apprehensive. "I don't know."

Val sighed. "I understand the need to do something. I do. But do you honestly believe the two cases are linked? Carol's murder and her Jane Doe?"

I lifted my shoulders. "It's possible. We won't know until we follow the trail and see where it leads us. I get Val's concerns. On the surface, it just doesn't jive. In the Jane Doe cases, all the victims were found dumped on backroads off I-85. And a lot of them have been there for several years, most a decade or more. Carol's identity isn't in question. No one dumped her up I-85, and she was found dead"—I motioned to myself—"in my house."

"Right," Val nodded. "It looks bad and will look even worse if you or Melanie are caught poking around."

"What are you saying? That Lyla or I had something to do with Carol's murder?" Melanie sounded aghast.

"She just said it looks bad, Mel." I shook my head. "And it does."

Val looked down and scratched her forehead. "I'm not accusing you or Lyla of anything. I'm simply stressing caution. And for us to stay out of the realm of fantasy. This isn't a novel, and Carol isn't just any victim."

Amelia looked abashed. She kept shaking her head in small movements as she stared at the fireplace.

"I agree with Val." Patsy rose and checked her watch as she shifted from foot to foot. "Let's let the police handle it. Trust them to keep us safe like we have all these years."

"They didn't keep Carol safe . . ." Amelia mumbled under her breath.

Patsy seemed to ignore her. "We all have enough to deal with, mourning our dear friend. And maybe this little group isn't the right fit for me anymore. Now that I have kids, it just seems too morbid."

"Patsy, don't say that. You're one of us." Melanie slid to her feet and hugged Patsy.

Emotions were running high. Everyone was scared and hurt.

"I don't know." She shook her head and leaned against Mel's shoulder. "I just don't know anymore." She gave Mel a pat and pulled out of the hug. "I need to get out of here. I have to get home to the kids anyway." She started down the hall. "I'll let myself out."

I rose. "Patsy, wait."

Val reached out and touched my arm. "Just let her go. She's upset like the rest of us."

Before I could even acknowledge Val's words, the front door closed. "Maybe we should all call it a night."

Amelia stood. Her conflicted expression troubled me.

"I appreciate y'all coming out here. We've all suffered a terrible tragedy. Our friend had a good heart and didn't deserve what happened to her."

Melanie sidled up next to me. "And we didn't deserve to find her the way we did. Like Lyla said, whoever was responsible had to know I was on vacation and that my luggage went missing." That caused silence to stretch throughout the room. "In most cases, victims know and trust their killers. I wonder if it's someone we know."

Val stared at Mel, squinting her eyes. "Are you saying one of us is guilty?" Val sounded appalled. "*Please*. Melanie, you posted a status about the airline losing your luggage on Facebook. Even if you're right, who knows how many people saw it? There's no way of tracking something like that." Val sounded as exhausted as I felt.

"I wasn't pointing the finger at anyone here." Mel's cheeks reddened. "I've had a long day and spent several hours at the police station. I was just talking through it like we do with our other cases."

"For the second time, this isn't one of our cases." Val's eyes welled up with tears. "This is Carol."

Melanie tucked one of her curls behind her ear as if attempting to hide the blush in her cheeks. I squeezed her hand. We were all out of sorts.

Val sniffed. "I'm the one who lost my best friend here."

Melanie stuttered over an apology.

I rushed to her aid. "Listen, let's all step back and take some time. We'll reconvene when we have more information. Agreed?"

"Agreed," everyone said in unison.

"I'll walk y'all out."

Chapter Ten

I made myself a cup of coffee and sat outside on the screened-in back porch. The meeting had resulted in nothing but frazzling my nerves further and causing dissension within the club. I didn't want to consider the ramifications to our friendships if something wasn't done swiftly. With crime being mostly nonexistent in our small town, Amelia had made me wonder if our police department was up to the task. Carol's husband, the judge, would be insistent they close the case. Perhaps, with his added pressure, the police would apprehend this guy—and fast.

While I waited for the folks to get home, another point of stress, I read more of the dumping grounds document.

The disclaimer: This story contains graphic images and details.

As I mentally prepared myself, I pulled the chunky, knitted light-blue blanket over my legs and allowed the porch swing to gently sway. I stared out over the herb garden, edged in boxwoods and illuminated by the strung outdoor lighting. Mother's parsley, sage, rosemary, mint, and lavender flourished this time of year. I sipped from the mug and glanced back down.

To date, thirty women have been discovered along the road you drive every day. The area "the dumping grounds" stretches nearly 200 miles along Interstate 85 in Georgia. Most victims were found in the northern Georgia section of I-85, where vegetation and hills in the rural areas hide the Jane Does. The victims' ages range from a few years old to the late sixties. From the youngest to the oldest, all were dumped and forgotten. The Janes are all someone's daughter, possibly someone's wife and mother, who were cast away to hide their unspeakable endings.

I took another sip from the mug and flipped to the next screen.

Do You Know This Jane?

A female was found in Cam County, a mile off I-85, where a car can easily disappear around a bend thick with brush in this dense countryside. The Georgia Bureau of Investigation had only a few items to identify the victim: a tattered, faded orange and blue scarf, a small angel necklace, and an antique spoon ring. Her identity became lost with each passing year of her exposure to the elements. She hasn't a name, a face, fingerprints, or a voice. She is mere bones. For now, she is Jane Doe.

For Special Agent Brad Jones, her story has just begun. The GBI agent is determined to unravel the mystery behind her life and tragic death. To him, the Jane Does found in the dumping grounds have become his total focus. To him, they'll never be forgotten.

But he needs your help.

My phone rang, and I jumped before glancing to see it was nearly nine and my uncle was calling. "Hey, Uncle Calvin, what's up?"

"I took the meeting with Judge David Timms."

"Not surprising. He isn't the type of man accustomed to hearing the word 'no' often." I took another sip of coffee. "How'd that go?"

"As one would expect. The judge is distraught and angry. He arranged for him and me to sit down with the chief, and there he presented the letter his wife received from her late grandfather's lawyer, informing her she, along with Kevin Richards, was to inherit his estate worth approximately seven hundred thousand dollars."

"Wow."

"Apparently she and Kevin had several heated discussions regarding his percentage of the inheritance. Judge Timms claims Kevin attempted to manipulate Carol, using her mental instability against her, to sign over more than the ten percent he was to receive on the sale of the property."

I froze, holding the mug midway to my mouth. "Carol was left ninety percent to his ten?"

"According to the documents I saw."

"Is he accusing Kevin of being involved?" I took another sip from the mug.

"He's presenting everything and letting me and the police sort through it."

"Melanie was really shaken up by her interview. At least it's over—her part, I mean."

"I'm not so sure."

I swallowed. "Meaning?"

"Apparently her ex-husband can't confirm the exact time she left his house. According to him, she borrowed his truck to make a run to the liquor store around two and took longer than it should have to return. Then they partied and he passed out."

"That jerk! He knows darn well Mel couldn't have done anything like this. Well, someone can check the cameras at the liquor store or speak with the clerk." Poor Melanie. Like she needed more humiliation.

"Have you received any strange texts or calls? Has any member of your book club?"

I shivered. "I haven't, and I just met with the group and no one mentioned anything. Why?"

"Well, that's good. Carol had been receiving calls in the middle of the night from an unknown number. The judge said he overheard her mention Jane Doe, and then sobbing from the other room after taking a call in the middle of the night."

My stomach lurched.

"Do the police think the murder has to do with our club? And perhaps that's why I received the suitcase—because I'm a member?" My thoughts went to the man in the car again, and my breath hitched in my throat.

"This case could go so many different directions, Lyla. Carol had many secrets. And the police are going to chase down every single lead."

I ran a shaky hand through my hair and wondered how much our Carol had been dealing with.

A flash of camo man in the car swam across my vision. What if I'd nearly been face-to-face with a cold-blooded killer? The mug slipped from my fingers and shattered against the brick floor. Coffee splashed the edged of the blanket.

"Lyla!"

"I-I'm here. Just dropped a coffee cup." I stooped and began cleaning up the large porcelain fragments and placing them in the decorative trash can.

"Have you spoken with James?"

"No, he isn't home yet. Why?" I had an idea what he was referring to. Not that I would say. I'd have to give up Gran if I did.

"I'll let him speak with you first. We can talk about it after, if you want. One piece of advice: don't get worked up when he confides in you."

"Should I be worried?" *Because I am.*

"We're all worried."

That didn't bode well. The silence stretched for a few heartbeats.

"Be careful and don't go anywhere alone. Especially at night."

"I hear you. I'll be extra cautious." I went inside and opened the drawer where the hand towels were.

I finished wiping up the spill. "If this has to do with the club, then it makes sense one of us found her. And I'm the last one to have seen her alive—and with the mystery passenger." This had to have something to do with her Jane Doe. *Had to!*

"That's what the police need to find out. People do crazy things when they're afraid. The chief also told me your house has been cleared. I have your spare key."

I wrapped up the blanket and went through the kitchen to place it with the dry-cleaning items in the laundry room. The front door opened.

"So, it's okay for me to go home now?" I hoped so. I wouldn't live my life in fear. I'd be careful, but I wouldn't retreat to my bed and stay there.

"There's no rush. You go back when you're ready. Relax in that nice house for the weekend. Let your parents spoil you with food you can't afford and sleep in five-hundred-dollar sheets. I'll be at the office after lunch tomorrow. You can come by then and we can have a talk, or wait until Monday if you want. You won't be failing anyone if you rest this weekend."

"I'll come by tomorrow. See ya then."

"Up to you. If you change your mind, no worries. 'Night, kiddo."

"'Night."

Chapter Eleven

As I searched for the Shout stain remover, my mind swam with everything Calvin had told me about his meeting. I didn't believe in a million years Kevin had anything to do with Carol's murder. He could be an ass sometimes, and they may have argued, but he wasn't a killer. I wondered who called Carol and if she confided in anyone regarding the calls. More and more, I began to ask myself if this did, in fact, have to do with the dumping grounds. Or maybe I feared it did. The words from the article, "cast off" and "forgotten," chilled me to the bone. Could this—

"Lyla."

I screamed, and my arms flew to my head.

"My ears, child."

I let my head fall back. "Mother, you scared me half to death."

"I'm sorry. I called and called for you. What are you doing in the laundry room anyway?" Mother glanced around, making sure everything was in its proper place.

"I spilled coffee on the blanket. Where's Gran?"

Mother rushed over to the hamper containing the dry cleaning. "She had a headache and went to bed. Leave it. It'll go out with the dry cleaning."

"I'm sorry about the blanket." Fatigue overtook me. The events of the day had taken their toll, and I needed to be alone to process the information I'd been given. "Gran has the right idea." I left the room and began climbing the stairs.

"Where are you going? Your father said the three of us were to have a conversation." She glanced at her watch. "He should be home any minute."

I'd gotten so caught up in my own head after my conversation with Calvin, the commitment had slipped my mind completely. Now, it didn't seem all that important, but I *needed* to know what happened to my friend. The grandfather clock in the foyer began to chime, and in walked my daddy.

I sighed, turned, and started back down the stairs. Daddy greeted Mother with a kiss on the cheek.

She took his jacket and briefcase from him. "James, you and Lyla go on in the family room. I'll put your things away. Have you had dinner?"

"Yes. I had Chinese delivered to the office. I'd love a scotch, though."

Mother nodded and turned to me. "Lyla, would you like a glass of wine?"

"Please." I followed Daddy into the family room.

I sat on the edge of the sofa. My father took up residence in his favorite chair and crossed his right leg over his left. Moments later, Mother handed him a glass filled with amber liquid. He thanked her.

"How was your day?" I asked Daddy as Mother handed me a glass of red wine and I thanked her.

"You're welcome, dear," she replied.

"My day was quite eventful. One of my patients had a psychotic episode, and if that wasn't enough, I received a visit from the police this afternoon."

I feigned surprise.

"Mrs. Timms had recently become a patient of mine," he said smoothly, and I widened my eyes. The police would certainly find out he'd been treating Carol.

Mother sat at the end of the sofa and turned on the lamp beside her. "Why would they want to speak to you?"

"Standard procedure. The woman died under unusual circumstances. I was her doctor, and Carol kept her treatment from her husband." Daddy took a long, deep sip. "On going through their records, he saw the insurance statement."

"Is that so?"

He inclined his head. "It is. And her husband was unaware she'd begun seeing me, which, as you can imagine, didn't go over well."

"Why?" Mother didn't look happy.

"The judge is a controlling type of man. He wouldn't be thrilled with Carol discussing anything outside the marriage," I informed my mother. I watched my father closely. "Her struggles with paranoia and paralyzing fear would be an embarrassment to him and his image."

My father studied me in return, and I pressed on. "We all worried Carol had begun an unhealthy relationship." Daddy's index finger twitched—a slight movement I happened to catch.

Carol must have mentioned whoever had her sobbing late at night.

"If she was having an affair, of course the relationship was unhealthy," Mother said.

"I'm not sure it was that type of relationship. Carol told Amelia she was frightened when she and the judge went over to the Kleins's house for dinner. The judge berated her right there at the dinner table. Called her awful names."

Mother's eyes widened. "Was she afraid of David?"

"Not that she told me. Amelia said she was definitely frightened of someone." Then I told them about the man I'd seen her with in the car that day.

Mother began shaking her head.

"I just feel so helpless, you know."

My father finished his scotch and placed the empty glass on the table beside him. "We have to accept the things we cannot change."

I nodded. "But there are some things we can affect. And some things shouldn't be tolerated. Carol was also digging into those cold cases up Interstate 85. That was the article you saw on my tablet this afternoon. She passed it along to me and the others in my club."

Mother shook her head. "That dead club should be dissolved. No wonder it's hard for you to find a nice young man to settle down with."

I ignored her comment. "I respect doctor–patient confidentiality, and I won't ask you to divulge anything. Could you at least confirm or deny if Carol mentioned anything about the cases to you?" I waited as my father ran his finger around the rim of the glass, staring at it as if mesmerized.

When he finally lifted his gaze to meet mine, I held my breath. He knew something. Something important. "I'm going to have to insist you don't involve yourself in any of those investigations. Dangerous sorts of people commit violent crimes such as those up I-85."

She'd told him something. And "insist" was the wrong word choice. "If you know anything, you should tell the police. Carol is gone, and as you well know, the police questioned Mel."

Mother gave a sharp intake of breath.

"They hauled her away in the police car right out in front of Smart Cookie."

"That's disgraceful! Her poor mother."

I threw my hands up. "What's her mother have to do with anything? They didn't question *her.*" I turned toward Daddy as my mother frowned. "And now there seems to be some discrepancy with Melanie's alibi. So if you know something that could help the police, you better tell them."

"Once the police provide me with a court order, I'll turn everything over. I have my reputation and the trust of my other patients to consider." My father got up and left the room.

"My word, I just don't know how in the world my own daughter could've turned out like this." Mother took a long, deep sip of wine; her brows were knitted together in worry. "It's terrifying. It's almost as if you're looking for trouble."

I massaged my forehead with my thumb and index finger, thinking, *I do not have the patience for this!*

"My friends' daughters who are your age are looking into preschools and potty training."

"Frances, this isn't the time." Daddy sat back down with a fresh drink.

"It is the time, James. Look what she's become."

I cleared my throat. "I know both of you are concerned for me. I appreciate y'all wanting to look out for me—I do. But it's my life, and just because in your eyes I'm a delicate female doesn't mean I'm unable to handle situations. Contrary to your way of thinking, women are capable of a great many things besides homemaking and child-rearing."

"Lyla, I believe we know a little bit more about life than you do. We were here when you had your little"—Mother lowered her tone—"setback. And we certainly don't need a lecture in existentialism." Mother made a distasteful face.

"I think you do." I glanced from Mother to Daddy. *They don't even know me.* Time to let them see the woman I'd become through the trials I'd lived through.

"I'm fine, Mother. I enjoy working for Uncle Calvin. My interest in solving crimes isn't going anywhere. Can I still become obsessive? Sure, sometimes. So can everyone else who's passionate about their career choices." I gave my father a pointed stare. "You dedicated your life to mental illness. It was your calling. This is mine."

"Honey, this scares us. We just want you to be happy." Mother scooted closer to me. "Isn't it possible the reason you haven't found the right man and settled down is because of this obsession with dead people? It's not normal. How are you ever going to raise a family with all those books and articles about murder and gore lying around the house?"

She isn't hearing me. I took another sip of wine, really wishing I could gulp down the entire contents.

"Frances, we're getting off topic here. This isn't about her marital status."

Mother frowned. "I think it's exactly on topic. If she were married and had a child to focus on, she wouldn't be obsessed with death all the time. Life is about the living, Lyla, not the dead."

I stood. "Okay. I love you both. Daddy, if you have information that would help, you should hand it over. Otherwise, you're impeding the investigation. Mother, I respectfully disagree with you. Seriously, feminism has made wonderful advancements in the last few decades. Women have more to offer the world than their uterus."

"Lyla Jane!" Mother put her hand to her mouth.

"Well, it's true. Just because we're women doesn't automatically make us baby-making factories. Our self-worth isn't tied up in such things any longer, thank God. We need more, not less, advocacy for women's rights on the basis of the equality of the sexes. Relegating women to being barefoot and pregnant isn't helping anyone."

"Don't talk to your mother that way!" Daddy said.

Mother's eyes were full of water.

"Please try and understand." I sighed, put my glass on the table, and sat. "I'm not saying women who choose that life are lesser. They're not. It's their choice, and I say more power to them. And I'm also *not* telling you I'll never find someone that makes me want to settle down and have a family." I took her hand. "Just not now, okay? Can you see me, Mother? Really see *me*?" The look on her face confirmed she didn't, and I hadn't a clue how to make her understand. "Is it possible for you to not think less of me because I haven't turned out like your friends' daughters?"

"I don't think less of you. You're a beautiful, smart girl. I want you to have a nice life. A safe one with love and laughter." She kissed my cheek and rose.

"Frances. Please sit down." Daddy gave me a look. "Despite our daughter's outburst, she needs our support."

I hadn't meant to hurt her feelings. I never did. It just always seemed to happen.

"No, it seems my opinions oppose the movement of my gender. How dare I want to have grandchildren and wonderful family Christmases before I die?"

"For heaven's sake." Daddy shook his head as she stormed from the room.

I got up. Danger or no danger, I was going home.

Chapter Twelve

"Sorry to ask you to come all the way back over to pick me up. I bought a new car, and they're supposed to deliver it first thing in the morning. I wasn't thinking. I should've left when you did. Why will I never learn that my mother will never understand me?" I said to Melanie, glancing over at her nightclothes, as she drove me home. She'd raced right out of the house when I called. I couldn't have asked for a better friend.

"Whose mother ever does?"

"True. Hey, I hope you don't have to be at the cookie shop too early. You sound exhausted."

Mel yawned. "I'm off tomorrow. I couldn't sleep anyway. After I left your house, I got a call from the police station, with a request to come back in."

"I'm afraid what I'm about to tell you isn't going to help us catch any more z's."

Mel took a right onto Cane Street, and I told her everything about my conversation with Calvin and my suspicion that Carol might have confided in my father.

"Oh hell."

"It's plain idiotic for the police to waste valuable time talking to you. And I'm going to do something about it."

"This whole situation terrifies me on so many levels." Mel turned up the heat. "I get trusting our law enforcement. But look where I am. One bad decision regarding my ex has landed me in the hot seat of a murder investigation. I can scarcely believe this is my life. These are desperate times, girl."

I stared at my friend, who sounded like a completely different person from who she'd been a week ago. "We won't sit by. And Mel, just to be safe, maybe you'd better speak to a lawyer. Daddy uses William Greene."

Melanie held my gaze at the gate and said, "Already taken care of. Teresa knows one." Then she punched in the code to our complex.

"Hold on a second, Mel." I leaned across her and waved to the security guard. "Hey, Al, you got a sec?"

The retired cop appeared to be in his late sixties and lived rent-free as payment for his duties at the front gate. The gray-headed man with a rather large middle emerged from the booth. "Hi, ladies. I heard you gals had an interesting couple of days."

Mel nodded. "Yeah, no kidding."

"Al, did you see anyone odd coming in or out that day?"

He scratched the back of his neck. "Not that I recall. I told the police the same and gave over the security footage from that night."

"Okay, just wondered. It's a little scary coming home after."

Al narrowed his brown gaze and stooped to peer into the car, his belly rolling over his belt. "Either one of y'all feel the least bit threatened, you give me a shout." He patted his sidearm. "I live about a minute from ya, and I'll haul ass."

"Thanks," we said in unison and meant it.

Headlights reflected off Mel's rearview mirror.

"I mean it. Don't hesitate, ya hear?" He patted the car.

"Yes, sir. We won't." Mel gave me a look.

With a final head nod, he waved us past.

"I'm going in to take an Ambien and crawl into bed. You going to be okay?"

I nodded. "I have to go back in there at some point. And the longer I wait, the harder it will become."

"That makes sense, and you're right."

I sighed as she pulled into her space in front of our building. Wasting no time, I opened the car door and stepped out.

Mel glanced around warily as she tied her robe back in place and glanced around. She was the most confident person I'd ever known. Melanie was the type of woman who could take on the world and challenge the status quo without giving the least bit of notice to how people reacted. She told me, after her divorce, she realized that not giving a damn about what others thought about her freed her. And she'd had no compunction about altering her beliefs in order to maintain her safety, sanity, and independence. Seeing her so terrified angered me on so many levels. She'd been through enough. Tomorrow, I would delve into Carol's life. Talk to everyone. Unearth all her secrets.

I hugged my friend. "It's going to be okay." I smiled at her. "Truly. You want to bunk with me tonight?"

Mel gave her head a shake. "I thought you might want to stay with me. They cleared my house right before yours. Didn't find anything." She wrapped her arms around herself. "I understand the necessity, but I'm not accustomed to having my privacy violated."

"I understand. I would stay with you, but I need to face this. You go try and get some sleep."

"Right." Melanie nodded. "'Night." She lifted her hand, and I watched her until she disappeared inside her home.

An owl hooted in the distance, and the wind rustled the trees; the smell of pine needles permeated the air. I dug through my bag for my keys as a car pulled into the space across from Mel's. I watched from the shadows of my front stoop as the man crossed the street and went inside a three-bedroom unit. I exhaled.

I put my key in the door and unlocked it. The door swung open. The smell of a strong disinfectant accosted me. I thought of Carol lying inert on the floor. The terror she must have experienced. I shivered.

My cell rang, and I glanced at my watch. I didn't recognize the number and clicked "Decline." Those telemarketers were working late tonight. I reached inside the doorway and flipped on the light. The room looked like it always had. Beige walls, a white bar with my wicker stools. The floor where Carol had been in the dreadful suitcase. Walking into my house proved more difficult than I'd anticipated.

My watch pinged as a text came through. Absently, I glanced down to read, and I did a double take. My breath caught in my throat.

I'm looking for Jane Doe. Are you Jane Doe?

I gripped the doorframe and took a couple of deep breaths. I looked to my right and then my left. Alone. I remained on this stoop alone. Calvin said Carol had received texts before she died. Was it related? Or some sick joke? A poke at the book club? I glanced next door to see if Mel came running out. Had she received a text?

As the seconds ticked on, my heart rate slowed when nothing happened. I stepped inside and turned to close the door and nearly leaped out of my skin. Through the small window of the catty-cornered building next to mine, someone stared at me through the blinds of a low-lit living room. A man. Kevin. Our gazes locked as he emerged from the front door carrying two large garbage bags. I was ashamed to say I felt better seeing a familiar face than I would closing the door and being alone with the text. As if transfixed, I stood frozen, holding the door with one hand as he made his way to my townhouse, wearing low-slung jeans and a thermal-style burgundy shirt. He was barefoot. His disheveled appearance and the wrinkle on the left side of his face alluded to the fact he'd been sleeping.

He momentarily lifted his free hand. "Hey, you okay?" His tone sounded gruff as he ran his free hand through his thick sandy blond hair. "I thought about calling, but . . ." He shrugged.

I nodded. "I thought about calling too. You alright?"

"I don't know."

I stared down the driveway.

"You want me to take your trash down to the street for you?"

I'd forgotten this week's trash pickup had been rescheduled to Saturday morning. Our family-run sanitation provider had sent out a notice last week. I shook my head, glad to be discussing something normal. "That's okay. There's not much in it." I left the door cracked, retrieved the garbage, and wheeled my small black container down to the end of the street. Kevin walked alongside me. Silence seemed to stretch for miles as I debated telling him about my scary message.

His receptacle, already at the street, was full of moving boxes and plastic bags. Of course, Ellen wouldn't concern herself about the planet by participating in the ongoing green movement. I'd seen her at the grocery store with her shopping cart full of environment-ruining plastic. She'd even been caught throwing her drive-through trash out her windows, and fined twice for littering. Ellen acted as if the world was her personal garbage dump. I shook my head, unsure of why I focused on that now.

He glanced over in my direction. "Since yours is empty, may I?"

"What?"

"Throw these bags in there?"

I could clearly read his uneasiness under my scrutiny, and yet there was something else swimming within his hazel gaze. Something odd, and I began to feel a little uneasy.

"Yeah, sure." I scratched my arm and let out a sigh.

He sighed too. Right now, our complicated past wasn't the most important thing in either of our lives, and it shouldn't matter that he'd decided to date my cousin, probably out of spite, and move right near me. It would again but for the moment, we had a truce of sorts.

"I hate what happened to Carol. And I hate that you're going through this." He enunciated the word "hate."

"Was it horrible?" He sounded much like the man I'd once been so close to. Kind, considerate, caring. I guessed it was true what they said about past relationships, like the one he and I'd had, the love/hate lines were sometimes hard to distinguish.

I swallowed. "So horrible. Every time I close my eyes, I see her."

"I can't imagine."

I shivered and ran my hand through my hair. "How are you holding up?"

He shook his head and shoved his free hand into his pocket. "When I found out, I sat on the couch, stunned for hours. I had no idea what to do or who to call. Her mom's gone, and Carol wasn't close to her mom's new husband, the one she married after Dad."

"She didn't deserve this. She was one of the most genuine people I've ever known."

He stared at his bare feet. "We argued, and I said some horrible things to her. Horrible."

I kept my voice low. "About the inheritance?"

He nodded and scrubbed his face with his hands. "I was pissed because Grandpa Jim was my biological grandfather, and he chose to leave the bulk of his estate to Carol. And I made some poor investment choices and was counting on the money to float me until I get my portfolio straightened out. When I received my copy of the will, I flipped."

I had no idea the grandparent Val referred to was Kevin's paternal grandfather. He lived on Long Island and never visited much. I saw him once five years ago, right before Kevin's dad died of stomach cancer. I had no idea he and Carol had been so close.

"Oh." I groped for words.

He shook his head and groaned. "I apologized, and we worked things out. I can take solace in knowing that. I loved her, and she knew I did. How's Melanie dealing? I heard about the police escort to the station."

"She's struggling." I hesitated as my voice caught in my throat. "We all are."

He nodded. "I'm sorry." He reached out and stroked his fingers down my arm to my hand. "I wish it hadn't been you that found her."

I focused on his face. He clearly had reservations regarding my fortitude. "No one should find a body that way, Kev. And God, Carol is the real victim here."

He held on to my fingers. "I know. I didn't mean to imply anything different." He shook his head as if regretting his earlier words. "I can't even imagine what that was like for you. Have you heard anything?"

I studied him. "Not really. I know there will be an autopsy."

He nodded. "Is there anything I can do? Anything you need, I hope you know you can always come to me."

"Kevin," I said, pulling my fingers free of his grasp, "I'm sorry for your loss. And not that I don't appreciate the sentiment, but we can't be close anymore." I lifted the lid and exposed a nearly empty can.

He dropped his bags inside, and they rested near the top. "I just thought we could comfort each other. We both loved her."

"We did." I gave him a small smile.

He hesitated. "Do the police know who did it? Do they have any suspects yet? I mean, like I said, I heard they escorted Melanie in for questioning, but that's absurd."

I studied him, feeling a little warier, yet at the same time the question wasn't out of left field. Anyone would want to know those things. He'd admitted to arguing with her, and I still didn't believe he had anything to do with Carol's death. Why did I get a weird vibe?

"Val said you're going into the police department tomorrow?"

"Yeah." He stepped closer, running his fingers over the arm of my sweater. "Quinn isn't exactly my biggest fan. That's why I—"

A door slammed, and a clip-clop sound echoed. Kevin jerked his head toward the sound. Ellen stood a few feet away. Her arms were crossed as she narrowed her eyes. Her face was flushed. The scene was almost laughable. My friend and Kevin's stepsister had died, and she thought I was trying to reconnect with her man. When she moved in, had she envisioned Kevin and I would never interact alone?

"Hi, hon. Just throwing out the trash and checking in on Lyla." Kevin retreated to her side.

Ellen wrapped an arm around his waist and glared at me. "Isn't he the sweetest? I'm so lucky."

"Oh yeah, you're one lucky woman," I said dryly.

She pulled his head down and slanted her mouth over his for my benefit. It was loud and awkward and completely uncouth.

The leaves rustled as the wind kicked up. One stray brown leaf swirled around and dropped at my feet. I had no idea their make-out session had ended until Ellen called out, "'Night, cuz. I'm going to get this poor grieving baby back inside."

I threw a hand up as the two of them walked back to their house. Kevin's shoulders were slumped forward, and where I could see he actually was grieving, Val had read Ellen incorrectly. She didn't appear the least bit bothered.

Alone in the coolness of the night, my mind went back to the text. The urgency to get inside rushed back. I closed the lid, and the side of the bag caught on something, tearing at the edge. I pulled the lid a little in an attempt to free the edge and tore the bag wide open. Papers spilled to the ground. "Terrific." I picked up the old grocery receipts and lifted the lid again and froze. Inside the bag was the camo baseball cap I'd seen the man in the car with Carol wearing. Well, it probably wasn't *the* cap. But he'd asked about the police and their suspects. The creepy Jane Doe text had come through while he watched me from the window.

I reached for the bag, then hesitated. My heart hammered in my ears. I glanced around. No one was out here or watching that I could tell. I snatched the bag out of the can and walked briskly toward the front door. A cat cried in the distance, and I stumbled over my own feet, and the bag flew from my grasp. I righted myself just in the nick of time, saving me from sprawling out onto the concrete walkway. The contents of the bag littered the ground. I went to my knees and began gathering everything up in my makeshift basket, with the hem of my shirt, as I'd done as a child. I carefully used a receipt as a barrier between my fingers and the cap. Once I'd collected everything, I hustled inside my house, closing the door and locking it. And just like that, the fear of being inside my home alone vanished. I feared what was outside way more.

Chapter Thirteen

I dreamed of skulls, leaves, and damp earth. On the mountain-side, I ran. Branches were slapping me in the face as I fled from a man in a camouflage baseball cap. His face was a black void. One second he was far behind me, and the next, his ice-cold fingers gripped my shoulders. He shoved me hard. I fell, arms and legs flailing as I attempted to scream. Not the slightest sound flew from my lips. A whoosh of air left my lungs as I hit the ground. Everything hurt. My extremities felt numb, and ter-ror had a viselike grip on me. When I rolled to my side, I saw Carol's lifeless eyes staring back at me.

A scream retched from my raw throat, and I sat straight up in my bed, drenched in sweat, with damp tangles of hair about my face. A nightmare. Only a nightmare—all the Jane Doe descriptions I'd been reading intermingled with Carol's murder, I reminded myself. I got up and padded to the bathroom, splash-ing my face with water, then patting it dry with a towel. Sleep no longer an option, a cup of tea would be in order.

My thoughts went back to what I'd discovered in Kevin's garbage bag. Did I really believe he could be involved? He could've been tossing out the cap because Ellen hated it, or maybe it'd been a gift and it wasn't his style. He'd never dressed in anything camo while we'd been dating. He'd openly admitted he and Carol had argued, and spoken about his troubling financial situation.

Then there was the text. I looked over it again. I put the number into Google search to no avail. What if Carol had discovered the identity of the Jane Doe killer? How, I was uncertain, unless she knew the person.

A pounding on my front door caused me to drop the hand towel. When I checked the peep hole, I spied a disheveled Mel. "Lyla! Are you okay?"

I flung open the door. Mel's eyes were wild, her phone gripped in her fist. She rushed in and hugged me.

"I'm fine. Sorry. Just a nightmare." I closed the door and locked up tight after she released me.

"I nearly had a heart attack when I heard you scream." Mel put her hand over her heart. Then paused, staring down at the floor.

"Go into the living room, and I'll make us a cup of chamomile tea."

Mel and I were on the sofa, our teas now finished. She was digesting everything I told her about the text I'd received. Mel sucked in a breath as I filled her in on my interaction with Kevin.

"The text is spooky as hell. And we should definitely take that to the police." She gripped the blanket tighter. "But you would know if the man in the car with Carol was Kevin, right?"

My shoulders rose, then fell. "Normally, I would say yes. But I don't know." I shook my head. "I mean, I don't believe it could be Kevin. But—"

"The inheritance," Melanie supplied.

"Exactly."

"Why would his grandfather leave the bulk of his estate to Carol?" Mel's brows drew together. "Spite?"

"Maybe. Who knows why families do what they do? Though, she was his stepsister. He wouldn't kill her. He's a jerk, but I just can't believe Kevin is capable of such a thing." I shivered at the thought. "I am glad the judge made the police aware of the conflict. They will investigate him for sure." I rested my arm on the back of the sofa, propping my head against my hand. "It does make you wonder where he was when Carol went missing. Was he at work? Packing with Ellen?"

"Well, as for alibis, look at me. I did find the proof I was at the liquor store. It was right there in my transaction history. Tim was pretty drunk, but it pisses me off how he all but threw me under the bus." Melanie tucked the blanket under her legs. "I mean, seriously, I could have been charged with murder for God's sake."

I shook my head. "Tim's a jerk. He never deserved you. I'll go down there with you tomorrow. From what I've gathered online, Amelia was absolutely correct. The way Carol was delivered to my house in a suitcase should have the department seeking outside help. A profiler or something. It's not your average offender who does something like that. I mean, the suitcase by itself should rule you out. Think of what type of deranged person they'd have to be in order to do something like that. Seriously, I get they must speak to everyone, and with the suitcase belonging to you it makes sense but come on. You're the gentlest person on the planet without even a single traffic violation."

Mel nodded emphatically, "Right! It's stupid. But I'd go through all the turmoil again to help Carol."

We sat for a few moments in silence, remembering our friend.

"If you're interested, I compiled a file." I pulled up the dumping grounds doc on my tablet and moved closer to Mel.

On the scene, Brad Jones is optimistic someone will be able to identify Jane Doe by the few remnants of clothing and her jewelry. Once the woman is identified, the investigators can move forward with victimology.

Half a mile off Interstate 85, off a service road, a short trek through the knee-high grass and thorn-ridden weeds, the remains of a likely Caucasian female, 18–25 years old and between 5'0 and 5'4", were found behind an abandoned country church. Most of her bones were recovered, along with a denim Gap jacket, a blue dress, Keds tennis shoes, a scarf, and her jewelry.

"This is the one Carol thought she could identify?" Mel's eyes were wide.

I nodded.

We took a look at the pictures. Skeletal remains in a mountain of detritus. The remnants of what might've been a blue dress. I zoomed in on the images of her scarf, necklace, and ring. The pictures weren't the best quality. The necklace looked to be a bit mangled, as if it'd been run over. The scarf had me squinting at the screen. The years spent outdoors in the elements had faded out the colors, and there were visible holes, but—

"Is that?"

"It could be Sweet Mountain High colors. Yes!" They'd given each member of the majorettes a scarf at the alumnae bonfire for our ten-year reunion. I stared at the image, unable to make out if it had our school's crest. Could the Jane Doe be a Sweet Mountain alumna? Someone we knew?

"I don't recall any missing person cases from our area. In fact, I'm not sure if Sweet Mountain has ever had such a case. I'll see what I can find when I get to the office."

Mel followed my glance over at the cap on the dining room table.

What kind of monster could be in our midst?

Chapter Fourteen

The second I entered the office, my phone chimed. I had
several messages from Mother. I'd placed my phone on
"Silent" when I went to bed, hoping to get a couple more hours
of sleep. I had finally, waking with a start at the realization of
how late it was. They were essentially the same message, containing her rambling concerns. I disappointed her; I got it. My
cell lit up with my uptown funk ring tone, and Gran's smiling
face flashed on the screen.

"Hi, Gran. I'm at the office. What's up?"

Gran's tone sounded tight and lacked her usual cheerful jol-
liness. "The police took James! I don't know what to do. I'm
afraid they're going to ask me questions, and I might crack. I
know too much."

I sat upright in the chair. *"What?"*

She began to prattle on frantically. As hard as I tried, I
couldn't manage to decipher anything other than that the law
had taken my father.

"Okay. Take a deep breath. Slow down and tell me what
happened. Leave nothing out." I stood and walked down
through the little hallway that led to Uncle Calvin's office.

"The Daniels boy—the one that was sweet on you—came by with one of his officers. They had some questions for James about your friend Carol. He told them he wouldn't be speaking with them without William present."

I rapped on my uncle's closed door.

"Officer Taylor—I think that was what was on the boy's name tag—got up in James's face. The Daniels boy pulled him off and shut him up. I thought they'd wait on William Greene, and the next thing I knew, they were hauling my boy out of here."

My heart began to race.

"Your mother is on the phone with William now. He's going to meet James at the station. What if they think he killed Carol Timms?"

"They don't. They're probably irritated by Daddy's defiance. He's digging in his heels on the doctor–patient confidentiality issue. It's standard practice, and the police should respect it. Someone will have to answer for this."

A door creaked and then shut. "I'm not so sure. Lord help us, there's a reason they might pick him up as a suspect."

"No, there isn't. You're just worked up. It's scary. I get it."

"No, Lyla! Listen. Carol had the hots for your daddy. And James hasn't been coming home at reasonable hours lately. I hate even to think it, but there it is."

"What in God's name are you talking about? Carol most certainly did not have a thing for Daddy. You've been watching too many soap operas. Daddy is adamant about having his attorney on standby. He wanted me to have Mr. Greene present when I gave my statement too."

"There's something I didn't tell ya. I wanted to spare you."

My heart hammered against my ribcage.

"There was a note about Carol experiencing transference."

"That's not unusual. If Daddy helped her make some progress, her gratitude might have confused her feelings for him. It isn't unusual for a patient to experience some confusion and misdirection of their emotions. It would've passed once she got to the root of her condition. I'm sure it was all handled in a professional manner."

"She tried to seduce him, Lyla. He made notes about inappropriate behavior." Of course, I realized, when Gran had told me she had a gander at the file, she meant she'd read it cover to cover. Now, I'm ashamed to say, I wished I had taken her up on doing a little snooping myself.

My parents had had their fair share of marital problems. Could it even be possible? Like Gran said, there it was to be considered.

I pounded on Calvin's door now. I didn't care if he had a client in there with him or not. After another second without response, I flung the door open. Empty. Maybe he was already at the police station.

"Officer Taylor said something about a wristwatch she had engraved for James."

Perhaps Carol had told her husband she had feelings for Daddy, and he jumped to conclusions. If so, that ruled Kevin out. Then why'd he thrown out his cap? So many conjectures, and now my father was in custody. "Did they arrest him, Gran? Read him his rights or anything?"

"I don't know. It all happened so fast. One minute James was shaking Quinn Daniels's hand and everything appeared to calm down and take on a friendly vibe, and the next he was leaving with him. James ordered Frances to call William Greene. I've known that Daniels boy since he was in knee pants. And even after the two of you called it quits, I liked him." Gran's voice hitched. "How could he do something like this? To think James would have anything to do with that girl's murder is ludicrous."

"Don't jump to conclusions. Let me speak to Mother."

"Okay, but don't tell her what I read in the file."

"I won't." My guess was still that our police chief wanted Daddy to share Carol's medical records because of pressure from the judge, something Daddy wouldn't do unless there was a court order.

"Frances! Lyla wants to talk to you. I told her about James," Gran called. Followed by "Frances! Frances!"

"For heaven's sake, Daisy. I haven't time for this," Mother shrieked, something my prim and proper mother never did.

"Listen, Gran."

More arguing.

"Gran!" I hurried back through the office.

She apparently hadn't heard a word I'd said. She and mother were squabbling, and now I heard Gran sniffling, and I instantly became angry with my mother. An emotion I had no room for.

Under the current circumstances, a level head was what was called for. "Gran!"

"I'm here. Y-your mother said—"

"Don't worry about her. She's upset. I'm going to go down to the station and see what I can find out. Stay calm. Everything is going to be fine. Trust me."

"I'll meet you there. I can call one of those Uber things you use." Poor Gran. We didn't have Uber in Sweet Mountain. She must've overheard Mel and me talking about our Uber driver in Atlanta last spring.

"Go with Mother if she decides to meet me down there, or stay put." I softened my tone and reminded her of days gone by. "You're my bestie, right?" When things got ugly at home, Gran and I would lie on my trampoline out back and talk about all the places we'd go when I got old enough. She said she'd always be there for me. It didn't matter where I was in the world, If I called her, she'd come running. We were going to travel the world together. I could talk to Gran about anything and everything, and she always understood. I loved her like no other.

"Always." Gran sounded a little calmer.

* * *

First Melanie and now my father. I wondered if there had been a larger crowd when Daddy arrived. Our family name carried a lot of weight in this town. And if indeed a Moody had been brought in for questioning, it would be fuel for the rumor mills.

The police station was silent when I walked through the white wooden double doors. I stood in front of the large, vacant mahogany desk in the poorly lit front room and waited. It occurred to me I'd hadn't set foot inside this building in years. Not since Quinn and I had called it quits.

The same large wooden plaque that hung above the glass that separated the desk from the waiting area. It read:

"The Sweet Mountain Police Department's focus is:

"To protect and serve our citizens with a high level of integrity
"To utilize a community policing philosophy
"To strive for excellence in all that we do
"To become less incident driven and more proactive in preventing crime"

The door swung open as I stared at the sign. In waltzed William Greene, our family attorney. His shoulders were back and his briefcase in hand as he filled the room with his presence. He and Daddy were roughly the same age. Both were tall, commanding men. Mr. Greene had practiced in Atlanta for years before moving his practice back home to Sweet Mountain.

His brown gaze landed on me. "Hello, dear. It's been a while."

"It has." I had a plethora of questions that somehow had managed to flitter right out of my head when the past crept in.

The man reached out and squeezed my arm. "Don't you worry about a thing. I'm here now, and I'm going to make sure your father is released and his rights upheld. But you have to promise me you won't speak with another person in law enforcement on any official capacity without me present. Quite frankly, I'd feel better if you would refrain from speaking with anyone in an unofficial capacity too. The lines get blurred sometimes. You understand?"

"Yes, sir." I wouldn't argue with him. I had no idea what was going on here, and I wouldn't do anything to hurt my daddy.

He handed me a card he'd taken from the front pocket of his briefcase. "Put my number in your phone. My cell is written on the back. Call me day or night."

I bobbed my head up and down, and the older man smiled. "It's going to be fine."

The door buzzed, releasing the lock on the door beside the desk, and out walked Quinn. "Mr. Greene."

My breath caught in my throat when our gazes met. Being in this building had me discombobulated.

"I'll be right with you, Chief." Thankfully, Mr. Greene didn't suffer from such compunctions. "Don't worry. I have this." Mr. Greene motioned for me to have a seat.

I nodded and sat down on one of the chairs, then fiddled with my bag on my lap.

"If you'll follow me, please, sir." Quinn took the attorney back without a word to me, and for a minute, a great sense of relief enveloped me. I had to get myself together before I uttered a single word. At this rate, I'd end up saying something damaging. I slowed my breathing and reminded myself I had the ability to handle anything thrown my way. Gran always said a woman could handle anything she had to. And I would, for my family, friends, and Carol. For a case to be effectively handled, every and all possibilities must be considered and ruled out. I didn't believe for a single second my father had anything to do with my friend's death. The notion was absurd.

Officer Taylor came through the front doorway and glanced at me, pausing. I wondered where he'd been. I'd assumed he was in the back room where Daddy was being questioned. At least from Gran's account, he'd been with his chief when they were at the house.

The arrogance on the officer's face caused my peaceful resolve to falter. "Still out harassing Melanie instead of looking for a suspect who might actually have the capacity to enact such a horrific crime? Or wait, now your department is going after a pillar of the community with a blemish-free reputation. Wow, that makes great sense. Stellar job there, Officer."

His face tensed and he moved closer. "I think you've confused our roles here. I'm the one with the badge. It's my job to focus on solving crimes. You and your little book club are just a bunch of bored women who think they know better than the authorities. In my opinion, I see all this interference as obstruction of justice. I'd lock you all up if I had my way. This isn't some book."

I fought to keep my temper in check. "Well, it's a good thing we have laws in place to prevent rogue officers from arresting innocent people then." My face flushed. "And I know it isn't a novel. I'm not an idiot."

He lowered his head, leaning down so close I could feel his hot breath on my neck. I turned my head away from his face. My skin prickled at his nearness. "Tough little gal, are ya?" I could see his sadistic smirk in my periphery. "Someone physically popped your friend's limbs out of joint and crumpled her up inside that bag."

My pulse sped up, and my eyes stung. I blinked to hold back more tears.

"Stop sticking your nose in where it doesn't belong." Officer Taylor rose and moved on as if I were of no consequence.

Chapter Fifteen

I locked my purse inside my car and checked the parking lot. I didn't see Mother's Cadillac rolling down the street, nor was it in the lot. Not that I was surprised. Mother wouldn't want to be seen causing a scene. In her mind, her reaction would give validity to the rumors that would soon be swirling like a funnel cloud during tornado season unless it could be handled delicately. Perhaps I shouldn't be seen around here either.

I strolled around the side of the building toward the creek, walking past the Sweet Mountain establishment sign. I wondered what troubles those early settlers experienced. Present-day Sweet Mountain was settled in the 1840s after Moody Mill was constructed on the creek that ran behind the municipal building. The mill was long gone, but the three historic buildings dating back to the same date, including the famous Sweet Mountain covered bridge, still stood, though they were no longer operational. The bridge was the state's oldest remaining covered bridge, listed on the National Register of Historic Places and part of the Georgia Covered Bridge Trail. A lot of photographers came from all over the states to photograph the rustic, wooden, lattice-covered bridge that crossed the creek. It was the only real draw to our little town unless you were a nature lover and enjoyed hiking, kayaking, and animal watching.

Unlike a lot of millennial residents, I wasn't itching to leave the area. Those who went away to college seemed to boomerang back after graduation. Our town seeped into your DNA and called you back when you were away too long. Until this thing with Carol, my life here had been peaceful.

I made my way down the gravel trail that ran under the covered bridge, and tossed a leaf into the creek, then watched it flow downstream over the rocks and pebbles as I took a seat on the metal bench. My mind flew to the many possibilities and the frustration of being kept in the dark. Calvin said investigating a person was akin to slipping into their skin and examining the world from their eyes. The ramifications of delving into the ongoing investigation seemed inconsequential. What I needed was hard evidence. I thought of my favorite quote—the one I had framed and hung in the office during my first week on the job.

"Physical evidence cannot be wrong; it cannot be perjured; it cannot be wholly absent. Only in its interpretation can there be error." ~ *Trace L. Kirk, 1974*

No truer words in the world of investigations had ever been uttered.

Pulling out my cell, I called my uncle. I had no idea where he was or why he wasn't here. When he answered on the second ring, I went into the developments without preamble.

"Calm down. It sounds like the police are just going through the motions of showing Judge Timms they're pursuing every possible lead. Your father's attorney is present, and you have nothing to worry about. How's your mother holding up?"

"Well, she's beside herself."

"She'll adjust. Franny is as solid as a rock." He sounded certain.

That made me feel a little better. "Where are you?"

"In Atlanta. The case got moved up. I left a voicemail on your phone as well as a note on your desk calendar that you never use."

Of course, I didn't use a physical calendar. Who did these days? It wouldn't send alerts or notify you of appointment changes. I'd asked Uncle Calvin to send me calendar invites in lieu of the old, archaic snail mail way.

"Okay, sorry. I've been a little preoccupied. Don't worry about a thing." Time to woman up! "I can handle things while you're away."

"I believe that, and it makes me feel better to hear the police are acting on leads. I'll be in and out of pocket. Just leave me a message, and as I said before, be vigilant."

"Always." I tried to make my voice calm and firm. "Take care."

As I slid the phone back into my bag, I let out a long, slow breath. I could handle this. Everything would work out. Yes, this was a good thing. If the police followed every shred of evidence to each lead, we'd find out who did this. With great difficulty, I pushed the image of her, from the last time I saw her, out of my mind, and the fleeting optimism began to fade.

"Lyla," a male voice said from my left.

My hands flew in the air, and I jumped, turning toward the intruder.

Quinn's hands were raised in a defensive posture. "I didn't mean to startle you. I kept my tone low." He shook his head as if he were inwardly chiding himself. "But not low enough. I could see you were deep in thought. I'm sorry."

My hand went involuntarily to my heart. "It's fine. You're right. I was in my own world. Not your fault."

He made his way down the path, his dark-blue uniform spick and span. Quinn had always had a swagger about him, an allure I'd always found irresistible until he showed his inability to compromise. If a man couldn't be supportive of my life choices, then he wasn't a man I wanted in my life.

"May I?" He motioned to the bench, and I scooted down. "I wasn't sure you were still here. There's a Hyundai in the parking lot, but last I checked, you drove a red Nissan."

He kept apprised on my mode of transportation. Hmm.

"It'd seen better days. I bought a new car." I stared at the creek, listening to the subtle sounds of babbles. "Has my father been charged?"

"No. We requested his cooperation with the ongoing investigation, and he adamantly refused. We brought him downtown to make the request more official. He left a few minutes ago, seeming to believe you'd done the same."

Daddy hadn't known about my new purchase either. He probably figured I went back to the house to wait with Mother and Gran. I was eager to have a word with my father and his attorney, if possible. Perhaps Daddy would confide in me. Whatever wasn't privileged anyway. Anything would help me. "I better go." I started to rise, when his hand rested lightly on my forearm.

"Stay, just for a minute."

Slowly, I sat back down and positioned myself so we were facing each other.

He ran his fingers through his salt-and-pepper hair. He had the beginnings of a beard. Flecks of gray sprouted down his jawline, standing out on his tan face. His blue eyes were soft as he took me in. "How are you?"

I met his gaze without a flinch. "Not great. What can you tell me? Gran said something about Carol having a watch engraved for my father. If she did, you know it was only because of transference. It happens when a patient feels her doctor understands her and wants to help."

"She did have one engraved. That's all I can say at present. I'm sure you can get more information from him and his attorney." He studied me.

"That's fair." I cleared my throat. "And Melanie?"

He shook his head. "We're focusing our efforts elsewhere."

Relief flooded me. Time to get back on track. "How have you been? I heard you were getting married."

He glanced away. "No. It didn't work out." When he didn't elaborate, I didn't pry.

"I do have something I should share with you."

"Oh?"

I dug into my purse and pulled up the text. "I received this yesterday. Calvin said Carol had received a few weird texts and phone calls as well."

Quinn glanced at the screen, and when he glanced up, he looked as if he could have spit nails. The annoyed expression on his face gave me a sick feeling in the pit of my stomach.

"Carol received disturbing phone calls. And I'm not sure if they had anything to do with her death." He cleared his throat. "Lyla, are you going around town discussing the Jane Doe cases up I-85? We heard all about your club's theories from Amelia Klein."

"No. Well, the Jane Doe Book Club has been discussing them, but Carol has been our main concern. Then when y'all hauled Melanie away like a common criminal, it got us riled."

"She was hardly 'hauled away.' Officer Taylor merely gave her a ride to the station. She was never handcuffed or charged. We have to look at everyone."

"Noted, and I agree. Like with the Jane Doe case. A lot of us wonder if there's a connection. It seems neither you nor your officers are taking into account how deep she was into those investigations. She told Amelia how scared she was and that she knew the identity of a particular Jane Doe." I started to pull my phone from my pocket, when he touched my hand.

"Carol Timms suffered from paranoia. And when you compile that personality type with the propaganda of those cases— well, it gets dicey."

Propaganda? "So, what you're saying is you don't believe there's any connection. Have you even glanced at the cases? Because, you might be surprised if you do." I shoved his hand away and produced my phone, ignoring his snort of protest. "See this? Look familiar?" He glanced at the image.

"It's a scarf."

"A scarf the exact colors and pattern as the one given to each majorette at our high school reunion. I received one, and so did Mel, Val, Ellen, and Carol."

He glanced at me, and I could tell he wasn't impressed. "Lyla."

I shoved the phone back into my pocket. "Fine. So, instead of looking into every possibility, you focus on my father. You brought him down here to intimidate him after you discovered Carol had gone to him for treatment of said paranoia and experienced transference." My eyes narrowed. "You actually believed you could break him. To convince him to compromise the doctor–patient confidentiality." I scoffed, my resolve rushing back full force. "Well, you know as well as I do that

Doctor James Moody doesn't shake easily. Never would he violate his ethics. He has his attorney on speed dial at home and in his favorites on his cell phone for just such an occasion. He thinks of anything and everything. Seriously, Quinn, it's lazy police work. Get a warrant instead of attempting to intimidate my family."

Quinn pierced me with his intelligent stare as he moved impossibly closer. I could detect the barest of hints of cologne. Ralph Lauren Polo Blue, the exact cologne I'd given him the Christmas before we'd split up. My heart raced, and my palms began to sweat. "This has nothing to do with my history with your family. I respect your father. Always have. I believe he's an upstanding man of the community. Still, I have to do my job. I'm trying to remain objective here. If I allow bias to creep in, I'll be unable to trust my findings."

That made complete sense, but I was rattled, agitated, and downright angry. "Is that why you had Officer Taylor show up at my house when I found Carol instead of showing up yourself?" The second the question fell from my lips, I regretted it.

He flinched, and his fist clenched on the bench next to my leg.

"Forget it." I rose.

He leaped to his feet, blocking my path.

"You don't owe me anything," I said.

"I'd just gotten back into town. I'd been on a fishing trip and heard about it after the fact. Then I had to let Taylor work the case."

"It doesn't matter. I have to go." I avoided his gaze and tried to maneuver around him on the tiny dirt path.

He didn't budge, and I slipped, nearly falling into the stream. Quinn grabbed my shoulders and pulled me back on the path.

Our bodies were so close. Both our chests were heaving as I stared up into his eyes, which were rapidly searching mine. "If I'd intervened and taken the case from my officer, with this being the wife of a prominent judge, and with our history, it would've been perceived negatively. And I will not taint this case. My hands were tied. Can you please try and understand?"

What was I doing? I sounded like a damsel hurt that her knight in shining armor hadn't come to save her. *I don't need a damn knight.* I pushed back, putting more space between us. I looked him straight in the face, irritated with myself. "I understand completely. You were doing your job. I can appreciate that. Expect it even. Because if you do your job, you'll find the person who did this to Carol. I want to ask a question—if I may?"

He nodded.

"Do you have any other suspects in mind, other than your old friends from high school and my father?"

He ran his hand through his brown hair and then dropped it, wiping his face of all emotion. "I can't answer that."

"Maybe you think I killed her."

"Don't be irrational."

Now I was angry. "Okay, so one of your official working theories is my father, a man above reproach in this community, would murder my friend and dislocate her joints." His eyes grew wide. "Oh, yes, your officer gave me a detailed description of what it would take to shove my . . . my friend into that suitcase"— I cleared my throat—"and leave her for me to find? All because she had a watch engraved for him."

His face flushed slightly.

"The affair angle is unimaginative and moronic. Plus, he'd never do that to me. Torture me by delivering my friend to my house."

"Lyla—"

I shoved right past him and marched up the path, past the covered bridge, into the parking lot, without looking back. I squared my shoulders and unlocked the door to my car. My mission now was to find out what transpired inside that little brick building called a police station.

Chapter Sixteen

"Lyla! Yoo-hoo, Lyla, dear," Mrs. Thelma Waters called from her front yard. Mrs. Waters lived next door to my parents. Next to her stood her friend Mrs. Ross, admiring her friend's prize-winning begonias. Mrs. Waters took every opportunity to show off her property. Actually, she recited her memorandum to anyone who showed the slightest interest. The woman lived for the Sweet Mountain Pilgrimage tour every year.

"Hello, ladies." I paused at my car, closing the door softly; then I smiled and waved a finger at them. "We sure are having nice mild temps this year."

Mrs. Ross darted to her car and emerged with something large. The two women hurried around the azalea bed to precariously tiptoe through the grass, something that, under normal circumstances, was a cardinal sin among their kind. That was what walkways were for. Mrs. Waters's neatly pressed beige slacks were wet at the hems, and her pearls bounced on her yellow cardigan. They slowed their advance, each with plastic smiles. Mrs. Ross held a gift basket.

"Lyla, dear, how lovely to see you." Mrs. Waters leaned in and gave me a single kiss on the cheek.

"Preparing for the pilgrimage?" I smiled, feigning ignorance.

"Well, I have worked in a new phrase." She swept her arm toward her yard. "Feast your eyes on our magnificent two-story Greek revival, circa 1918, tucked peacefully among gorgeous Southern grounds of massive magnolias, towering oaks, mature pecan groves, and varieties of ageless, historic flowering shrubs, hedges, and plantings."

"Feast your eyes?" Mrs. Ross crinkled her nose.

"Too much?"

"Indeed." Mrs. Ross turned her attention back to me. "Honey, we were so terribly sorry to hear about your troubles. Must've been a shock to find your friend the way you did. Your mother has been worried sick about you."

"Yes, ma'am. It isn't something easily recovered from, but I'm coping." I adjusted my gray tunic and smoothed out my high ponytail before positioning myself between the ladies and the house. "Is there something I can do for you, ladies? Mother isn't feeling well or I'd invite you in."

Mrs. Ross's mouth contorted in what I assumed meant sympathy. It was more reminiscent of a pucker. That reddish-brown lipstick did nothing but pull out the orange in her foundation, which had settled in the creases of her chin and neck.

"Maybe you could give this to her." She passed the basket full of beauty products over to me.

"With pleasure. It's so very kind of you both." I studied the faces of the two women and saw genuine concern marred with something I'd call a little more than curiosity. I wondered if word of Daddy's ordeal had already spread.

"Think nothing of it." Mrs. Waters clasped her hands in front of her pink mohair sweater and shook her head. Her nut-brown hair was curled so tightly it barely moved. "You let her know that if she needs us, we'll drop everything and be over in a jiffy. With everything going on, she's bound to need her friends close by."

"Mother is blessed beyond measure to have such caring friends. I'll be sure to deliver your well wishes to her. She'll be so pleased." I gave them a brilliant smile. "Have a wonderful day." I turned on my heel and started up the drive, suddenly realizing how much I'd learned from Frances Moody. *Convey nothing of your distress and they'll second-guess everything they've heard.*

I turned at the front door and waved again. The two women still stood in the driveway. Both ladies waved. Well, that was done—score one for the Moodys.

"Calm down, Frances. I refuse to have a conversation with you when you're behaving in such a sloppy manner," my father was saying as I opened the front door and quickly slipped inside.

"Sloppy. How dare you? My behavior didn't land us in this mess. Yours did."

Oh no. I glanced around for Gran as I passed by the formal sitting room.

Mother didn't sound like herself. "James, I've put up with a lot in my life and managed to scrounge together a semblance of a well-adjusted, functioning life for myself and our daughter. I clawed my way out of the gutter, and I've never allowed my past to seep into my present. Lyla deserves nothing less. I refuse to allow you to destroy everything I've worked so hard for. You better come clean to me now, or, so help me God, if I find out—" A glass shattered.

I stood still as a statue in the archway leading to the family room. A deluge of emotions overwhelmed me, and I had no idea how to react. Daddy had his hand on his forehead, and Mother was on the balls of her feet, with both fists clenched. Red wine streamed down the bricks of the fireplace; shards of glass were scattered on the hearth.

"Don't you turn your back on me, James Moody." Mother hissed through her teeth as she reeled.

I gave a soft intake of breath. Never in my life had I seen such a display. My mother had always had such control over herself. Both sets of eyes turned toward me.

Mother's shaking fingers went to her parted lips. Daddy dropped his hand and squared his shoulders as he attempted a smile. "Lyla, we didn't see you there."

"I-I . . . I brought over a basket from Mrs. Ross."

My mother's eyes were wild as she glanced from the shattered glass to me. Not wild—desperate. "Are you okay, Mother?"

"She's fine. Emotions are just running high." Daddy put a hand on her shoulder, and she visibly fought her instinct to jerk away.

"I'm going to lie down for a bit."

I stood there, numbly staring after the ghost of the woman I knew while she made her way toward the back stairs.

Once she'd gone, my blood began to boil as my father casually poured himself a scotch and sat in his armchair. He hadn't even gone after her.

How dare he!

She'd given her entire life to him. She donated her time at his stupid hospital fundraisers, hosted his dinners, and made a home for us. She practically sacrificed her entire life to enrich ours. And he, fully aware of her past, hardly seemed bothered.

"What did you do?" I bit out in a tone I'd never taken with my father before.

"Lyla, please."

"Lyla nothing." I dropped the basket on the sofa and stood several feet from him. I didn't trust myself to go any further. His demurely calm demeanor fueled my anger. "You're being a gigantic jackass!"

His head whipped up, and he pierced me with his cool blue glare. Intimidation wouldn't work.

"I've always been on your side. Always. I heard all the hushed arguments during the night growing up. Kept silent about the archaic practices. No more! I know you haven't been coming home some nights. And that Carol had some sort of thing for you." I made sarcastic finger quotes around "thing."

"Yeah, girls talk. Surprise, surprise!" I wouldn't throw Gran under the bus. "And the next thing we know, you're being taken to the police station for questioning. Transference or not, there wasn't a way to avoid such a scene? You couldn't give them something to spare Mother more embarrassment?"

His eyes narrowed in a silent dare for me to continue my rant. As if I were the one with the problem.

Dare away! "Gran is beside herself, and now Mother is— well, coming unglued. So, I'll ask you again, what in the hell did you do?"

"Don't talk to me that way, young lady. I won't stand for it." His tone dripped with warning. He sipped from his glass and then stared at the flickering fire.

I didn't budge. "Not this time. You want my respect? You're going to have to earn it."

To my surprise, he sighed and waited a beat, running his hand through his hair. "It isn't what you think. David Timms found out about his wife's therapy. Apparently, she wrote my name down in several places in her address book and had a watch engraved with something like 'You saved me, James. All my love.' Or some nonsense. He assumed the worst."

He gulped the scotch. "I told Quinn I'd protect patient privilege until he presented me with a court order. My hands are tied when it comes to my practice." He shrugged a shoulder. "That young officer Taylor is full of himself. He tried to strong-arm me. Pressure from Judge Timms." He stared into the amber liquid. "William shut it down."

"That's it?"

He lifted his head; his eyes were hot. "I did not have an inappropriate relationship with your friend. I'm insulted you'd have to ask. Initially, I wasn't even going to treat the woman, but she insisted. And she needed treatment."

"Why? There are plenty of other shrinks she could've seen. She could've even gone out of town to protect herself from being found out if she didn't want the judge to know about it. Why you?"

He took a deep breath. "She claimed she felt comfortable with me because I was your father. She had trust issues when it came to men. And she needed to be sure I wouldn't violate her trust." No wonder with the Neanderthal she was married to.

My palms began to burn, and I unclenched my fingers. I hadn't even realized I'd dug my nails in. I perched on the ottoman in front of him. "You swear to me nothing is going to come out? There isn't the least bit of evidence to question impropriety?"

"I swear." Daddy's gaze never left mine.

I nodded. Okay, okay. "When they get a court order, and you're forced to turn everything over, will it help them close the case?"

He shook his head. "I honestly don't know."

"Did she say anything about Kevin? Or the dumping grounds?"

He raised his brows. "You're referring to the news report about the Jane Doe found up I-85?"

"Well, there are thirty Jane Does, to be exact, but yes, Carol believed she had information on a specific Jane. All this craziness began after she passed the information to my book club."

He studied me but said nothing.

"She told me people believed she was paranoid," I lied, and received no reaction. "And Amelia said she was petrified. I've known Carol for a long time. She never struck me as a paranoid or delusional person. Add that to the man I didn't recognize with her that day at the gas station, followed by her body showing up on my front stoop, and we have a scary situation dumped into my lap."

Daddy reached out and took my hand. "Don't go down any rabbit holes. Let the police do their jobs. If I wasn't bound by privilege, I would have turned over everything this afternoon. My patients must be able to trust I will honor their privacy, no matter what." He gave my hand a quick squeeze and sat back, rubbing his forehead—his one and only tell indicating his high stress levels.

I could appreciate his dilemma. Still, Mother needed peace and security. It would've been nice if he could've made that a priority. I shook my head, and my shoulders slumped forward. "I won't lie to you. I'm scared to death."

"Move back in here, sweetheart. I can't keep you safe if you're not under my roof. And I won't lie to you either and say this situation doesn't scare the hell out of me too."

I met my father's gaze. I didn't say he couldn't protect me anymore. I had to protect myself. "You know I can't do that." I sighed. "Where's Gran?"

"Once I got home and reassured her, she caught a ride with Sally Anne. Tonight's the widow's banquet at the church." He started to stand. "I better go check on your mother."

"No." I rose. "Let me."

Chapter Seventeen

As I mounted the steps, I mentally rehearsed the soothing words I could say to the woman who gave birth to me. I had a renewed appreciation for how she'd managed to start anew in order to give me a better life than she'd had. I'd always viewed my father as the strongest one in the family. Now, I knew different. She'd constructed her life to give me what she never had. Her defense mechanisms of never allowing people to get too close made complete sense to me now.

I rounded the banister and walked down the hall, which was lined with a blue and beige runner, past half a dozen doors, toward my parents' room. All along the hallway were family photos. Some of mother's equestrian years when she was younger had always been favorites. She gave it up after I was born, and I never understood why.

I tapped on one of the French doors, left slightly ajar, and slowly creaked it open. Mother was lying on her bed, on top of the covers, with one arm draped across her eyes and her long, slender legs crossed at the ankles. She didn't stir as I entered the room. The entire scene looked like something from a painting.

Mother certainly fit in this bedroom decorated in French countryside creams and blue floras.

"Come in, Lyla, dear."

Softly I closed the door and made my way over to the bed. "Are you alright? I'm worried about you."

She reached out with her hand and took mine as I sat. "Your mother is made of steel. It takes an awful lot to make me pliable, and it's only when I expose myself to the right amount of heat." She'd always told me that, and God, now not only did I believe her, but loved her even more for it.

"I hate that you've had to be that strong. I'm sorry life has forced you to harden." I returned her squeeze.

She dropped her arm from her eyes, looking years older. "Don't be." She sat up against the pillows. "If I hadn't walked through fire, I wouldn't be who I am today. I'm sorry you saw my outburst. I never wanted a scandal or trauma to jade you." She forced a smile, "My job, to protect you from such goings-on, has always been my priority. To give you a life I only ever dreamed of. Now, well, you see, there are fissures in my armor. Does that make you question everything I ever taught you?"

I lifted my chin and smiled, despite the ache deep within my chest, while I kept my eyes wide so I wouldn't cry. "On the contrary. The difference between my childhood and yours is I'm strong because of how you raised me." I smiled. "What my adult life has taught me is that sometimes life is messy, and you can control it about as much as you can control the wind."

She laughed. A glorious tinkling kind of laugh that warmed me from the inside out. "Don't I know it. Though, some of the trials can be prevented. Your father could have refused to treat Carol Timms." Her eyes narrowed slightly. "As you have complete control over which field you choose to work in, and you could be a little more cautious with the hobbies you engage in."

I started to pull my hand away.

She held on with the strength of Samson. "Lyla, my path has been chosen, and I regret nothing. I've always wanted to be a wife and mother. To keep house and raise a well-adjusted child. To give her everything I never had growing up."

I settled closer to her. "And I'm so grateful. Why won't you ever let me in? Truly in? You know I love you and have always longed to be close to you. Yet, even now, you don't confide in me about your past. Uncle Calvin doesn't speak of it either. When I ask, he immediately shuts me down."

Her eyes softened. "Dear, it would only bring heartache. Let the past stay where it should, buried. Neither my brother nor I desire to relive those days, especially not through your eyes."

An awful thought ran through my mind. I wondered if there were any records of their past. Could it be as easy as a few strokes of the keyboard, and voila, enlightenment? Perhaps I'd understand her better. It might even bring us closer. Staring into my mother's intelligent eyes, I decided, no, it wouldn't. It would be a betrayal.

I nodded to let her know I agreed to let it drop. "Understood. But please don't worry about me. I appreciate all you've given me. Trust you've raised a determined young woman who can make her own decisions and mistakes. Mistakes aren't the end of the world. Like Gran says, it's how we grow and learn. I want to make a difference. If I can affect change in even the smallest of ways, my life will mean something. Not only with Carol's case but also all those Jane Does—"

"Lyla—"

"Please, listen to me."

She sat back with a sigh and motioned for me to continue.

"I understand how disturbing my desire to investigate cases of dead women is to you and Daddy." I gave my head a small shake and licked my lips as I groped for the words to reach her, to make her understand. "Those women couldn't pull themselves out of the gutter, nor were some of them even given a chance to discover which path life would take them down. Their identities were stolen, and their lives simply erased. Someone has to care. I care."

"And that's so noble of you, sweetheart. It's a dangerous and morbid sort of life to choose. I want more for you. I want happiness that comes from watching your child take her first steps and say her first words. The glorious sound of giggling on Christmas morning." She had a faraway look in her eyes, as if remembering her time as a young mother.

"The life you gave me was akin to a fairy tale, and I'm so grateful."

She shook her head, her gaze intense. "I'm not after gratitude. I'm advocating for you to reach your potential. For your life to be good. This dead club isn't good. Your obsession with murder victims isn't good."

She loved me and meant well, but we would never see eye to eye on this matter.

I sighed. "I don't want to cause you problems. Or to fuel rumors about our family."

"That's on your father at present. He's aware of how I despise scandal." She rubbed between her perfectly arched eyebrows with her index finger, and just like that, we were back in a familiar realm. "Please, honey. I understand you want to help those who need justice, and your friend is on that list now. Just be careful and give this club a rest. This isn't one of your little games where you guess who the murderer is. This is real life with upstanding folks' reputations on the line. Are you truly so naive you can't see the danger you're in?"

"Let's just agree to disagree. This isn't about my club or my decision to work for your brother. My friend is dead. Someone took her life and crumpled her up as if she were garbage. I'm no fool."

Time to get real. "Could the fact that Carol was delivered to my house have been some sort of message? Sure. Likely even. Is that going to make me shy away from helping the authorities hunt down the SOB and lock him away? Not a chance."

Mother pursed her lips, and I rose. At least she'd regained her strength. I'd accomplished that, at least.

Chapter Eighteen

M onday, Gran called as I unlocked the office door.
"'Morning. You're up early." I'd left my parents' house
shortly after Gran returned Saturday night from her banquet.

She'd come home with a widower from church, instead of
Sally Anne. The old man had looked to be a hundred and was
bonier than even Gran, and that was saying something. She'd
had her arm looped through his, and they waltzed through the
house giggling like school kids. Gran offered him a piece of
pound cake that "she" had baked. And he made little kissing
sounds while they ate from the same fork. Daddy hadn't even
had the energy to make a fuss as he usually did when Gran
brought a man home. I was just happy she'd found some joy
after the brutal day we'd had.

"Yes, I'm in love." Gran giggled on the other side of the line.

I laughed despite myself. "In love that fast, huh?"

"When you're my age, fast is the only way to live. He's a real
looker, don't you think?"

"Uh-huh. Sure." I put a pod in the Keurig and pressed for a
strong brew. The dripping began, and I placed my earbuds in my
ears and my purse under my desk. My grandmother had gone

from the depths of despair about Daddy to madly in love in record time. She'd always been the carefree sort, but this was something, even for her.

"I thought maybe we could double-date sometime. Let him get to know you." Crunching came from her end of the line.

"Oh well, when I get a date, we'll have to do that." The image of Gran and me out on the town with our dates in tow was the levity this morning needed. I sipped on my black coffee.

"You'll get a date. You're like your ole Gran. We have this aura that draws the opposite sex like moths to a flame."

Pounding on the office door startled me, and some coffee sloshed over the side and onto the sleeve of the green cashmere sweater mother bought me for Christmas last year. "Shoot! Gran, I have to go."

"Okay, sugar. Think about the double-date idea. I'm comin', Frances. Hold your horses. I'm just chatting with my granddaughter."

"I'll think about it. Bye." I disconnected the call and snatched some napkins off the bar and began to blot as I went to the front door. I opened the blinds, and there stood Mrs. Ross, banging with such intensity that her chunky necklace and bracelet bounced around on her neck and wrist.

I unlocked the door and met the frantic gaze of my parents' neighbor. "Mrs. Ross, please come in." I moved to allow her to pass.

"Is Mr. Cousins here?" She stormed past me and began pacing, glancing behind her as if she feared she'd been followed.

"No. He's working a case in Atlanta." I closed the door. Her behavior had me on full alert.

"Good. You're the one I want to speak with, and if at all possible"—she lowered her tone as if someone could overhear her—"I'd like to keep this confidential."

I nodded my head and tried not to act alarmed.

"Well, I wanted to talk to you about this yesterday, but Thelma was there, and you know what a gossip she is."

I motioned to the chair opposite my desk. "Please have a seat and tell me how I can help you."

She sat on the edge of one of the chairs across from my desk. "It's my daughter-in-law Chelsea." She dug a Kleenex out of her purse and put it up to her well-powdered nose. "She's got herself involved in something awful. I just know it!"

I pulled my chair from around the desk, to be face-to-face with her. "Take a deep breath and explain."

She vigorously nodded. "Okay." An exhale. "Well, the day after Carol Timms was found, I had my son Trace and Chelsea over for dinner. Chelsea had a little too much wine and got to talking about Carol. They were tennis partners."

I hadn't known Carol to play tennis.

"She said Carol gave her something to hold for her."

She had my attention.

"Now I'm terrified. I went to the police, but they told me to have Chelsea come in and speak to them if she were concerned. They brushed me off as if what I had to say was completely inconsequential." She leaned forward, her eyes narrowing. "If you ask me, I bet Carol Timms would still be alive if the police had moved faster. Don't you?"

I opened my mouth and closed it again.

"I know you can't speak to the specifics of that particular case"—she waved the tissue—"but folks talk. I heard how she was brutalized after being held in confinement for several days.

And then how she escaped and fled to the safety of your home because it was the closest." She shook her head. "Only for it to be too late in the end. Her poor heart couldn't take such treatment, you know, with her heart condition. And I won't have it be too late for Chelsea."

I swallowed. "Mrs. Ross, I'm not sure you have the facts." I made a "whoa" gesture with my hands. "Let's not jump to conclusions." Now I understood why people weren't looking at me sideways. Instead of being demonized, those who heard the rumors saw me as the person who had tried to save Carol.

I stared at the jumpy woman before me. "What did Carol give your daughter-in-law?"

"Oh." Mrs. Ross began digging through her oversized shoulder bag and pulled out a crumpled manila envelope.

I had my hand on the envelope when the office door opened and in walked the chief of police. I stood, and before I could address Quinn, Mrs. Ross was on her feet and wagging her finger at him. "Chief Daniels, you should be ashamed of the pathetic job your department is doing. Ignoring a concerned citizen when they come to do their civic duty. That poor Timms woman would have lucked out if she'd died in a different county."

"Mrs. Ross, I understand you're upset. I heard from my officer you weren't happy when you left. I assure you the safety of our citizens is our highest priority." Quinn shifted on his feet and maintained eye contact with the older woman. "Have your daughter-in-law come in and I'll speak to her personally."

"Ha! Now you want to help. What are you doing here sniffing around Lyla when you could be out there" —she flung her hand toward the window—"searching for whoever is responsible for that poor Timms girl's death?"

When Quinn blinked at the mention of sniffing around me, Mrs. Ross smirked.

She put her hands on her narrow hips. "Oh yes, we all know how you're still hung up on her."

My eyes went wide, and I glanced from Quinn, who stood as if frozen, but only his mouth opening and closing, trying to get a word in.

"Mrs. Ross, please. I'm sure the chief is here on an official capacity."

"Pfft. The entire department is out of their depth! And I won't stand by doing nothing. You hear me?"

This was quickly escalating, and I had to put an end to it. "Quinn," I moved to his side and placed a hand on his forearm, "if you have business with Calvin, he isn't on the premises at present. You might try him on his cell phone. Otherwise, it might be best if you come back another time."

"Yeah, get outta here, you worthless good for nothin' waste of space!"

Both Quinn and I swung our heads toward Mrs. Ross, who, moments before he entered, had seemed so feeble and lost. Now she looked stark raving mad.

"Perhaps it would be best if we speak at a later date." He walked over to my desk and reached into his pocket, took out a card, scribbled something on the back, and left it on the desk. "Mrs. Ross, please don't hesitate to reach back out or have your daughter-in-law come by." He nodded to us and left.

I didn't have time to focus on Quinn or ponder what he'd come here to discuss.

Mrs. Ross grabbed her shoulder bag. "I better get goin'. Now that I've turned this over to you, I can put my mind to rest."

"Could I perhaps have Chelsea's contact info? I'd like to have a word with her."

She narrowed her eyes. "Why? I told you everything. You have whatever it is." She motioned to the envelope in my hand." I could clearly see that she'd snooped through its contents.

"Like you just reminded our chief of police, this is serious. I need to speak to her directly. I'll be discreet. You have my word on that." I gave her a smile. "And of course, I appreciate y'all's help."

The old woman dithered momentarily. "Look, Chelsea doesn't know I took that from her house. And to be perfectly honest, I did look through it." She raised both her hands. "But only after they were so rude to me at the police station. That's when I knew I had to come see you." She snatched a pen off the desk and jotted down her number on a sticky note.

"Thank you, Mrs. Ross."

Mrs. Ross straightened and nodded. "I will expect you to keep your word. I don't want to hear you've blabbed to Frances. Chelsea is an upstanding young woman, and I plan to keep her that way."

Chapter Nineteen

I sat at my desk and dialed Chelsea's number while I began opening the envelope. I got her voicemail. Expecting as much, I left a detailed message. With all the spam risks out there, if you don't recognize the number, straight to voicemail it goes.

I pulled the seal free and my heart skipped a beat. Inside was a scarf—our majorette alumnae orange and blue scarf. A sticky note fell out of the envelope. In Carol's handwriting, it read, *Give to Lyla Moody before there are ro—*.

The rest of the message was smudged with what appeared to be bronze foundation, making it difficult to read. It looked like Mrs. Ross's shade of choice. Was this Carol's scarf? Someone else's? Not Chelsea's. She'd never attended Sweet Mountain High.

My mind raced back to the picture I'd saved from the dumping ground doc. I pulled it up and compared the two. They were so similar. It would be difficult to make a definite determination without viewing the one they had in evidence. Carol had hidden this. *From who?*

Panic flooded me, and I shoved the scarf back into the envelope and stuffed it into my bag. I had no idea what to make of this.

My cell rang. I'd hoped the caller was Chelsea but was disappointed. "Uncle Calvin, how's it going?"

"It's going. What's happening there?"

"We have a few new developments. Daddy's back at home. He and I had a long talk, which was good. Mel is no longer being harassed by the police." I fingered the envelope. "And Mrs. Ross came in, concerned about her daughter-in-law."

"What about her?"

"Carol left something at her house." I debated how much to go into. "A scarf. She thought it might be important."

"And was it?"

"Yeah, I think it might be. I'm going to do a little digging. Have you heard from Judge Timms?"

"Actually, Lyla, that's why I'm calling. He's keeping me updated. There's been a development in the case."

My shoulders tensed. Maybe that's what Quinn had come by to discuss with me. "Do the police have a suspect in custody?"

"I'm afraid not. There's no easy way to say this."

"Don't even try to make it easy." My tone sounded strong, even to my own ears, and I steeled myself for the worse.

"Very well. With the unusual circumstances surrounding the case, Carol's heart condition, and the way she was discovered, the coroner has ruled the cause of death undetermined. They're releasing her body for burial."

"Wait a minute. You mean they're not ruling the death a homicide?" No ruling, no crime.

"No, they're not."

"That's bullshit!"

Calvin coughed. "It's how it goes sometimes in cases, Lyla."

"So, the most we can expect is unlawful disposal of a corpse?" I couldn't believe my ears.

"From the information I was given, yes. Without a homicidal cause of death, legally there aren't many more options."

"Wait a minute. I thought the judge was vying for a second opinion or something." I gripped the envelope containing the scarf. Could this even help us now?

"I'm not sure if he obtained one or not. What I do know is, with no hard evidence and taking into consideration that all the alibis of those who could have had involvement checked out, it doesn't look like we're going to have answers any time soon."

"You're saying they're not investigating anymore. That's it?" My tone rose higher than I intended.

"The investigation is ongoing."

But not as a murder investigation.

"They're releasing her body to her husband this afternoon. Keeping her in the morgue won't change the findings."

"And what will the guy get who did this to her? I mean if they even find him. A slap on the wrist? A felony that might bring three years after good behavior?" I scoffed. "Pathetic. That coroner should have his license revoked."

"It isn't easy when a case doesn't go your way, especially when you have a personal relationship with the victim, but that's how it is. Hold on a minute." I heard him talking to our newest client. I made a mental note to remind Calvin about the mute button on his phone. "Okay, I'm back. I've only got another minute or so."

"But what about the man I saw with her? Did they ever locate him?" I massaged my temples.

"You're the only eyewitness that such a man even exists." Calvin hadn't softened his tone, and I took that as a point of pride.

"They don't believe me then. I just fabricated the entire ordeal. My ruined dress must have appeared out of thin air too." *Is that what Quinn wanted to speak with me about?*

Mrs. Ross was right! Carol should have died in another county. I wouldn't waste my breath on sharing my theories or what I discovered involving the Jane Doe case with our chief of police.

"It isn't that they don't believe you. You have to understand resources in our small town are scarce. Even if they wanted to, Sweet Mountain doesn't have the manpower to hunt down some random individual who may or may not reside here. The person could be from anywhere."

"And Judge Timms is in agreement with the police?" I stood up and went to get a bottle of water. What I really needed was a stiff drink.

"No. He has his own theory, and I don't have time to go into it now. Listen, I'll be out of pocket for a few days, maybe a week. Leave me a message, and I'll get back at my first opportunity. And Lyla . . ."

I twisted the cap of the bottle too forcefully, and a little water sloshed out. "Yes?"

"Don't go doing anything stupid before I get back. Leave this alone."

I swallowed the sip I'd taken. "I have to find out what happened to her. You know that."

"Dammit, Lyla. As your boss, I'm ordering you not to do anything until I get back."

I huffed, then said, "You can count on me."

"Why don't I believe you?"

"Because you're an intelligent yet notoriously suspicious person. I get it. I'm the same way. That's why we make such great business partners." There was no way in hell I was letting this drop.

"Let's stick with receptionist, for now, who helps me out on occasions while she learns the ropes."

"Suit yourself. I have no qualms proving myself." I'd do whatever it took to get to the truth. "Seriously, Uncle Calvin, I'm not an idiot."

"You're hearing me."

"Yes. Speak soon." I disconnected the call, and stalked outside, taking in a deep breath of brisk air. The historic square was alive with pedestrians. The slight coolness in the air was welcome after the brutal summer we'd had. The maple trees strategically positioned around the square swayed in all their glory. Carol had loved fall. God, I was so angry, I didn't know what to do.

My phone buzzed. I glanced down and read the text in green on my screen.

Want to play a game, Jane Doe?

The bottle of water slipped from my hands and crashed against the ground.

My heart pounded.

"'Morning, Lyla." A woman I recognized as one of Mother's friends said with a smile. She had a little toddler in pigtails with her, and they were heading for Smart Cookie. I couldn't recall her name.

"Good morning." I groped for it. Nothing. "I . . . I better get back."

Back in the office, I texted back.

Who is this?

The little dots were moving on the screen, signifying the sender was typing, and I waited for the text to come through.

The other Jane lost. Will you?

Something knotted in the pit of my stomach. Dear God, . . . help.

Chapter Twenty

The Jane Does were gathered at my house. Everyone except for Patsy. Her twins had colds, so she joined us virtually. Amelia propped her tablet up on a pillow next to her. "The book was terrific up until the end. I mean, I didn't buy that the little girl would be able to manage to climb out on the roof and around into the attic. Come on! My niece is that age and would be scared senseless by the height, let alone the creepy attic space."

"It's possible." Amelia turned to face the tablet. "It would depend on the kid, I guess."

"No way, and another thing that bothered me was when Rowan went into the poison garden and got a rash on her forehead. They never once mentioned how she treated it or if anyone noticed the blisters." Patsy shook her head. "I mean really, who's not going to at least ask a pharmacist about a rash like that or, at the very least, put some hydrocortisone cream on it. That's totally a plot hole."

Val snickered. "I don't think that constitutes a plot hole, Pats."

"What do you think, Lyla?" Patsy's image froze on the screen.

"Huh? Oh, I didn't finish it." If I were to be honest, I'd never even started.

Amelia sucked in a breath, "It was a DNF—did not finish—for you?"

I shook my head. "No. I've been a little preoccupied."

"Yeah, with real life," Mel added. I'd already shared with her what transpired today.

"What's going on, Lyla? Is this about your dad?" Val took a sip from her glass.

"Oh, we lost Patsy." Amelia put her tablet back into her purse.

"No. That was a complete misunderstanding. It's all straightened out now." I felt a tad relieved when I stood and told the club what I believed would be easier coming from me. Patsy was too emotional to have to deal with all of this. Her words, not mine. I informed my club of the coroner's findings and how the police would proceed.

"That's it then? There'll be no justice for Carol. Whoever murdered her gets to walk around living their pathetic life while she rots away in the ground!" Amelia's voice quivered with what sounded like a combination of outrage and heartache.

"According to the law, if homicide isn't the cause of death, then, at this point, the most we can hope for is unlawful disposal of a corpse."

"Corpse. It's Carol, not a corpse." Amelia sniffed.

Melanie moved closer to Amelia and hugged her.

"I didn't mean it to come out that way. Of course it's Carol."

Val crossed and uncrossed her legs, with her hands in her lap. "I agree on the outrageousness of the judgment, but the funeral is scheduled for this Thursday. We should cool it on the insistence the police do more."

Everyone gaped at Val, who responded, "Out of respect. Her family needs time to grieve, and so do we."

No one here knew better than I did that time was of the essence. If we "cooled it," as Val suggested, then it could go cold for good. I ran my hands through my hair. Everyone was upset, and emotions were still running so high, I had to be careful what I said next.

"Val, we don't want to cause the family any grief," Melanie said softly as she and Amelia sat next to each other on one end of the fit group, staring at Val and me seated on the other side. "It's just difficult for us to fathom, from the way Lyla and I found her, that the coroner could rule the cause of death as he did. They sure were hot to trot on the investigation a few days ago, hauling me in and then Lyla's dad. Now all of a sudden it isn't top priority? All those cases we've studied where, after all these years, families are forced to carry on without any closure. We don't want that for Carol's family or for us."

Val nodded. "I get that—I do. And if it were one of us that had died, Carol would stop at nothing to see the responsible party was brought to justice."

I bit my lip and debated whether I should share what Mrs. Ross had given me at this juncture. I knew I would tell them about the texts. They needed to be warned about the madman who seemed to be targeting me and, if I'd read his reference to the other Jane correctly, Carol before me. Or maybe he meant the one who he'd dumped up I-85. Either way, it was scary as hell.

"What is it, Lyla?" Of course Mel would recognize my inward-debate face.

"Yeah, what are you staring at?" Val asked with narrowed eyes.

153

We were all in this together, especially if they became a target next. Plus, my club would care what I discovered. Decision made. "Okay, two things. One, I had someone come into the office today and hand something over that Carol left for me."

The eyes of all the women in the room were big as they listened.

I went and retrieved the envelope, dumping the contents out. Eyes got impossibly wider.

""Before there are ro'?" Val furrowed her brow. "'Ro'? That doesn't make any sense."

"It's all smudged. maybe with makeup. But it clearly says, 'Give to Lyla,'" Amelia added.

I pulled up the image of the scarf from the Jane Doe file for the others to give their input. While they were arguing among themselves as to whether or not it matched, I continued, "Now what I'm thinking is this: my uncle has an IT specialist he works with. If Carol visited the Jane Doe site in the days leading up to her death, I should be able to prove it by having her watch or phone history tracked by the location of the tower it pinged. Then maybe that would force the police department to consider the two crimes linked."

"Oh! What a brilliant idea! Carol had a smart watch with cellular." Amelia sat forward. "She was so excited about her upgrade because she could play tennis and receive texts and calls."

I nodded. "There wasn't a watch on her wrist when we found her. If—and it's a big if—she had been wearing it before the, um, the end, according to the IT specialists I spoke with, we can track the last tower it pinged, giving us a location."

Val's mouth gaped. "That's possible?"

"Apparently. It can be done with her phone too, but the judge said she left that behind. If her watch is still at her house, then we're out of luck there."

"I never saw her without her watch." Amelia sounded encouraged.

"We didn't see her without her purse either, and she didn't take that when she left." Val chewed the side of her index finger. Something I never saw her do. "I'd call David right now if I didn't believe he'd crumble. I mean, how much is a man expected to take? And now the police aren't going to be actively searching for whoever harmed her." Val got up and began pacing. "Do you really believe the cases are connected?"

I nodded. "I'm sorry, Val. She was your best friend," I said as Amelia, Melanie, and I exchanged a worried glance.

Our poor friend was struggling more than we realized, and we were harping on finding out the truth and hadn't considered whether it was Val that needed a break.

"I should have waited to share."

Val tucked her dark hair, straight as a board tonight and split down the middle, behind her ears. She blew out a breath and straightened her shoulders, and the controlled Val we were all so familiar with reemerged. "No. Don't be sorry. I don't want to be kept in the dark. I want to find out what happened to Carol as much as y'all do. Do you know if the police attempted to track her location?"

"I don't think so. If the judge told them about all of her belongings being at the house, I don't see why they would." I lifted my hands. "But don't quote me on that. I'll need to speak to the judge to confirm." I sighed. "That's another reason why I said it was a long shot. She may have left the watch behind too."

"What else? You said there were two things. What's the second?" Val stared straight at me.

"I've been receiving texts. Ever since I started digging, these texts began." I laid my phone on the coffee table for my friends to read.

"This is getting freaking spooky," Mel said tremulously.

I nodded.

Val tapped the screen with one of her long manicured nails. "Game? What game? Is Carol the other Jane Doe?"

"I think so." I swallowed, and Mel let out a little whimper.

"This is really scary. Maybe we should back off." Val shivered. "If this psycho thinks this is a game, he might come after all of us."

"Sweet Jesus," Amelia gasped. "You mean, like, one by one?"

"I know it's frightening. But if this guy is coming for me, I must be on the right track or getting there. And I, for one, think this is the same scarf. It's our majorette gift. The one we all received at the alumnae bonfire."

"Me too." Melanie pointed back at the image.

"Oh my God. The Jane Doe went to high school with all of you?"

I lifted both my palms up as I met Amelia's gaze.

Val began shaking her head in what appeared to be disbelief. "I don't see it. This old worn-out thing appears to have a similar pattern, with the stripes of burnt orange and navy blue, but in its condition, it's hard to tell."

"Carol thought so because she left it with someone to pass onto me. I'm thinking now I better contact the agent on the case. Maybe Carol reached out to him."

Val asked, "Who did she give it to?" At the same time Amelia blurted, "As in Special Agent Brad Jones from the article?"

I nodded to Amelia and said to Val, "I swore to secrecy—sorry."

"That's stupid. You're telling us everything else."

I sighed. "If I divulge when she came to Cousins, it might reflect poorly on the business. I swear its inconsequential, and if that changes, y'all will know."

Val didn't look happy, but she let it drop.

"Also, we have to consider that Carol had been fighting with her stepbrother a lot. And she was scared of someone."

"Oh shit!" Mel's hand went to her mouth. "Yeah, and you found the camo baseball cap. Plus, he was staring out the window at you when you received the first text. Could it be Kevin? It fits now."

"What?" Val sounded even more on edge.

"He was?" Amelia asked in shock, and I nodded.

"What baseball cap?" Val asked.

I rubbed my forehead with my thumb and index finger. "Kevin threw a bag of trash away in my can the other night. The bag ripped on the edge of the lid after he left, and a camo cap the exact style of the one I saw on the man at the gas station that day, in the car with Carol, was exposed."

"All this, and the police can do nothing?" Amelia was outraged.

Mel was on her feet, gesticulating wildly, flinging her arms toward Kevin's building as she ranted. "And the killer could be nearby! Did you speak to Quinn? My God!"

"I did speak to him. Not about what I just found out, but the text. He didn't take it as seriously as I would have thought. He seemed to think it was a joke because I'm interested in the Jane Doe case and"—I shook my head and glared at the floor—"because of our club and my obsession with finding Carol's killer." I sighed and faced the others. "And it could be a complete coincidence about Kevin and his cap. We mustn't rush to judgment."

"Yes, but that was before the texts and this new information. Now"—Amelia flung her arm toward the table—"you have the cap and the scarf. Carol must've discovered not only the identity of the victim but also the killer. This needs to be looked into. He's practically living next door to you and Mel. I'm scared for you both."

"Lyla's right. We can't rush to judgment here. There were more than twenty scarves given away at that bonfire. And I bet half of them were donated to Goodwill or something. I know I donated mine with several bags full of fall clothing years ago. And that's *if* it's the same scarf." Val dug through her bag and began tapping on her phone as she paced the floor.

"Who are you texting?" Amelia wanted to know.

"Greg. We need his help."

"Who's Greg?"

Melanie shifted in her seat. "It's Officer Taylor's first name."

Val glanced over at me. "I'm going to see what he knows," she continued. "If we can get him on our side, maybe he'll listen to you"—she shrugged—"since Quinn won't."

I stood and put my hand on her phone. "No. We need to be careful who we talk to. And I'm not a fan of Taylor's. He's a real jerk."

Val studied me. "He's always been so nice to me."

"Let's get all our ducks in a row before we speak to anyone else in the Sweet Mountain Police Department. I want to have a word with the judge first. He's working with Calvin, so it'll be easy for me to approach him on this."

Val nodded and put her phone away. "You're right. If we have him go to the police, it'll hold more validity." She stared down at the scarf. "Like you said, someone has to do something, for Carol." Val's crystal-blue gaze had a wild glint to it. Clearly, she'd been thrown by what I'd found.

"I wonder if this department is up for the task," Amelia huffed.

Val ignored her and perched on the edge of the coffee table, facing me. "I also don't want another one of my friends come to the same end. I can't do it, Lyla. I can't take another b—" Her voice quivered, and she wiped her eyes and rose. Her cell phone chimed. "I must have accidentally sent it to Greg. But don't worry. I can fix this."

I cast a glance toward Mel and Amelia.

While Mel looked uncertain, Amelia nodded her head and said, "My suggestion would be to go to the press. But I'll relent and agree we should try this first."

I rose and gathered the scarf and camo hat and put them in the envelope. I registered how difficult all this was for everyone.

"I appreciate y'all trusting in me." I smiled at my friends.

Val let out a shuddering breath, "God, I miss her." She started for the door. "I'll find out if she left her watch behind when I check in on David tonight and see how he's feeling about the new developments."

"You don't need to do that. I'll speak to him." I was on my feet.

She shook her head. "My mind is made up. Carol and I were best friends. He won't find it odd for me to ask. I'll share everything with the club when I find out the particulars. Now, I'm going home and getting plastered. This is all just too much, and if I don't let loose, I'm afraid I'll blow a fuse. I'll see y'all Thursday." She put her hand on my shoulder. "Walk me out."

The rain had cooled the temperature to the high fifties, and with the howling wind, it felt slightly chillier. Val had been quiet as I walked her to her shiny red BMW. Both of us kept glancing over to where the flickering of the television lights lit up the living room window of Ellen and Kevin's place. I shivered and prayed the cap meant nothing. This was just too close for comfort. Yet I was fully aware that most murders happened by the hand of someone the victims knew and was close to. And the time frame worked out. Kevin and Carol would have lived under the same roof through high school. Kevin graduated only a year before we all did. She would know if he had something to do with the Jane Doe. Carol would know more than anyone else. My pulse raced.

"I can't believe this. Everything is spiraling out of control." Val turned and hugged me, squeezing tightly.

I couldn't hide my shocked expression and was glad she was unable to see it. Val wasn't as affectionate as the rest of us. In fact, she sort of reminded me of Mother in that way.

"It's going to be okay." I hugged her back.

She let out a throaty laugh. "Why do people say that when obviously the situation isn't okay?"

"I guess because we need it to be. If our brains don't somehow normalize and find a way to justify what transpired, we fracture."

A dog began barking in the distance.

She nodded. "Promise me you're going to be careful. I know you're eager to delve into this PI business, and I respect that. But you could make yourself a target by getting in too deep. They've already sent you warnings."

"I promise. You don't worry about me. Sweet Mountain is still safer than the majority of cities in Georgia."

"And yet, look what happened to Carol. Right here in our sleepy little mountain town. You're not as tough as you think you are. Or as invincible. You've never had to be. Be thankful."

She clearly was speaking from experience, and again I was reminded of Mother.

"I hear you. And you promise me you'll take care of yourself. I know how independent and strong you are; we all do." I leaned back, holding on to her hands so she would be able to read my sincerity. "It's okay to be weak sometimes, to lean on your friends. I know you, and I haven't been as close as you and Carol were, but I'm here for you. We're here for you."

Something flickered within her gaze. It moved so swiftly I couldn't detect what it was. "Do you ever wonder what my life was like before I moved here?"

Surprise overtook me, and I stumbled to respond.

She smiled. "You've never asked."

"I . . . I figured you'd tell us if you wanted us to know." In the beginning, I had wondered. I recalled the little dark-headed girl in pigtails, dressed in a pink dress, with white knee socks and patent leather shoes, sitting alone at lunchtime. Mother had warned me not to speak of her past or ask questions. It would be rude and unfeeling to upset the new girl at school. She'd been so quiet at first.

I recalled the day Carol had decided to leave our lunch table and go over to where Val sat alone, eating her lunch. Carol pulled up a chair and chatted away. She gave Val a friendship bracelet. The two were inseparable after that, and then a few months into the school year, Val became a different child. The shy, timid girl had been replaced by an outspoken social butterfly.

Val had a dazed expression. "My early childhood years were hell. My birth parents shouldn't have been allowed to procreate."

I'd never seen Val as a victim before. Out of nowhere, tears began streaming down my cheeks.

"No! Don't weep for me. The one thing those assholes gave me was my iron will." Iron—Mother always used that expression. "Weakness is an impossibility for me now." A ghost of a smile played on her lips, and she glanced off. "Carol understood me. It's why we were so close. She's the only one in this town who ever asked about my birth parents and how I came to be adopted by the Heinzes."

"That must've been so difficult. A little girl in a strange new place."

She shrugged and her eyes glazed over. "The Heinzes were wonderful people. And this town offered security and safety. Life here was simpler, you know. I honestly thought I could live happily ever after here. Then, well, people just ruin things, don't they?"

I nodded. "Yeah, sometimes they do."

She blinked a few times, then turned and slid into the driver's seat of the car. "I'll call you."

Chapter
Twenty-One

The next day, while at the office, Mel and I were having a cup of coffee and biscotti between her shifts at Smart Cookie. I'd contacted Judge Timms first thing, and he'd agreed to meet me at the office. I'd finally spoken to Chelsea as well. She hadn't any information other than that she and Carol were tennis partners, and Carol had asked her to hand the envelope over to me if she had to leave town for some reason or another. I believed her. She had, however, expressed her annoyance with her mother-in-law.

"So, you left a voicemail for Brad Jones? Weren't you nervous?"

I dunked her shop's new flavor, pumpkin spice with white chocolate chips, into my dark brew. "It was early when I called, and no, not really. He's a GBI agent, sure, but he's just a person like you and me. He put a call out for help identifying victims." I shrugged. "I'm answering his call. Plus, there's a great probability he spoke with Carol."

"Makes sense. Still, I'd be nervous about being in a room with a man who'd seen that many horrors. It has to take its toll."

I ignored the fact she hadn't seen the link between the agent and us. We'd seen a few horrors in our life as well.

"Any more spooky texts?"

"Nope, and I blocked the number, so I'm not expecting any." It had felt good to add the sender to my blocked list. Sort of like a "Take that!"

I had grit. I wasn't helpless.

"Good." She let out a deep sigh of relief. "It's all I thought about last night. Do you see Kevin killing anyone? I mean, his own stepsister?" She scrunched up her face.

I finished chewing. "No. And I approached it with an open mind too. But what if we're wrong?"

"That's bone-chilling."

We settled into silence.

"Too many white chocolate chips?" She'd been waiting for me to comment.

"Sorry." I shook my head and put my fingers up to my mouth to cover how full it was. "It's perfect. I'm going to have to hike every day if you keep bringing these to me."

Her brown eyes sparkled with pure delight. "Good. I needed something to focus on this morning. Experimenting with a new flavor did the trick. It didn't exactly take my mind off all this, but it did help. I wonder how the rest of the Jane Does are holding up. Val seemed really shaken last night. Amelia too, but not to the extent Val was."

My shoulders rose and fell. "I hope so. I think Amelia will be okay. I'm worried about Val. I've never seen her so rattled."

"That's the problem when a person appears to have nerves of steel. You never consider they're breaking down." She sipped from her mug and perched herself on the edge of my desk. "Well, actually, now that I consider it, appearances can be deceiving. Think about it: Val is a capable woman, yet she's never actually worked. Amelia is different; she runs her medical transcription business from her home and still has time to organize dinner parties, host her husband's out-of-town guests, and keep up with book club. So really, she's the one with nerves of steel. And wow, besides you and me, she's the most invested in all of this. Patsy—well, I have no idea what's going on with her."

"Amelia is amazing. Patsy just has a lot going on with the twins, and Val has a job. She works in her parents' flooring company." I wiped my hands on my napkin.

Heinz Flooring was big business around these parts, with locations all over the state. The corporate office had and would always be, according to the Heinz family, located right here in Sweet Mountain, which brought ample jobs to our residents.

"Not really. She's a sporadic employee at best. It's almost like she pops in a couple of times a month to appease her family. Why wouldn't she want to do something with her life?"

"Mel, that isn't fair."

"I know, I know. She had a troubled past. Her biological parents died in some fire. It's awful." She raised her free hand. "I'm just saying, she hasn't chosen the life with a husband and two-point-five kids with a golden retriever either. Why?"

"I don't know, and it isn't for us to judge. She had a hard beginning before she moved here. I saw clearly last night how she and Carol were so close."

"My point exactly. She clearly struggles, or wouldn't she have pursued some sort of career? And now I'm wondering, since she and Carol were so close, why didn't she leave the scarf with her? Maybe Carol didn't think she could handle it. Why leave it with—" Mel raised her brows expectantly.

"I'm not divulging that information, Melanie Smart." I gave her a scolding glare.

"You'll have to tell the GBI guy and the police. Why not tell me?"

"It's not going to happen." The last thing I wanted to do was gain a reputation for divulging client information.

Melanie, like me, had the gift of gab. Sometimes her gift became a curse. Technically, neither Chelsea nor Mrs. Ross had been clients, but I'd given my word.

"Oh, come on . . ."

Judge Timms walked through the front doorway, and Mel slid to her feet while I allowed the chair to roll backward as I rushed to stand up and swallowed the last of my biscotti. "Judge Timms, sir."

"Good Afternoon, Judge Timms." Melanie giggled a little and covered it up by faking a cough.

I shot Mel a warning look. I loved her to death and understood her weird giggling quirk, but this man before us wouldn't.

"I beg your pardon," she rushed to add.

He nodded. "'Afternoon, ladies. Is Calvin around?" The heavyset man had thinning, wavy gray hair and a full gray beard in need of a trim. He had bags under his fawn-brown eyes and wore a brown tweed suit that didn't appear as if it had just come from the cleaners. In his hand, he had a gallon-sized Ziploc bag.

"No, sir. He isn't at the moment. Um, I asked you here so I could speak with you."

He stroked his beard absently and glanced away. "Oh yes. I remember Calvin mentioning the case in Atlanta."

"That's correct." I gave him a small smile.

His attention returned to me. "Valerie mentioned on the phone last night that you and Calvin were interested in searching for Carol's last whereabouts via her devices. Something about your own personal IT specialists who might be able to find out more detailed information."

Val had majorly overstepped by dropping Uncle Calvin's name. But I knew she was only trying to help.

I moved around the desk. "That's what I wanted to discuss with you. It's possible if she had her devices on her at the time of her disappearance. We could see the last location where each device pinged. Perhaps gain some idea of who she might've been with." I crossed my hands in front of me. "But I can see from the bag you have that she indeed left everything behind."

He nodded. "Yes, but what if we traced where she went before she went missing. Perhaps that would give me some idea what my poor wife got herself into. I offered to release my records to the police, and they agreed to contact my cellular provider, but once the coroner ruled her death undetermined, well, we no longer had a case that would warrant such records. They may have a preliminary report. I don't know."

"You're offering to release those records to us? And agree for us to contact Calvin's IT specialists?" I didn't technically know if Calvin had his specialists on the payroll per se, but I was betting he used him often enough they were on a regular pay-per-case basis. I felt confident I could enlist the services of the friendly man I'd spoken to.

"I was and spoke directly to Calvin a few days ago, offering him the job at double his usual rate."

That I hadn't been aware of. But I'd planned for this. I skirted around the desk and retrieved the print.

"He claimed to be too busy and gave me the name of another private detective he trusted. I don't know that man, and I don't do business with someone I haven't run a check on or am not familiar with personally."

"You can trust Lyla to handle it!" Mel piped up. "She has access to everything her uncle has. She just cleared her first case the other day. She'd do a terrific job, Judge Timms."

I scowled at Melanie. There hadn't been another job, and she knew it. Her gaze quickly shied away from me.

Turning to Judge Timms, I squared my shoulders. "Under the circumstances, I can understand how you might have reservations working directly with me, without Calvin, on this case." I cleared my throat and plowed ahead, not wanting anything to deter his trust in my ability to do this job. "For more than one reason. The obvious one is I'm new here, but I have a vested interest in seeing justice be done in this case. Two, the fact that Carol went to my father for treatment." I raised my free hand. "Although, I can assure you, there wasn't the slightest impropriety between my father and Carol. It was strictly a doctor–patient relationship."

The judge studied me for a few long seconds, and something about his intense scrutiny made my skin crawl. "Your father and I had a long conversation, and my suspicions were put to rest." Thank God Almighty for that. "And I might be willing to give you a shot. You seem to be a capable young woman, and Carol respected you and your decision to work here."

I felt genuinely stunned.

I must have shown it because as he handed the bag over to me, he said, "If Calvin allows you to work my case, let me know. If not, I'll come back and collect those. I'll also have a file in a day or so that I'll want to share with you. One of my underlings did a little investigating for me, and I should have everything we need to move forward. He doesn't have the resources Calvin does, but he claims to have found some valuable intel."

"I understand." I held the document out to him. "If you wouldn't mind signing this authorization to release all records to this office."

He took the paper, giving it a once-over.

I cast a glance over my shoulder to Melanie. She gave me a thumbs-up, beaming proudly when he grabbed a pen and signed the document atop my desk.

Judge Timms handed it over and pointed his finger at me. "If Calvin agrees."

"Yes, sir." I nodded as he turned to leave. "Um, Judge Timms."

He paused, and half turned in my direction.

"I'm terribly sorry for your loss. Carol was one of a kind, and I'll do my best by her." I clutched the bag to my chest.

"I believe that."

"But I must caution you, it might get messy. I may have to dig into your personal and private dealings. And there's no guarantee either one of us will like what I find." I insisted that our arrangement would be aboveboard.

He couldn't expect me to shy away from anything, no matter how insulting or embarrassing.

"I understand how investigations work, Miss Moody." He gave me a nod. "Feel free to reach out to me with any questions you may have. Contrary to popular belief, I want answers. I don't care about the consequences."

I shuffled the bag to my left arm and extended my hand. "We're in agreement then."

His large sweaty hand engulfed mine. "We're in complete agreement. Now, let's just hope Calvin is."

He left, and I turned around to face Mel, who had both her hands over her mouth, her eyes wide.

"I can't believe you lied like that. What if he wanted a reference? I should be so angry with you."

"You can't be. This is what you wanted, and now you have complete cooperation from Judge Timms. It's official for you to work on this case now." She came around the desk and hugged me and sniffled. "Carol would be so grateful to you. Now I've got to go to work before I get all weepy again."

I fought emotion for a moment as well. "You're right. We both need to get to work."

She waved goodbye as she left. "Love you."

"Love you too."

I left a detailed message for my uncle, explaining the specifics of the potential case. Until I heard a hard no, I'd work it as a definite yes. I began a file and followed that up with a call to the IT specialist.

Chapter
Twenty-Two

After the call, I had a good grasp of how our cell phones are traced. Cell phone towers in wide-open areas could provide service for up to a twenty-five-mile radius around the tower. Each of these cell phone towers had a precise location, with latitude and longitude coordinates. Each time a cellular phone attached to a particular cellular tower, the records indicated which sector the cell phone pinged and captured what was referred to as a call detail record.

The big takeaway for me was that if your phone was on—and let's face it, our phones were always on—they were constantly using data service, especially with all the apps we have running in the background. Therefore, we were all traceable.

Another takeaway was it would take time to get our hands on the records, and since the police should have copies after being granted access from the judge, it might speed things along if I made nice with officers and asked for copies.

I got organized. I pulled out my messenger bag and filled it with essentials: my tablet and stylus. The computer was secured in its rightful place. I had a couple of legal pads and pens, just in case. Then I slid the Ziploc in the outer pocket. I'd searched the bag while on the phone and was sad to see Carol's smartwatch. What I wondered, though, was if she'd gotten another phone. Perhaps on a completely separate account from the one she shared with her husband. Though she certainly could've bought a phone from the superstore so that no one would be able to track her, like the person who texted me. I'd attempted a trace and gotten nothing other than that the number was linked to a cellular device. She clearly didn't want anyone to know where she was going. Leaving all her devices behind was a glaring clue.

When I pulled up to the police station, the butterflies were building, and I made a conscious effort to slow down. I'd gone home and changed into something more flattering. I took care to enhance my cheekbones and curl my lashes. To make nice, I needed to look nice. I had to do whatever was necessary to find answers and right wrongs. I did wonder if I'd gone a little overboard to dress up as much as I had. Would Quinn see right through me? I couldn't focus on that now. What was done was done.

By the time I made my way up the steps and opened the door, I'd managed to tamp down some of the nerves and slow my breathing. I had my hand on the door when, to my astonishment, Ellen came waltzing out.

Her eyes widened when she nearly ran me over. "L-Lyla," she stuttered. "What are you doing here?"

"I have an appointment with Quinn." I smiled despite my lie.

She smirked. "All gussied up too. Well, well."

I hefted my bag higher on my arm. "It's business. What about you?"

"I came to check on the case. Unlike you, Carol and Val were friendly to me. We had dinner on occasion, and I wanted to see if there was anything I could do to help." Was she serious? What could she possibly do to help out with the case?

My skepticism must have shown on my face because she all but snarled.

"You're such a bitch. You always think you're smarter than everyone else." She threw up a hand. "I don't have to stand here and take this."

"Ellen." I frowned.

She stormed past me and marched toward her car.

Oh well.

A woman in uniform sat at the front desk. She must have been new since I'd never seen her before. She scowled as I approached, but slid the panel window open.

Not that I would allow her "stay-away" glare to deter me. I was a woman on a mission, an official private investigative mission. "Is this about the Carol Timms case? Everyone wants to talk about Carol Timms. Everybody has an opinion, a theory, and a suspect."

Yikes. I didn't care for her tone. I smiled. "Hi, actually I'm here to speak to Chief Daniels. I'm Lyla Moody. Is he available?"

The woman scratched her head with the back of her pen. She had her hair pulled back in a tight braid. "I'll see." She closed the window, and I realized it was soundproof and, I was betting, bulletproof.

The door buzzed and she waved her hand for me to go through. Not a chatty gal. I walked past the two small metal desks in the large room with beige walls and ratty, green, threadbare carpet. Both desks were vacant. I rounded the water cooler and saw through the windows and the half-closed door with "Chief Daniels" stenciled on it. He sat at the desk, on the phone, his back toward me. I crept closer.

"I took care of it. Yes," I overheard him say. "There isn't anything else that can be done at this point. If she comes by, rest assured, I'll handle it. This squares us."

Something inside clenched for a moment. *She? Ellen? Or someone else.* I hesitated and almost turned back. He slammed his phone down, and I jumped. My heel caught on a worn spot in the carpet, and I stumbled, my bag hitting the door, opening it further.

When he whirled around, I immediately lifted my hand in a friendly manner. His face flushed; his eyes roamed my body.

"Sorry." I tucked one of my long, wavy locks behind an ear. "The officer at the desk said I could come on back. If this is a bad time, I can reschedule."

"No, it isn't a bad time. I told Officer Clarence to send you back." Quinn stood and waved his hand swiftly. "Come in. Please."

"Okay. If you're sure." I slipped through the doorway. Perhaps he thought he'd be finished with his call before I made it to his office. "May I sit?"

"Oh yes—yes, please." He settled back in his chair as I took a seat in one of the armchairs with red padding.

His office had wood paneling and an artificial plant in the corner. Other than that, it lacked any other descriptive pieces.

I found the space depressing. "I saw Ellen leaving."

He pointed to the paper on his desk. "Shoring up her statement."

"Ah." She said she'd come by to help. Ha!

"You never called," he said softly.

"With circumstances being what they were, I didn't feel comfortable." I let the messenger bag slide from my shoulder to rest on the floor against my feet. "Quinn, Cousins Investigative

Services has been retained by Judge Timms to look into his case. In the spirit of full disclosure and to show how invested we are in working with the police department, I have evidence to share."

Quinn raised his brows.

I pulled the envelope containing the scarf, note, and camo hat and placed it on the desk. I gave him a detailed account of everything.

"And you believe this scarf is linked to the Jane Doe case Carol was supposedly interested in?"

I nodded.

"And the note? Doesn't make much sense."

"No. That one puzzles me too. The note being smudged doesn't help things." I'd spoken to Mrs. Ross after speaking with Chelsea, and she swore up and down the note was written exactly as she delivered it. I cleared my throat, "I also realized I'd behaved a little unfairly toward you." I smiled. "You have a job to do, and my feelings shouldn't be the focal point. It isn't as if we've been close in years. I shouldn't have expected you to come rushing to my side. It's a ludicrous notion, to say the least. I apologize."

He folded his hands on his desk. "If I'm being honest here, I was sort of flattered you looked for me. I've often thought back to how we ended things. Sure, we were kids and all, but I wished we'd ended things better."

I nodded. "So here we are. Working together."

"Here we are." He smiled. "What can I do for you?"

"Judge Timms came by the office and updated me on the case, and with the coroner ruling the cause of death undetermined, he's concerned."

He inclined his head. "Is that right? Did he also inform you that he, your father, and I had a long meeting when your father turned over Carol's patient file."

I raised my eyebrows in question. "He mentioned having a discussion with my father and how he no longer believed there to be any impropriety."

He studied me. "Interesting. The court order came through before the cause of death."

Huh. I wondered if I could take a gander at those files. Judge Timms obviously had. Daddy kept audio files too. It would help me on this investigation to have a listen.

"The day I came by your uncle's office, I wanted to explain, in limited terms, of course. I know how disturbed you've been about losing your friend, not to mention finding her in that way."

"Of course." I crossed my right leg over the left and folded and laced my fingers over my knee. "You still have no idea why they left her for me to find? It's odd, you have to admit."

"It is odd. I've seen and studied a lot of stranger cases than that, though. One never knows what's going on inside the head of a person on the verge of insanity. And Carol had some strenuous relationships."

"Like?"

He gave his head a shake. "I can't discuss an ongoing investigation."

"You're still actively involved, then?"

He nodded.

"Will the case change directions with the discovery of new evidence?" I nodded toward his desk.

"Could be. Have you received any more texts?"

I swallowed. "Yes."

I pulled my phone from my bag and showed him. His face tensed as he read the text, and I was sure the word "game" was what had him unnerved. No one wanted to even consider dealing with a serial killer playing a so-called game. He jotted the sender's number down and pierced me with his gaze. "If you get another one of these texts or if you feel the least bit threatened by anyone, I want to know about it."

I nodded, surprised and pleased he was taking it seriously.

"Tell me about Kevin." He leaned forward; his eyes were intense. "His name has come up more than once. He would know about your past obsessions, and he and Carol had a dispute regarding an inheritance. Was your breakup amicable?"

"Well, 'amicable' isn't exactly the word I would use to describe it." Needing something to do, I smoothed my skirt with my hands. "I thought so until he moved in by me. And . . ."

"And?"

"Well, it might be nothing, but when the first text came through, he was watching me through his front window." I raised both hands. "It's probably a coincidence, but he asked about Carol immediately after. And about how I found her. In light of the camo cap, I'm only divulging this so nothing is missed. Not accusing."

"Was he ever violent with you?" There was an edge to Quinn's tone I didn't care for, and I feared Kevin had just become his sole focus.

I kept my expression blank. "No. He never became violent. He isn't a mean person."

"He isn't? He's dating your cousin and moved in by you. That seems unkind to me."

I shrugged and removed my phone from his desk, clutching it in my lap. "Well, the breakup you and I went through would lead people to believe you weren't the kindest person either." He opened his mouth and I held up a hand. "All I'm saying is you can't go solely on how people behave during a relational breakup."

"You can't compare what we had to your fling with Kevin." He sounded incredulous. "And I was never hateful to you. I've heard from others Kevin was nasty. And was livid when you broke up with him. It makes a lot of sense for him to want to make you pay."

I couldn't hide the shock. My mouth dropped open. "I beg your pardon?"

"Getting rid of the evidence and forcing you to find the remains. Two birds, one stone."

Disliking the scenario he laid out, I closed my eyes and shook my head.

"I'm sorry. I shouldn't be pressing you like this. Finding a deceased before decomposition is tragic in itself and enough to deal with."

I took the out he offered. "Yes . . ." My voice trailed off as my phone rang. I used it as an excuse to catch my breath and focus on why I was here. I recognized the number: Mr. GBI, Brad Jones. I couldn't believe he was calling me back so soon.

"From the look on your face, it's someone important."

If I went running from the room to take the call, it would make Quinn keenly interested in who had called, and I'd either have to lie or explain my intention to hopefully bring this man in on Carol's case. In light of the new evidence they possessed, thanks to yours truly, they'd probably be contacting the man themselves and might see my reaching out as interfering. I sent Mr. Jones to voicemail and hoped he would answer when I returned his call.

"No. Just a number I didn't recognize." I slid the phone back into my bag and straightened. "Can I ask you something?"

"Yes." His eyes narrowed in suspicion as my recovery might have come a little too quickly.

"Don't close yourself off. I'm here because the judge asked me to take a look into Carol's whereabouts before she went missing, by looking at which cellular towers her phone pinged. He claimed your office has some sort of preliminary report. I would like a copy of it as well as the medical files."

He didn't respond.

"I shared what I knew. Gave you information about Kevin and passed on valuable evidence."

He folded his arms and studied me intently, and I found him changed somehow. The years on this job had caused him to question everyone and everything. His scrutinizing gaze nearly had me fidgeting, and I felt certain he would turn me down.

I did my best not to squirm as he continued to search my face. For what, I didn't quite know.

"Okay. If Judge Timms has given consent, which I'll need in writing, of course, I'll hand over what we have from the cell phone provider and the files your father provided us. It isn't much and is probably not what you're looking for. But, Lyla, this isn't an open invitation to utilize this office for your personal investigations."

"I understand. I wouldn't be here if Judge Timms hadn't sought our help." I reached into my bag and retrieved the signed waiver, presenting it to Quinn.

Quinn inclined his head, his piercing gaze holding mine captive as he took the form. "The judge is in his rights to seek out a private investigator if he so chooses. It isn't as if I question your uncle's abilities. I just really don't see what he'll find that we haven't. He was smart to send you." Reaching in his desk, he handed over an envelope labeled "Carol Timms" in my father's handwriting. "I'll have to get back to you on the phone records."

I let out a quiet exhale as I put the envelope into my bag. "He didn't send me." I rose. "Thanks for the cooperation and thank you for speaking with me." I started for the door, eager to return Mr. Jones's call.

He hurried around the desk, his hand lightly brushing my arm, "Hey, I didn't mean to offend you."

I turned to look into his luminous baby blues. "You didn't." I smiled.

"Will you have dinner with me?"

I blinked in wonderment as I attempted to regain my composure. This wasn't what I'd had in mind when I set out to make nice.

His tone softened. "I know, I know—it's out of left field and probably the worst timing on the planet. But I'm not seeing anyone, and, from what I heard from your mother, neither are you." *Oh, of course: Mother.* "Just dinner to catch up on each other's lives. I've hated how we've avoided each other for all these years. It's childish, and neither one of us are children anymore." That was true. "What do you say? Friday night? Around six?"

"Well, . . ." My phone chimed with a voicemail alert. It was just dinner. I smiled. "Sure. Why not." It could be beneficial to be on friendly terms with the local chief of police. And it would also be good not to have to avoid him like the plague any longer.

He rocked back on his heels, and his face creased in a giant grin. It was a genuine smile that made its way up to his eyes. "Is there any place special you'd like to go? We could go into the city if you want."

"How about Trail Head Grill?"

His grin still hadn't faltered. "Sounds great to me."

I left the police station with a bounce in my step. Confidence that I could do this job successfully began to bloom. I darted across the parking lot and around the building toward my car. The sun had long set, and the air reflected the drop in temperature. Wind whipped my hair around my face, and something flapping on my windshield caught my attention. I snatched it off and unlocked the door. I could hardly see as I slid into the seat and started to put my bag beside me—and froze . . .

The odor of death accosted me. Something was seeping into the back of my cotton dress and my steering wheel was covered in something dark red. *Blood*. A scream ripped from my throat as I struggled to free myself from the car. I slipped on the drenched leather seats, feeling the stickiness on my thighs. I fell to my knees hard, glancing around wildly. A figure came up from behind my car.

I scrambled backward in the darkness, screaming bloody murder.

The next thing I knew Quinn was in my face, gripping me tightly by the shoulders. "It's me! It's only me."

Chapter
Twenty-Three

I stood in the lady's room in my bra and panties after scrubbing the blood from my body with paper napkins. Quinn had informed me during his questioning that a dead possum was found in my back seat, and the blood in the car came from it. Someone was sending me a harrowing message. At least now Quinn was taking this seriously. They'd canvased the area, asking everyone eating in the little restaurant in the neighboring lot if they'd seen anyone suspicious. The police department's cameras hadn't picked up anything, a fact I found highly suspect. Officer Taylor had warned me off, and now I wondered if he was somehow involved.

I glanced up in the mirror and, with shaking hands, attempted to smooth out my long, frizzy hair. Nervous blue eyes stared back at me, and I exhaled a slow, controlled breath. How could this happen? In the parking lot of the police station! I began to have more concerns regarding whom to trust.

Goose bumps erupted across my skin as I pulled on the gray sweatpants Quinn had given me. When I reached for the police-logoed sweatshirt, a crumpled piece of paper fell to the floor. I must have fisted the flyer on the windshield and brought it in with me. I smoothed out the blood-smeared paper and read, *Game on, Lyla. Ready to play? Six little Jane Does started to pry; one's heart gave out, and then there were five.*

I dropped the paper. My breath came in pants. In that moment it hit me. Carol tried to warn *me*. She hadn't written *before there are ro*; she'd written *before there are none*. A reference to *And Then There Were None*, our book club pick. Terror gripped me. The killer somehow knew she'd referenced the book, and was now using it to play with me. Were all the Jane Does in danger? I'd have to warn them.

*   *   *

I sat in the parking lot in front of my building, on the phone with Mother, while I waited on Melanie to get home. Quinn had dropped me off at my parents' house, where I borrowed Mother's car. I'd avoided her completely, with no desire to explain my appearance, and had Gran sneak me her keys. I'd left another message with Mr. GBI, citing the urgency for a callback.

"What happened?" Mother sounded impatient.

"Nothing. I had an accident with my car and didn't want to bother you and Daddy this late."

"Are you okay?"

"Yes. I'm fine. Don't worry."

"I heard the coroner ruled Carol's death as undetermined."

I rubbed my forehead. "Yeah. I heard that too."

She coughed. "That idiot wouldn't know whether to wind his butt or scratch his watch. And he does the worst makeup jobs. Last Sunday, when I went to Christa Wakefield's viewing, she looked like an Oompa Loompa."

Our coroner/funeral director certainly seemed to struggle these days. The man was getting up in age, and I wondered if they'd decide to hire someone a little younger.

"Well, that's terrible for the poor woman, but sometimes these things happen. There aren't always answers for everything, and it'll be good to get things back to normal around here."

"I guess." I didn't have the strength to argue with her, and supposed we were back in the realm of "I'm okay, you're okay, and if we keep this charade up, it will be."

"I heard about Betty Ross's daughter-in-law." Mother clucked her tongue, feigning astonishment. Mother forgot I could read her tells. In fact, she didn't even believe she had any. Her speech sped up when she fought a cunning emotion. She fanned the flames of the rumors to deflect the ones circling our own family. "I can't believe the gall of Betty. Chelsea got involved in some sort of scandal, and she wanted to pawn whatever it was on you."

"It wasn't like that, Mother." Another call came through, and I checked to see if I recognized the number. Didn't.

"Lyla Jane Moody, are you listening to me?" Mother asked.

"Yes, sorry, Mother."

"I said I saw Valerie Heinz at the country club this afternoon."

"You did?" I rubbed my aching neck.

"Yes. She was having lunch with your friends Amelia and Chelsea, of all people."

I frowned. Had Val figured out who Carol entrusted with the scarf?

"Well, actually, they were finishing up. Amelia was meeting her husband for a round of golf. I spoke with Valerie about her parents. Her mother has just been diagnosed with a touch of dementia. Bless her heart."

"Val didn't tell me about her mother's condition." Perhaps that was another reason why she'd been so out of sorts the other night.

"That child was lucky to be adopted by such a respectable family. She came from poor white trash. I've always rooted for her."

I shifted in the leather seat. "What do you know about Val's past? She told me they were horrible parents."

"Drug addicts, I think. They abused the poor girl and her older sister. Their house burned to the ground when Val was about ten, I think. She and her sister were the only ones who survived. Her birth parents were passed out, and their drug paraphernalia caught fire."

"What happened to her biological sister?" Val had never mentioned her. Maybe she was adopted by another family.

"She had problems." Mother lowered her tone, "I think she ended up in one of those homes for troubled kids."

I stared at the flickering yellow streetlight. Poor Val. The crosses she bore were enough to manage, and now she'd lost her best friend in such a tragic way.

Another call came through, and this time I recognized the number. "Mother, I have to run."

Not expecting him to call back so quickly I stuttered, "H-hello, Mr. Jones?"

"Yes, Miss Moody?"

Thankfully, I recovered, saving a little grace. "Yes, this is Lyla Moody. It seems we've been playing a bit of phone tag. I wondered if you had spoken to my friend Carol regarding one of your Jane Doe investigations."

A short pause. "I have spoken to Mrs. Timms on a couple of occasions."

"Oh, well, I'm not sure if you've heard, but she passed away."
Another pause.

"No, I hadn't heard. I'm terribly sorry to hear that."

Why hadn't he heard? "The Sweet Mountain Police Department hasn't reached out to you?"

"No. Any reason they would?"

Melanie pulled into the space next to me and lifted a hand. I returned the gesture.

"Well, the circumstances surrounding her death were highly suspect. She had been really wound up about the article 'The Dumping Grounds.' She seemed to believe she was able to identify one of your Jane Does."

"Suspect in what respect?"

Did I relay this sort of thing over the phone or hold back until I felt certain he would aid me? It took less than a few seconds for my mind to run down the pros and cons list since it wasn't very long. "Well, sir, . . ." This man and I had something in common. We were both as consumed with Jane Doe cases as Carol had been. I went with my instinct. "I'm actually the one who found her. It's going to sound crazy, but she was, um, in a suitcase on my front stoop one night when I came home from work."

Dead silence.

Unclear about the appropriate amount of time you gave a person to digest such things, I fiddled with my nails as I waited for him to respond. It wasn't the kind of news one delivered every day—not someone like me, anyway.

Mel knocked on my passenger's window, and I unlocked the door for her. When she slid inside, I mouthed, "GBI."

Mel's face was drawn with concern. I'd given her a full rundown on what happened over the phone and how Quinn had checked out my apartment. I worried about her safety and had insisted she stay over at my apartment tonight since hers hadn't been cleared. After my insistence, Quinn agreed to send an officer by to check her place in the morning.

"Mr. Jones? Are you there?"

"I'm here. I'm going to want to sit down with you at the first opportunity. Are you free tomorrow? I can drive up." He sounded more intense than he had a moment ago.

"I have Carol's funeral at two tomorrow, so if we can meet really early, I can make it work."

"Yeah, okay. I can move some things around. How's seven?"

"That works. Sir, can you clue me in on why the urgency in our meeting face-to-face?" My heart fluttered in my chest when he didn't respond. "I trusted you, and now I'm going to have to ask you to afford me the same courtesy."

"That's fair. The case your friend and I were discussing has an ugly similarity to what you just told me."

"I'm afraid I'm not following."

"The Jane Doe was discovered in a suitcase."

Blood thrummed in my ears, and my face began to tingle. I hadn't recalled reading about that in the article, which meant it must've been kept from the public. The acrid taste of anxiety filled my mouth, and I nearly lost the contents of my stomach.

"Miss Moody?"

"I'm"—I cleared my throat—"I'm sorry. I just didn't expect . . ."

"Like I said, it's best if we speak face-to-face."

"Okay. I'll text you the address of where I work. Is this a good number, or is there another you'd like me to use?" My hands continued to shake, and I had to force my knees still.

Melanie reached over and took my hand, her eyes wide with worry.

"This number is fine. Don't talk to anyone about what I told you. I'm trusting you on this."

"I understand." I rushed to add, "I'll text you the address. Goodbye."

Chapter
Twenty-Four

I'd spent a few hours listening to some of Carol's therapy sessions. So far, they hadn't shed any light on the investigation. I had noticed with each session her increasing paranoia, and that troubled me. Uncle Calvin had left me a voicemail with a winded message that I listened to on my way into work. He'd given me his approval to work Judge Timm's case. Not that it mattered now; I was going to do it anyway.

I'd parked down the street from our building to get a visual on Brad Jones before he had one on me. I suspected he'd be here first thing since we'd discovered the commonality between his Jane Doe and Carol. My nerves were still frazzled from last night, and it'd been difficult not to confide in Mel what I'd discussed with Mr. GBI. But I'd given my word. She'd stayed over last night, and we'd both slept on the couch. Not that either of us got that much sleep.

We had a conference call with the other club members explaining what happened and my suspicion that Carol had been using our club pick to warn us. Everyone was freaked out. Especially regarding the note.

"Oh my God, it's bone chilling." Mel kept repeating. "How are we just supposed to go about our day with some lunatic out there gunning for us?"

"Because we can't live our lives in fear," I'd told her. "If we do, then he's already won." If I were to be honest with myself, I was more pissed than afraid. This creep was not only threatening me but could also go after those I held most dear.

We'd tried to make sense of it all and never were able to. It wasn't until this morning that I recalled Officer Taylor's words. In his opinion, we were all guilty of obstruction of justice. Was that enough similarity to the novel? The characters were all guilty of a crime in the book.

I sighed and scanned the area. Sure enough, I'd been correct. Mr. GBI wasn't waiting in front of the office like I'd expected. He was sitting on the bench across the street, between two large maple trees. He seemed lost in thought as he stared at his phone, either reading e-mail or checking social media. I would bet e-mail. Mr. Jones didn't look like a man who had much use for Facebook. I took advantage of his distraction to size him up. He was in his late thirties, I guessed, with thick black hair cut close to his scalp, a sharp nose, and eyes a little closer together than average. He wore a blue blazer over a thin gray sweater and had matching blue slacks. As if he sensed my scrutiny, he raised his head, our gazes met, and recognition hit. He rose, and I lifted a hand, turned, and continued toward the office. I had the door unlocked and partially open when he approached.

"Special Agent Jones, I presume." I extended my hand, and he took it.

He had dark-brown irises that were almost black, making him appear somewhat intimidating. "It's nice to meet you, Miss Moody."

I pushed open the door. "Come on in." I flipped the lights on and went to the Keurig. "Coffee?"

"No, thank you."

"Make yourself at home." I made myself a cup, and when I turned around, he was sitting with his back straight against one of the chairs opposite my desk. He had his little pad and pen out. Unsure why he made me a tad jumpy, the edges of my mouth jerked up in a tense smile.

"Shall we jump right in?"

I sipped from my mug. "Sure."

"From what I gathered from the local police here, they're viewing this as an accidental death and unlawful disposal of a corpse." He looked at me.

"Yes. The coroner ruled Carol's death as undetermined. She had a preexisting heart condition. Since her husband isn't thrilled with the direction of the investigation, he's enlisted our services to see if we can dig up more info in an attempt to persuade the police to reevaluate." More sips to calm my nerves. I should've chosen decaf.

"It's a puzzle for sure, though. Since speaking with you yesterday, the suitcase makes sense in a twisted way. Why someone would do that to her, and out of all the places they could've placed her, why my house?"

His gaze bore holes into mine. "Yes, why indeed," he said ambiguously.

I wiped my upper lip that had begun to itch. "Right. Well, as stated in the police report, I was also the last to see her alive, other than her killer." I recounted in detail everything from the morning I saw her at the gas station. "And now, with what transpired last night, I have a theory as to why my house was chosen."

He seemed to listen but didn't react much. Training I supposed.

"I placed my mug on the desk and pulled my phone from my purse. I told him about Carol's warning note, scarf, the cap, and the texts, plus what had happened to me last night at the police department. I swiped my finger across the screen, thankful I'd had the presence of mind to take a picture of the note before handing it over to Quinn.

He sat back stoically. "The police are looking into this?"

I nodded.

He raised his brows. "You belong to a book club called the Jane Does?"

"Yes."

"The same club Carol belonged to?" He asked these questions with such a demurring, calm delivery it mesmerized me. I believed I could learn a lot from him.

"Yes. And our last pick was Agatha Christie's *And Then There Were None*. Her note said to give the scarf to me before there are none. Well, technically, as I'm sure you could tell, it looked like 'before there are ro—,' but it'd been smudged by the woman who passed it along to me when she read it."

"Did the woman who passed it on to you recall it reading 'before there are none'?"

I shook my head. There it was. That look of careful consideration. *"Is she crazy?"* I could almost pick it up from his thoughts: *"Could she have sent all this to herself for attention?"* Now, I understood all too well that those who didn't share our enthusiasm in murder mysteries could perceive our group as odd. But the man before me spent his life neck-deep in murder.

"The police didn't mention any of this to me." He held my gaze, and I shifted in my seat. "You're keenly interested in Jane Doe cases."

I fought to keep my facial expression passive. "Yes. And before you decide to pass me off as a lunatic, the note wasn't made public, nor was how we found Carol."

"Did you tell anyone how you found her? Did your friend"—he glanced at his pad—"Melanie Smart?"

I pursed my lips.

"I'll take that as a yes. Did Carol share with you about the Jane Doe found in a suitcase?" Again, with the deadpan stare.

"No. I hadn't spoken to Carol about any of the cases. Before she died, she e-mailed the members of our club. I found out about the scarf from the image posted in the article. It wasn't until I discovered the scarf Carol left with a friend that I made the definite connection."

"This scarf you turned over to the police. Why do you think it's the same as the one in the image with the Jane Doe?"

I explained about our alumnae majorette scarf and where I found it. I tapped the screen on my phone and drew his attention back to the picture. I wasn't a fool. There would be no way I'd turn something over without documenting it digitally first.

"Again, I find it odd they didn't mention it to me. I'll have to stop by there and speak with the chief."

I nodded and wondered right along with him why they hadn't shared the information. It was his case. I began to get uneasy as I thought back to overhearing Quinn's conversation. Willing my resolve to stay in place, I rolled forward to sit under my desk and took another sip of coffee.

"Want to tell me about discovering your friend?" he asked with calm aplomb.

Wow. This felt more like an interrogation or a character assessment than two people sharing their intel. *Is there some prerequisite for those working in law enforcement to all have the same sparkling personality?*

He shot me a sideways glance. "Well."

"You have access to the police report."

"I'd like to hear it from you." His face showed no emotion, not even a flicker or a nerve twitch. I did notice he had a scar above his right eyebrow that ran down to his temple.

"Okay, then." I went through the discovery in detail yet again.

He scribbled more things on the pad. "The similarities between the Jane Doe and Carol cases are difficult to ignore. And I just don't happen to believe in coincidences."

"Me either. And what an awful way to go." My thoughts shifted, grateful my friend hadn't also suffered such a fate of being forgotten after she was discarded. "How did Carol react when you told her about the suitcase?"

He studied me for a few seconds. "She told me."

Chills ran up my spine. How could Carol have known about the suitcase unless she visibly saw the body before it was reported? Or she found out about it after the fact from an active participant.

"You look pale."

"That's what happens when all the blood drains from your face and you feel like passing out. Either my friend was directly involved or had knowledge of who the killer was. And said killer or partner or whatever might have decided to send a message to anyone else who decides to poke their noses where they don't believe they belong." I got up and paced, fighting wooziness. "It all makes sense. I told you she was using the book as clues. She knew any one of us would be able to put that together. And it terrifies me that now the killer does too!"

"Calm down, Miss Moody."

"Calm down!" I turned around and waved my hands toward him. "I'd be a fool to believe I haven't poked the bear. The person who killed a possum and soaked my car in its blood fears I'm getting closer to the truth." My mind went to a very dark place. It had to be someone I knew, someone with access to my gated community. Someone with access to the police.

"Miss Moody?"

"What?" I stopped pacing and faced him. In my inward panic, I almost forgot he was sitting there.

"You might be right. Want to take a ride out to the Jane Doe's crime scene? Maybe something will stand out to you."

"What could you possibly discover after all this time?"

"You never know."

I checked my watch. I could do this and still make the funeral. Our gazes locked as my heart raced. I could do this. I had to do this.

"I'm in."

Chapter
Twenty-Five

A melia, Mel, and I sat near the back during the funeral while
Val sat on the same row as the family. Patsy sat with her
husband several rows in front of us. The judge had an enlarged
portrait of Carol positioned at the front of the sanctuary of
Sweet Mountain Methodist Church. It had been a beautiful ceremony, and now we sat wiping our eyes and sniffling as the pia-
nist played "Amazing Grace." Our friend had been cremated
two days ago, and I'd been touched to see the church packed by
those who loved her. Faces in the crowd were creased in masks
of sympathy. How I wished Carol had come to me immediately
instead of leaving instructions with other people. Maybe she'd
still be alive. I would have encouraged her to take everything to
the police immediately. Then an ugly thought occurred to me:
Why hadn't she?

I scanned the sanctuary; the local police had attended.
Quinn, dressed in uniform, stood at the back of the room, his
officers spread throughout the pews. He gave me a single nod
when he saw me looking. I returned a small, sad smile and cer-
emonially ducked my head. My mind spun with worry and
fear.

A sob echoed from the left side of the room, and my heart ached. I'd given anything to prevent this tragedy. Flashes of the scene where Carol's Jane Doe had been found came flooding back. Brad had driven me slowly down the service road behind the rundown, whitewashed Baptist church, overgrowth so tall you could get lost in it. The area was littered with detritus consisting of beer bottles, drug paraphernalia, old tires, and burn barrels. I'd hoped to see or find something, anything that could help us solve this. We found nothing.

My initial impression of Brad Jones from my short time with him was that he was dedicated to his work. There was a doggedness about him I'd never recognized in another human being before, and I admired the trait.

Everyone began to rise and file out of the church. Weeping and soft music filled the space. I mopped my face with a tissue as I followed the person in front of me, and we all filed out into the cloud-covered afternoon.

Amelia gave my hand a squeeze, and we shared a commiserating glance.

"Is that him?" Mel motioned with her head to the right.

I was surprised to see Brad standing under the canopy of a large pine at the edge of the small cemetery on the church's property. Like me, he'd changed. Now he wore a black suit, a white shirt, and wraparound sunglasses. He looked suspicious and dangerous.

"Yes, that's Brad. I'll catch up with y'all," I whispered to Amelia and Mel.

"Wait a minute." Amelia had a death grip on my arm. "Special Agent Brad Jones?" On my nod, she gripped tighter. "I take it you've met with him."

"Yes. But we can't talk about it now."

She searched my face with great urgency. "Does he agree with us that there is a connection with the Jane Doe case and Carol? How scared do we need to be?"

People were starting to notice, and I hugged Amelia and patted her back in a consoling sort of way. "Yes," I whispered at her ear, "but we have to keep it between us for now. Okay? And just be careful. Don't go anywhere alone." I wished I could involve Uncle Calvin, but he was still deep into the new case that would keep him out of town until late next week.

"You have my word." Amelia whispered. I nodded, and she said in a reverently low tone, "I'm really getting scared now."

I released her, and Mel said, "We all are."

Patsy and her tall, thin husband walked toward us. She had her hand tucked in the crook of his arm and wore cat-eye glasses. They paused, and Patsy whispered something to her husband, and he went off ahead. "Hey, y'all. Wasn't that a beautiful ceremony?"

We all nodded.

"I was a wreck this morning. I couldn't even get my contacts in." Patsy's eyes were bloodshot.

"Your glasses are lovely." I smiled at her.

"They're not, but thanks. I still can't believe all this. Bill and I got into it about the book club. He thinks we're asking for this negative attention."

"What?" Amelia hissed.

"That's crazy!" Mel scrunched up her face.

"Let's not do this here." I smiled at a few guests passing us, and I noticed Brad appeared to be watching us. "And Bill's entitled to his opinion."

Patsy squared her shoulders. "I've got to go—Bill's waving to me. See y'all at the house."

Gray skies and dense clouds were overhead as we dispersed, and I crossed the grassy patch on tiptoes. My heels sunk into the soft dormant Bermuda grass.

Brad moved to the left to make room for me. "How was the service?"

"It was nice. I think Carol would've liked it." I wiped my nose.

"Nothing of consequence to report then?"

I snorted in a very unladylike way. Mother wouldn't be pleased. "No one threw themselves in front of Carol's painting, wailing and begging for forgiveness, if that's what you're asking." I pulled sunglasses from my little clutch and put them on. I didn't need them, but it afforded me privacy as I watched the crowd interact.

I spied the judge receiving condolences on the large stone porch of the church. Judge Timms's face contorted in a distasteful way as he conversed with Kevin. I honed in on them when Kevin's head whipped backward, as if he'd been slapped. He must've said something equally harsh to Judge Timms because the man tensed up, looking fierce and ready to fight. My heart hammered against my ribcage. My cousin Ellen walked out, adjusting her purse strap on her shoulder, looking around. She spotted Kevin and sauntered over, pulling him down the steps of the church.

"You know, in the book the judge was the guilty party." I shivered.

"I think we'll need more to go on than a hunch from a novel." Brad sounded unimpressed.

I cut my eyes his direction. "I understand that. There are lots of cases where weirdos reenact crime novels or use them as research. What about that man in the UK who offered a hitman two hundred thousand pounds to kill his partner? He claimed he planned to use it as research for his new crime novel."

Brad didn't respond. Quinn walked out mid-conversation with Officer Taylor, and both men turned, saw us, and stopped cold. Quinn was better at hiding his surprise than Taylor. I tried to get a handle with my warring emotions. I should be grieving the loss of my friend, not worrying about a killer among us.

"Chief Daniels said the scarf was misplaced?"

I turn to face Brad. "What? That's absurd."

He didn't return my gaze. "Indeed. They're in possession of the camo cap, but the scarf I need for my case has conveniently vanished."

"Oh, my God," I breathed, and my gaze skated back to the church. I also shouldn't be wondering what secrets these men sworn to uphold the law were hiding behind closed doors. Mother's constant insistence that respectable folks in Sweet Mountain didn't air their dirty laundry took on a whole new meaning now. I really wished my uncle were here.

"I believe you about the cases being linked. I think it's highly probable your friend was killed for the knowledge she possessed. And if we're right, then you are the next target."

As his words sank in, my thoughts drifted back to the phone call I'd overheard. *"There isn't anything else that can be done at this point. If she comes by, rest assured I'll handle it. This squares us!"* Quinn had said, and I whispered my concerns to Brad, relaying the phone conversation.

"Hmm," Brad said. "He also warned me to be careful when it comes to you. He claimed you had compulsive issues regarding Jane Doe cases."

I fought a wave of anger. "How dare he!"

"He did, however, sound genuinely worried about you getting involved. He's taking the threats you received seriously."

Well, that is his job!

"I'm supposed to have dinner with him tomorrow." I took an inadvertent step closer to Brad, the outsider's presence more than welcome now. "I haven't been out with him in over ten years. I'm not sure I even know him anymore. And right now, I don't trust anyone."

"Good. That might keep you alive. But you should keep the date. He's interested in you, that's for certain. He acted territorial when I inquired about you."

"He may not be interested in me much longer. He's shooting daggers my way as we speak."

"Those are directed at me. He doesn't like that I didn't go back home and wait for him to send me whatever he deems is related to my cases."

"Should I be worried about the department acting shady? I know you don't know Quinn. What I'm asking is if you have a hunch or whatever. You get senses about people, right? Your profession requires it. I usually trust my own instincts." I tried to calm down by taking in some timed breaths. "Now, I just don't know."

"That's smart. Your senses are rattled, skewing your judgment. And someone wants you to stand down."

I swallowed as Quinn whispered something to Taylor and then stalked toward us.

"Be careful. The threats you've been receiving have escalated. First texts, then the dead possum." He didn't tiptoe around my sensitivities, didn't worry about my feelings or speak to me as if I would break at any moment. I liked that about him.

"I'm aware, and I will."

I nodded and left him standing there and lifted a hand when I reached Quinn. I had no intention of stopping.

My head spun in astonishment as Quinn blocked my path. "You have a minute?"

I nodded, and we moved a few steps away from the others.

"We processed your car and I had it sent to be fully detailed. We didn't find any prints—not surprising. The camera positioned at the side of the building had been tampered with." Chills broke out over my body. "If you receive any more threats or at any time feel threatened, call me. I care."

"I appreciate that." Unsure how to act, I simply wiped my nose with the tissue I had in my hand and wiggled a little distance between us. "It's all just so awful."

"I'm sorry you're having to go through this. Watch out for that guy." He jerked his chin toward Brad. "He'll stop at nothing to close his case, even if that means destroying everyone's lives within his path."

I glanced up in surprise and got another shock. Quinn's lips brushed my forehead. Nonplussed, I stumbled back, and he caught my arm, steadying me. *That's weird.*

"I'll see you later." He rose to his full height before continuing his advance toward Brad. In that same direction, I saw Val walk past Mother's car in the parking lot. When she made it to me, she hugged me and held on for a moment longer than I'd anticipated.

"Hey. You okay?" I put the sunglasses up on top of my head.

"I just can't believe she's gone. It's hitting me harder today. Funerals are so final."

"I'm so sorry." Weddings and funerals had a way of bringing all the emotions home to roost, Gran always said. "It was a beautiful service."

She pulled back, wiping under her eyes with the sides of her index fingers. "It was. Thank you for coming. I know how you feel about these rituals. It was nice of your parents to come too."

They had? I glanced around and didn't see them anywhere. Huh. I must have missed them, though I wasn't sure how. "I wouldn't be anyplace else."

The wind kicked up and blew, making me second-guess my choice in wearing my somber gray V-back sheath dress. I rubbed my arms.

"You still going to work the case? After that incident with your car? And those notes?"

I nodded. "I have to."

"I've been thinking about what you said. About the book. If Carol knew the killer and the book rang true with her, it could be—"

"The judge. Yeah, I had that thought too."

She nodded and wrapped her arms around herself.

"I suppose all the club members had that though. But he's pushing for us to find answers. We should be careful around him though."

"And I also heard he's been seen at the Catfish Diner with Officer Taylor," Val said. My eyes went wide.

"So his reach could extend to our police force."

Val glanced around. "On the one hand, yes. On the other, I've been around him a lot, and I just don't know what to think. I mean, I could be all wrong, but Carol never acted afraid of the man. And she never confided a fear for her life to me."

We settled into silence. "Lots to think about. I guess I'll see you at *his* house. I won't lie, it makes me nervous. You need a ride?"

She tucked her sleek, straight hair behind her ears. "No. I'm going to run by and pick up my contribution from Joe's."

"Okay. I'm going to run by and pick up a bucket of chicken."

She lifted a hand, and off she went.

Chapter
Twenty-Six

The parking situation at the Timms's residence was overflowed onto the street. Cars lined up next to the curb forced me to park several houses down. I was arriving a little late.

The large, faceless, two-story brick home with an L-shaped, three-car garage situated at the front of the neighborhood seemed to be the largest on the street. I rapped lightly on the double-paned stained-glass window in the front door. Someone I didn't recognize opened it, nodded in the way of greeting, and moved on. I closed the door behind me. The large traditional staircase split the first floor. On my right was a large formal dining room, and to my left, a living room. The house filled with cacophonous noises felt a little jarring. Idle chitchat from one corner. Sobbing and sniffling in another. Laughter came from another portion of the house from what I assumed or hoped emitted from those sharing humorous stories about their life with Carol.

People were seated at the cherry-wood dining table with small plates of food. I navigated through the dining room—nodding sympathetically as I passed anyone who made direct eye contact with me. I placed my offering on the large granite island in the kitchen. Women were fussing around, laying out additional plates and silverware.

"Can you believe that Heinz girl?" one of the elderly women said to the small group. "She's buzzing around Judge Timms like a honeybee on an azalea bush."

"Shameful. I heard from his housekeeper that she's been coming over after dark to visit him," another woman added.

All three women began shaking their heads. "Shameful."

I turned to them and wagged my finger. "'Judge not lest ye be judged.' Carol was Val's best friend, and I can assure you there is absolutely no impropriety going on between them. They are simply helping each other get through Carol's death."

A couple gasps and a few huffs went up as I brushed past the gossiping old biddies.

Through the curtains of the French doors off the breakfast room, I spied Val sitting across from the chair Judge Timms occupied. He had a long black cigar between his fingers.

She spied me through the window and cast me a small smile as she rose. I cracked open the door just as Judge Timms reached out and grabbed Valerie, behaving effusively, squeezing her hip and attempting to lay his head on her chest. Val visibly flushed.

"You're too good to me. I don't know how I would've gotten through this without you." Val fought to pull his hands away and free herself.

"Okay. Someone has had a little too much to drink." She made a face in my direction.

The judge must be coveting rumors because this behavior would certainly fuel them. "Val, could I see you for a moment?" I asked in an attempt to draw the judge's attention.

"Lyla!" He drew out my name. "So good of you to come." The judge waved me over, and Val shot free.

She embraced me, and over her shoulder, Judge Timms grinned at me. Now I could see he'd already had more than a little too much to drink. The scotch glass on the garden table in front of him contained melted ice cubes.

"I'll just go inside and see if I can be of any help. Be careful. He's sloshed."

As Val slipped through the doorway, the judge stood, reached out, and took my hand, pulling me over to where he sat back down. I squeezed it and strategically took the chair opposite.

"How are you holding up?" I asked and tried to look pleasant, even though my mind constantly went back to the guilty judge character in the novel.

"As well as can be expected. I just can't believe I'm alone. Again." He picked up the glass and sucked loudly on the contents.

"Nice to have so many caring, um, . . . friends," I said ambiguously.

He balanced the glass on his knee. "You're referring to Val. She's a good little gal."

"She loved Carol for sure." I nodded.

He let out a sigh and stared off at the yard, which was full of hardscapes. "Carol wasn't much into gardening or flowers."

I glanced around the red-bricked patio and firepit that, despite the lack of plants or color supplied by flowers, remained lovely. And the upkeep would be a lot easier.

"I heard you had a little trouble at the police station the other day."

"Yes."

He rose and waved for me to follow him. I reached out instinctively when he stumbled. He laughed and wiped beads of sweat from his forehead. "I trust you won't allow some stupid threat to keep you from looking into what happened to Carol."

"No, sir. If anything, it's spurred me on more. Terrified me but fueled my desire to make someone pay for what they did and stop them from killing again." As I followed him down the brick steps, off the patio, to another glass-paned door at the side of the house, I fought my inward trepidation. He dug into his pocket and unlocked it. He left it open, and I tentatively ducked my head inside to see that this was his office.

"Come on in and shut the door behind you."

I did as beckoned, and he walked over to a large painting of a heavyset nude woman. The painting left nothing to the imagination.

"Good. I'm glad to hear it." He shook his head as he set the frame on the floor, exposing a safe in the wall, and I averted my gaze to the floor to afford him privacy.

"You work for me now. No one will mess with you. I'll put the word out."

Is he serious? I swallowed the lump in my throat.

"This safe is the best on the market today. My thumbprint is the entry code. Unless someone chops off my thumb, it's uncrackable."

Yikes. "Wow. Um, I haven't received the data on Carol's movements yet. I'm expecting them any day." I turned away, not wanting to invade his privacy.

"I'm not too concerned about that now."

When I heard a distinct click, I turned back around.

He held an envelope and thrust it to me. "Val said you produced evidence showing that low-life Kevin was with my Carol before she died. These will help."

"I'm not sure it's conclusive evidence. Lots of people have camo caps." With steady fingers I felt proud of, I took the envelope, and he moved to the small bar in the corner of the room to refill his glass. The man really didn't need any more alcohol. But who was I to judge the actions of a grieving man? Even one such as he.

Inside were copies of affidavits. Kevin had challenged the last will and testament of his grandfather. And after Carol's death, he had petitioned the court for the entire sum. I felt ill. There was also a set of photographs. Carol outside of the motel off I-85 with a man. Their heads close together in one shot—the man gripping Carol by the shirt collar in another. Her face was stricken with fear—Carol in the car with what appeared to be the same man in a camo hat. *Kevin*.

"Sweet Jesus," I breathed, and glanced up to meet the blood-shot gaze of Judge Timms.

"That about covers it. And by your reaction, I take it Carol hadn't confided in you about her struggles with mental health or her stepbrother manipulating her for money."

I shook my head.

The judge leveled his gaze, measuring me. "Not a word?"

"No sir. She did leave a note and a scarf for me." I kept my tone even, controlled.

"So?" He sat on the leather love seat and slung one arm across the back. "She never was attached to her wardrobe. Keep it."

Okay. Steeling myself, I moved closer and perched on the edge of a chair. "It's regarding the Jane Doe case. Something Carol discovered terrified her."

He made a distasteful face. "She was frightened of everything toward the end. Just ask your father. She was losing her mind." He leaned forward, his tone dropped, and—I swear—so did the temperature in the room. "Move. On."

My pulse raced, and my stomach did a flip-flop. "Yes, sir." I cleared my throat. "Did you show these to the police?"

"I did." He leaned back, and the tension in his sweaty face began to ease a little. "Those are copies. They have a set."

"And?"

"And nothing. I thought for sure, with the evidence of Kevin's cap, that would be enough. Idiots. Quinn said they'd keep me apprised as needed. The man owes me."

The room spun a little. The judge must have been the one on the phone that day.

"Well, if Quinn won't do something, I'll take matters into my own hands. We'll fight dirty. You used to date Kevin. It shouldn't be any trouble for you to work your pretty little ass back into his bed and coax a confession out of him."

My skin began to crawl, and I rose, my cheeks burning. "You've got me all wrong. If the police are investigating, perhaps we should sever our agreement now."

He set his glass down and leaned forward, his manner intense. "I'm not looking to sever our agreement. I'm after justice. That man"—he pointed to the picture still clutched in my hands—"is trying to steal my money. With Carol gone, the money is rightfully mine by law." He clamped his mouth shut in agitation. His eyes were full of fire.

The killer in the book And Then There Were None *had been the judge!*

Time to go. I started backing toward the door.

"You do as I tell you, and I'll make you a rich woman, you hear?" He rose to his full height and gritted through clenched teeth, "I hate feeling a fool. I earned that money. I'm not some chump!"

"Of course not. No one would think you were a fool. I'll speak with Quinn." I took another step backward and ran into a small table.

He flung his arm toward me; it was a sloppy motion. "You would have thought that since you found her on your doorstep, you'd have found out more than you have. A murder buff obsessed with those damn Jane Does, like Carol, and working for a private investigator, I'd put money on it." His words were heavily slurred now, and I wondered if he'd remember any of this in the morning.

I should've recorded this conversation. *A stupid mistake I couldn't afford to make!*

"Are you keeping things from me, Lyla? Did she tell you about the case she believed she could solve? Some damn suitcase killer or something."

"No, sir." I fumbled with the doorknob behind me. The door clicked open, and cool air rushed in.

"Oh, hell." He raked a hand over his mouth.

Relief flooded me when he made no advance forward and seemed to read the room.

He'd gone too far. "I'm sorry . . . I—"

"You're grieving. I understand. I'll do what I can. You have my word."

His body seemed to sag on his bones with the weight of his predicament. "Fair enough."

I backed out with a consolatory smile.

I stepped out into the coolness, hurriedly shut the door behind me, and rested my hand over my heart, thankful to be out of the lion's den.

Talk about being a fool. I felt like the biggest one on the planet. Now that I knew for certain it'd been Kevin with Carol that day, and fairly certain it had been the judge I'd overheard Quinn speaking to, not to mention the connections the judge had with Officer Taylor, I understood now more than ever that deadly, vile secrets riddled this town. *Trust at your own peril.*

Chapter
Twenty-Seven

Melanie called after me as I ran for my car. I hadn't even gone back into the house, running through the shrubbery, leaving dirt and wet spots on my dress.

"Lyla, what is it?" Melanie grasped my arms. She looked panicked as I attempted to catch my breath.

For a few minutes back there, I feared I might end up stuffed in a suitcase. Amid the man's ramblings, I got the impression he'd left his wife for me to find so I'd investigate. I told Mel everything through timed gasps.

"He's such a cretin. Anyone who treats a sweet person like Carol the way he did could be nothing less than a monster. Now he wants to pimp you out for gain. Just like the novel! It's him! It has to be."

We huddled together next to my car.

"You don't think he'll do anything nuts, do you? Like mow down everyone in the house? Or come after you in the middle of the night?"

I shook my head. "I don't think so. His vendetta lies with Kevin and his attempt to fight the will over the inheritance. He might have killed her." A tremor shook my body. "As long as he thinks I'm on his side, I should be fine. What purpose would my death serve? I keep trying to make sense of everything he told me. His words were tantamount to a confession. But if he's behind the threats, they should stop now."

Mel's fingers dug into my flesh.

"That's not all. He claimed Quinn owed him, and just a little while ago, Brad told me the scarf has gone missing from evidence at the police station."

Her mouth fell open. *"What?"*

We'd been keeping our voices down, but because of the way we were clinging to each other conspicuously, we were receiving sideways glances from the new arrivals passing by, our intense colloquy attracting the wrong kind of attention.

"We need to leave."

Mel nodded in agreement. "What about the others? Val, Patsy, and Amelia are inside. I rode over here with Amelia. I just came back out to see if I could find you."

"Text them and let them know we're leaving. Have you seen Kevin?"

"Yes. He and Ellen just went inside. He . . . he asked where you were, and Val told him you were meeting with the judge and taking over the case."

The sky opened up, and the bottom fell out, drenching us. People scurried for cover.

Amelia pushed her way through the small crowd, waving her arms at us. "Wait up!"

I hit the key fob and unlocked the doors. The three of us piled in my car. Amelia was nearly in tears. She thrust a photo at us.

The blood in my veins nearly froze.

It was a picture of the book club. One we had taken for the library newsletter in hopes of increasing our membership. Amelia, Patsy, and Carol in the front in chairs; Melanie, Val, and I standing behind them. We all sported our Jane Doe Book Club T-shirts Carol had made up. There was an X over Carol's face.

"What the hell?" Melanie squeaked.

"T-turn it over," Amelia gasped.

Five little Janes won't leave it alone; who will die next and be the new Doe?

"So much for no more threats." Mel's voice quivered.

"Where! Where did you get this?" I turned and stared into the back seat at Amelia.

She visibly shook. "It . . . it was taped to the bottom of my cake plate."

"Who could have done this?" Mel clutched her purse to her chest.

"I thought it was Judge Timms." I kept shaking my head. "But now, it's looking more like Kevin."

Amelia leaned forward, "Who else would know about our theory that Carol was using our club read? Like the note you received—this is obviously written to the rhyme like the 'Ten Little Soldiers' poem."

"Well, all of us." We all exchanged a wide-eyed glance. "Plus, Quinn—well, actually, the entire police department—Brad Jones, and I never said a word to Kevin, but—"

"It could have gotten around." Mel hugged her purse tighter.

I nodded. "Yes. And I'm not sure Judge Timms was in any condition to do this today."

"He could have accomplices," Amelia added.

"Maybe. But the judge wanted me to investigate. This"—I waved the picture—"says someone else doesn't."

"It certainly appears that way." Amelia leaned back against the seat.

With trembling fingers, I started the engine and turned on the heat. "Although the threats didn't start off using the rhyme. It could be something to throw us."

"Like Kevin!" Melanie turned in her seat. "He was there when the first text came through. And he's here today."

But the judge knew about the suitcase! I couldn't share it with them.

"What should we do? If it's Kevin, then he might hurt someone else if he thinks they suspect him. Our friends are in that house." Amelia's eyes couldn't get any wider.

"Something doesn't fit," I said.

"Let me see the pictures," Mel requested.

While Mel and Amelia inspected the images, commenting about Kevin's venomous facial expressions, I tried to make sense of everything. The version of the judge I'd just witnessed could have murdered his wife. His admission, regarding his belief that I would have investigated anyway, despite not being hired, made me worry. Yet Kevin wanted the inheritance and had a temper; those pictures spoke for themselves. He'd never been abusive or physical with me. And now someone had left a threat, in the form of a picture, for Amelia. We needed to share the picture with the police, but right now I wasn't sure I trusted them. They'd done nothing up to this point. I shoved the picture into my clutch.

I relayed all of these thoughts to my fellow club members, who had just finished staring at each and every image with great detail.

"What if this is all some freak accident after a heated argument, and Kevin tried to cover it up? He could've had Carol in the moving van and just rolled her right over to your place. And maybe he heard about you getting involved and decided to play games to throw the police and you off the trail," Amelia said staring me straight in the face.

I rubbed my eyes. "It's possible and I hate it. I've known Kevin most of my life. And I'm trying to see this objectively. I just can't wrap my head around it." The police didn't have any intention of investigating the crime as a murder, and Quinn could be in Judge Timms's pocket. But Uncle Calvin thought so highly of Quinn. Everyone did. My head ached.

"You should try talking to Quinn again. I really don't believe he's crooked. Judge Timms could be stark raving mad. We're all caught up in this and aren't seeing straight."

I dropped my hands and faced my friends. "I just don't know anymore."

Melanie sat back against the seat and stared straight ahead. The rain pelted down, and the wipers moved squeakily across the windshield. People filed up and down the street—some were leaving, and some arriving.

I felt numb as I put the car into drive. "Text Patsy and Val, Amelia. Make sure they're okay. To be on the safe side."

As my friend began a group text message to the other Jane Does inside, I pulled away from the curb, coasting down the street toward the Timms's residence. Flashing blue lights ahead caused me to slam on my brakes, sending Mel bouncing forward but missing the dash, thanks to her seat belt.

"Geez," Mel braced her hand on the dashboard and craned to look.

"Oh my sweet Jesus," Amelia breathed.

Flashing blue lights were also in the Timms's driveway, and the front door was wide open. Out came Quinn, followed by

Officer Taylor and another officer I couldn't recall from this distance. Quinn had Kevin cuffed behind his back and headed toward the police car.

"Guess we have our answer." Melanie had her fingers to her lips.

Astonished, I didn't respond. Kevin jerked at the restraints and shouted something vile to Quinn. I thought I'd caught my name, though I couldn't be positive. Blood thrummed in my ears. Ellen came running out the front door, screaming. I lowered my window, ignoring the rain dribbling inside.

"What the hell is going on here? Release him this instant, Quinn Daniels, or you'll be sorry you were ever born!" Ellen screamed.

Mel leaned over to my side to get a better view out the window. The crowd around the front door of the residence grew despite the pouring rain. People stood with umbrellas, watching with great interest like they were viewing an episode of the show *Cops*. Ellen pitched a hissy fit, stomping her feet and shouting obscenities. Her heel caught in soft, wet ground, and she stumbled forward, plowing into Taylor's back. He turned around and gripped her by the arms, righting her. His head bent and moved with sporadic jerks. He must be giving her a stern talking to, and I wished I could hear what he was saying.

Taylor released her, and I thought it was over. The crowd spread out into the front yard. I gazed around, searching for Judge Timms. He was nowhere to be seen, and I surmised he was sleeping it off in his room.

The next thing we knew, Ellen's arm swung around, and she landed a slap across Taylor's face. Even from this distance, I heard the wet clapping sound. Both Mel and I sucked in loud, sharp breaths. Grumblings were audible from the crowd, along with a few snickers. Taylor's face reddened to an unhealthy shade of puce. For a second, I believed Ellen would join Kevin in the back seat of the police car. Quinn stomped over and said something to Taylor, then addressed Ellen with his finger pointed at her. She stormed back into the house.

Chapter
Twenty-Eight

L ike my fellow Jane Does, I stared into my mostly full mug. I fought to still my trembling hands. I'd barely even nibbled the cake. The shock had rocked us all. The picture left for Amelia lay on the coffee table. It had been the consensus that Kevin must have been responsible since the photo had belonged to Carol. Val recalled seeing it framed on Carol's desk. He could have easily swiped it, and when I wasn't around, used it to threaten Amelia.

"I just can't believe it," Patsy said over and over again. "Lyla, was he ever violent with you? Is that why y'all broke up?"

I glanced up from where I sat on the love seat. "No." I took a sip. "We argued, and he had a hot temper at times . . ." I shook my head. "But nothing like you're referring to."

"First the baseball cap, and now he's been arrested," Val reminded me. "It confirms your findings. Sometimes love is blind." She wrapped the afghan around her shoulders and settled into the recliner. "He killed our Carol over a few hundred thousand dollars."

"Three hundred thousand, to be exact. The dollar amount was listed in the copy of the files Judge Timms gave me." I took a sip of coffee. "It's a lot of money. And money is a common motive for murder." I still struggled to comprehend the turn of events.

"Well, I can't believe I brought him a housewarming gift," Val said. "I wish I'd cracked him over the head with the lamp when I had the chance." Her eyes flamed. "If it wasn't for him, my best friend would still be here!"

Eyes widened.

Amelia moved her head back and forth. "I can see how he could be guilty. It makes sense. But after speaking to Special Agent Jones, I'm beginning to wonder if we missed something." Amelia was referencing the dumping grounds again. "The similarities in the cases are terrifying."

I wondered if Brad had told Amelia about the suitcase. I couldn't very well ask her here, in front of everyone. I'd promised to keep that to myself. "I know he looks guilty. I do. I just can't shake the feeling I need to keep digging. What if the police are wrong? And Kevin serves time for a crime he didn't commit? It happens all the time."

"Please." Val blew out a breath. "Please, just stop. It's over. And even if we did miss something in regard to the Jane Doe, did y'all ever consider Kevin was at the alumnae bonfire? He could have snatched one of the many tossed scarves on the ground. Everyone was laughing at the stupid scarves, remember?"

"Even if that's true, don't we want to know who she is? The Jane Doe. Finish what Carol started? We have a GBI agent eager to solve it." Amelia looked at each person.

"Carol would want us to." Melanie cradled her mug between her palms.

"That's my point exactly. What does it hurt to continue to investigate? If Kevin's guilty, he'll go down for another crime." Amelia put her mug on the coaster.

"It's crazy how we think we know someone." Patsy wrung her hands. "Trust them, even. And then they just turn out to be the most wicked person on the planet."

We sat in silence for a few long minutes. "I'm not sure anyone can truly know what a person is capable of in a moment of passion. It's just difficult for me to process. And before anyone starts claiming I'm in denial, I'm not."

"Really? It happens all the time with girlfriends of killers. What about Ted Bundy's girlfriend, Elizabeth Kloepfer? She never suspected a thing. If the person is intelligent enough, like Bundy, they can live among people, and no one is the wiser."

"Kevin isn't stupid, but he isn't a genius either," Melanie argued. "Besides, I have to disagree. Kloepfer knew. She might not have wanted to believe it. Still, she knew. If she'd never reported him to the police all those times, he might have murdered a dozen more women."

"For God's sake!" Val exploded. "Why are we even discussing this?"

Shocked faces stared at one another.

She closed her eyes and took a deep breath. "I'm sorry. I'm overwhelmed."

"Of course you are. We all are. This probably isn't the time to discuss the Jane Doe anyway," I said, placating. The Jane Doe could wait.

She rubbed her forehead and blew out a breath, opening her eyes. "No. Y'all are right. Carol started the dumping ground mess by e-mailing us. I understand that. And if Kevin is involved, it might be what we need to lock him away for good. He deserves nothing less for what he did to our Carol. I want to help. Truly. Look, David and Greg meet every Tuesday at the Catfish Diner.

Maybe there's some connection I'm not seeing." She turned to Mel. "Greg likes you; why don't you see what you can find out."

"Greg?" Amelia raised an eyebrow.

"It's Officer Taylor's first name." Mel began vehemently shaking her head. "I can't, Val. I'm sorry, but I just can't. He creeps me out, and if I give him the first inkling I might be the tiniest bit interested, he'll never take no for an answer. I can tell. I'll do anything else."

Val rolled her eyes. "Fine. I'll do it."

Mel let out a sigh of relief.

It would be good to know where the police were going with this case and if they were attempting to link the crimes.

"Lyla, you have a handle on this GBI fella?"

"Well, I wouldn't say 'handle,' but we communicate. And I'm having dinner with Quinn tomorrow at the Trail Head Grill. I plan to see if I can get anything from him. Perhaps give him a nudge." The idea of Quinn being dirty caused a pang of anxiety.

"I'll do more background digging." Amelia looked happy to have a purpose. The possibility of change always gave her a sense of calm, she'd told me.

"Good. That's good. I'll plan my date for the same night. We'll do this for Carol." Val smiled as my phone chirped.

Everyone waited to see if I'd share.

"It's Judge Timms. He's apologizing for taking a nap." *More like passing out.* "Kevin's been charged with illegally disposing of a body and kidnapping." My gaze darted around the room. Eyes were wide and heads were shaking.

"You'll be called as a witness, you know?" Val said when my gaze landed on hers.

"I've thought about that. I'm the only eyewitness that puts him in the car with her before she died, and can attest to her state of mind. Or at least my perception of it." I felt now more than ever I had to speak to Kevin. I needed to look him in the eyes and read him, and preferably before we were in a courtroom. I wouldn't inform the others just yet.

"Mel, prepare yourself to testify as well."

Melanie nodded at me.

"Let's nail the bastard! Whoever is guilty should pay." Amelia sat forward. "I was terrified when I found the picture. More terrified than I've ever been in my life. No one has the right to make me or any of us fear for our safety."

"I don't believe my ears," Patsy huffed. "This isn't a game, and y'all can count me out! I, for one, am glad I'm not involved with people who could do such a thing. It's shameful. Those of us with children have been on edge ever since the news broke."

Those of us without children have been on edge too. Not that I would remind her of that fact.

"And, Lyla, I hope there aren't any skeletons in your closet because of that man," Patsy cautioned with a manner that edged on judgmental. "No dirty bondage nudies or anything. I find it hard to believe that a man like that one day just suddenly became violent and vile enough to stuff a woman in a suitcase—his sister, no less. They're going to be unearthing everything to make a case, and whatever you're hiding will come out." She waved her hands toward me. "And I can't be associated with all that."

"That's mean, Patsy. Why are you turning on Lyla? She doesn't have control over Kevin." Melanie sounded incensed.

"I'm just saying those of us in normal, healthy relationships and with families frown on activities that lead to violence." Patsy rose and brushed off her skirt.

I'd be lying if I said her snooty air didn't bother me.

"I know you didn't just say that!" Melanie appeared livid.

"Mel, it's fine." I waved my hand. I wasn't the least bit worried about skeletons.

"Well," Patsy said, drawing out the word. "I suppose now is as good a time as any to inform y'all that, after a long conversation with my husband last night, I've decided this group isn't for me anymore. I'm not even going to read for a while except maybe some lighthearted romances or humorous chick lit. I'd planned on waiting so I didn't hurt feelings, but after Lyla enlightened us with her little investigation plan, I need to make my position clear. Don't try to involve me in your lunacy."

"Lunacy? That's harsh." Amelia folded her arms.

Patsy shook her head and held up a hand toward Amelia. "Whatever, I'm out."

"Suit yourself," Val said dryly. "I'm having a beer. Anyone want one?"

We all waved her offer away. She shrugged and left the room without a glance at Patsy.

In my humble opinion, Patsy could've been more tactful. She'd been Carol's friend too. But I suppose there was no accounting for people and their reactions.

I rose and crossed the room to give her a hug. "Well, we'll certainly miss you."

She stiffened in my embrace, and I immediately let go. Kevin's arrest had given her a new perspective on me. A wrong view, in my opinion. Why wasn't she blasting Ellen instead of the person who'd thrown her a baby shower and brought food when she had her twins?

Amelia had risen with me, but after the way Patsy behaved, she sat back down and avoided Patsy's gaze when she glanced at her expectantly.

"I guess this is goodbye."

"So long, farewell," Mel sang with a curled lip and a snide tone.

This isn't the way I wanted this to go down. "Listen, Pats, I'm sorry the fact I dated Kevin gave you the willies. I understand if you don't want to continue being part of the group."

"Not everyone is up for real criminal investigations." She pointed to the picture of all of us with the X over Carol's face. "It's not worth it to me. And if y'all are smart, you'll back off too. This whole business is plain scary. Like my mother-in-law says, don't go hunting for evil or you'll find it." Her voice became shrill.

I took a step back and lifted my hands. Mel and Amelia gazed at her as if she were mad. Her behavior did verge on the hysterical side.

"We aren't a cult, Patsy," Amelia said softly. "We aren't hunting evil."

Val came back in the room in a pair of sweatpants with a six-pack of Corona Light. She was quickly consuming her bottle. I wished I'd taken her up on her offer now. "Nope. Evil came hunting for us."

"Damn straight!" Mel grabbed a beer.

"Y'all are crazy. Too into all this." Patsy glowered at us.

"Patsy, come on. Don't be like this," Val said.

The door slammed, and I sat down next to Amelia. "Well, hell."

"Yep." Val lifted the pack and put it on the coffee table.

We all helped ourselves.

"To Carol."

We clinked bottles. "To Carol."

Chapter
Twenty-Nine

I had my sticker pass stuck to my shirt, and I'd gone through the metal detector. Had my shoes checked by the correctional officer, making me glad I'd worn my black Mary Janes. Now I sat under the florescent lighting, in chairs bolted to the floor, waiting with a half dozen others for our names to be called.

I'd never visited anyone in jail before, and I had no idea what to expect. Around the room, a little girl skipped up and down the back wall with a tiny doll. She appeared quite comfortable in the environment, and it grieved me. To have to visit your family member in this place as a small child must have some negative effect on her development. Not that she was showing evidence of it at present.

Another older woman with white hair and a pink sweater sat in the chair opposite me. She was knitting, or maybe it was crocheting, some sort of baby blanket. Perhaps for her daughter or granddaughter. She hummed a tune I'd heard before but simply couldn't place.

An older bald man sat in the corner of the room on his own. He had his head in his hands. When he raised his head, he involuntarily met my gaze with his bloodshot eyes. The pain he clearly felt was palpable.

Names were being called, and I directed my attention toward the uniformed officer with a clipboard. Everyone began to line up, and I followed suit when my name was announced. I couldn't imagine doing this on a regular basis. Going through the same song and dance every week while attempting to maintain normalcy would be maddening. Although, as I took in those in the line, to some this must be their normal. The doors opened, and we were hustled into a small room with the same tile floors and several booth-type areas separated by small partitions. There were two cameras recording where the walls met the ceiling on opposite ends of the room. I went to my designated booth and sat down on the red enameled chair and waited behind the piece of glass.

Last night I'd continued listening to the audio recordings of Carol's sessions with my father. I almost felt as if I were invading her privacy, but persevered. She definitely sounded paranoid. Her fear of dying and her body deteriorating slowly over years came across in graphic detail. I could see how the police, her husband, and those close to her would believe she suffered from some sort of psychosis.

I jumped as the doors opened on the other side of the glass, and in filed inmates wearing orange jumpsuits. They weren't shackled or cuffed, as I had expected them to be. When I spotted Kevin, my breath caught in my throat. He had a black eye, and his right cheek was swollen. He seemed relieved to see me. I'd been surprised when he called me from jail, on my way home from Val's, and begged me to come see him.

He picked up the black phone connected to the wall on his side, and I picked up mine. "Thanks for coming."

"What happened to your face?"

He slanted his eyes to the left and then back to me. "Some guy in here. I've got to learn to keep my head down until I get out on bail. I did some time in juvie when I was a teen for petty stuff, but this—well, nothing prepares you for this."

I hadn't known anything about his prior juvenile record, but there was no reason I would've.

He gave his head a small shake. "I didn't do this. And that stupid Quinn loved slamming me into the wall. He's always hated me because of you."

Quinn certainly wasn't a fan of his. But there was a niggling worry in the back of my mind because this had more to do with what I'd overheard. "Why do they think you did it? What evidence do they have?" I didn't want to show my hand. I needed to see if he would be honest with me.

Kevin rested his elbows on the table attached to the glass. "My lawyer says it's all circumstantial stuff mostly. We fought over the inheritance. I told you about that. Her husband is pissed because he wants what's mine. He's actually planning on fighting me in court. Now I'm in here. Coincidence? I think not."

"You think you were framed?"

"It's crazy, Lyla. Like something straight up out of the movies. They can plant things, you know. I watch the news. I know how things like this go down. Especially if the cops have it in for you."

"That seems a little paranoid. They must have something solid. They can't arrest you without cause." My mind went back to the photographs. He'd looked like a raving lunatic. It wasn't a stretch to make the leap to murder or accidental death based on those.

Kevin rested his head on his arm and held the black receiver against his shoulder for a moment. "I told you, Carol and I got into it a few times. It got ugly." He met my gaze, and his eyes flared. "It isn't what you think! I didn't hurt her."

"Tell me what it was like." I kept my mind open and my eyes watchful. If he came across as defensive and edgy, I'd worry more. Although, one could argue, that could be attributed to his situation.

"If I do, will you help me?"

"If you tell me everything without leaving anything out, I'll talk to the judge." I held up my finger. "Everything, Kevin."

He nodded. "Carol called me a few weeks back to discuss the inheritance. We met a few times privately at that motel off the interstate. She'd just come back from looking at some old crime scene on I-85 each time, and she acted freaked out."

My pulse sped up. I leaned forward. "Freaked out by?"

"I asked, but she wasn't making sense. She went on and on about some wolf-in-sheep's-clothing nonsense. Carol was petrified. She would reference 'the person,' but never gave me a name, claiming it would be safer for me if I didn't know." Kevin rubbed his discolored cheek. "I thought she was losing it. Carol was seeing your dad. He was treating her for paranoia."

When I didn't react, he nodded. "You already knew that. Okay. Well, we'd come to an agreement. She planned on splitting the inheritance with me. So, you see! There isn't a motive to hurt my stepsister. Even if she hadn't agreed, I wouldn't have hurt her. You know me."

"It was you I saw with her that day in the car?"

His eyes blazed again. "That wasn't me! I swear to God! I did see her the day before, though. She was hysterical. She said she planned on running away with someone, a killer, she said. To keep those of us safe from him. She wasn't making sense. I asked her why she would run away with a known killer. She just kept saying, 'before there are none' over and over again. And like I said, I didn't really believe her." He was leaning so close to the glass it fogged up in a round circle at his mouth. His eyes were glossy. "I should've, and I didn't."

"Did she give you any clue as to who the person was?"

"I honestly don't know. I think he was her escape plan. She was crying and carrying on about being conflicted. She loved the guy, the killer. And she couldn't believe they were capable of such a horrible act and how she believed it was a dream."

Chills ran up my spine. "That's all she said?"

He stared me straight in the face. "Yes. I swear. And I didn't do that to her! I'm being railroaded." He lowered his tone. "You know me. I'm not capable of that. Stuffing her in a suitcase. That would entail a lot of shit I don't even want to consider. Plus, I didn't even know she'd been in a suitcase or that you found her that way until they showed me those pictures. Lyla, I swear to God, I would never do that to her or you."

I narrowed my eyes. "Have you been texting me?"

He shook his head.

"Did you kill a possum and smear blood in my car?"

His face held shock. "What? No. Somebody did that to you?"

I nodded my head.

"Well, it wasn't me! I didn't do this! I mean it!" He let out a shuddering breath.

"Did she say anything else? Think, Kevin, think."

He turned his head side to side. "She said a lot of shit. Oh." He lifted his head. "I think she said something about leaving the evidence somewhere for safekeeping. I told the police that too. They think I'm making all this up. I'm not even sure my lawyer believes I'm telling the truth."

I felt my eyes widen. "What evidence?"

The corners of his mouth turned down, and I could tell the motion caused him pain. "I don't know. Something about pictures she took or found or something."

"Think, Kevin!"

"I don't know, Lyla!" He thumped the glass with his fist, and the guard gave him a stern warning. "Sorry. Won't happen again," Kevin said compliantly.

When his eyes focused back on me, I blurted, "I found the cap."

"What?" He shifted in his chair; hope visibly began to fade from his eyes.

"In the trash. I found it," I said tersely.

His eyes were wide with panic. "I was afraid! After she died, I heard from Ellen that you told the police you saw a man wearing a camo cap like mine in the car with Carol. I was afraid that after the disagreements I had with Carol over the inheritance, they would use it to try and pin this on me." He motioned to himself. "Case in point."

Ellen? How did she know about my statement?

"Throwing it away made you look suspicious. Why else throw it away unless you were identified as the person wearing it with Carol before her death?"

The correctional officer announced a five-minute warning.

"It was stupid! Yeah, I get it. I did not do this. Please, Lyla! Please. You have to help me. If you find out who's behind this, they'll have to let me go. I was a jerk to you. I should never have let Ellen talk me into moving by you. We could've chosen another unit a few streets over, or she could've moved into my place instead of me renting it out."

Their move *had* been vindictive. "Listen, Kevin. I don't care about that anymore. If you want to be with Ellen, fine. I don't hold a grudge against you."

Time was called, and Kevin started to rise, his eyes shifting to his left, where one of his fellow inmates was sneering his direction, and then to the guard.

"I'll do what I can. For Carol. And if you're innocent, for you."

"I am. I swear I am."

I placed the receiver back on the hook, and as I watched him file out with the other inmates, a look of desperation on his face, I wondered if I could believe him.

Chapter Thirty

My mind reeled with so many things as I showered and dressed. I was going for nice without being over the top and giving Quinn the impression I was trying too hard to impress him.

I spoke to Brad briefly before my shower and told him about my conversation with Kevin. I let him know about the picture Amelia had found. He'd told me he would be having a discussion with Kevin after his arraignment. The Sweet Mountain Police Department would allow him the professional courtesy in due course.

After I hung up, I listened to more of Carol's sessions. I stopped midway in the last session to get ready. She'd rambled for most of it, listing famous killers—Jeffery Dahmer, Son of Sam, Ted Bundy, and Aileen Wuornos. She stressed how they just continued on, living essentially normal lives as if their behaviors were completely sane. She kept alluding to the evidence left in plain sight with each case.

So, even though everything in me screamed, "Cancel and race over to the lion's den," which is how I thought of Carol's house now, and search for whatever evidence she left behind, I decided not to break the agreement; I'd just go over after dinner.

The police had searched the Timms's residence, I was sure. And if they'd found anything, perhaps Quinn would mention whatever it was. Or maybe it eerily went missing like the scarf, I thought. That was if Kevin had been truthful with me and there was even anything to find.

I'd still not heard from Uncle Calvin, and I tried not to worry. Since I'd gone to work for him, he'd never not returned my calls. With something this important, I couldn't imagine what would keep him from doing so. I even went so far as to call Mother to see if she'd heard from him. She hadn't, of course, and told me he vanished for weeks at a time, sometimes months. He had, sure, on jobs he couldn't discuss, but he'd never gone MIA when I'd called him. There were too many things and people to worry about, and my brain ached. I sat on the sofa and opened my laptop.

The triangulation the IT specialists sent wasn't as challenging to read as I'd anticipated. He'd included a summary I found highly useful. I put the coordinates into Google, and I watched as it traveled up Interstate 85 and took a service road that ran directly behind the abandoned Baptist Church in Cam County, Georgia. The exact location Brad had taken me to. Kevin had been honest about Carol's whereabouts before each of their meetings.

"Oh God," I breathed as realization dawned. How would she know? I knew for a fact she hadn't gone with Brad. Had someone else taken her there? Kevin? Had she gone on her own because she knew the place? My pulse quickened, and I grabbed my tablet off the end table, pulled up the dumping grounds doc, and scrolled to the article "On the Scene." I needed to see if the article gave more clues to the location than I initially believed.

Nothing specific. If Carol was really determined, I bet she could've figured it out. A few more searches would probably do the trick. There had to be local reports and news broadcasts of the discovery.

While I waited on Quinn, I put my earbuds in to continue the session, and poured myself a glass of wine.

"Carol is there a reason for the fixation on killers in fiction this afternoon?"

"You said discuss my thoughts. These are my thoughts. Dr. Moody, did you know that when the average person thinks of a killer, their brain likely conjures up an image of a monster? When in actuality the person looks like you or me."

"Yes, I imagine that is true."

"If I were to write a novel, one that my club, the Jane Does, might read and discuss, I'd have my protagonist, um, Maggie, hide evidence about a murder in plain sight. Like in a framed print!"

I froze mid-sip. Did Carol believe I'd ever hear this recording? Was this her way of leaving me a clue?

"Maggie would be really creative. Perhaps in a bath—"

The doorbell rang. "Just a minute," I called, closed my laptop, and stood.

Carol, did you leave evidence behind?

I took a glance in the mirror over the sofa and smoothed out my long hair. I exhaled a long, slow, controlled breath. Something I was getting good at these days. My pale skin and shaken appearance wouldn't do. I grabbed my brown leather carryall and dug through it to find my coral blush lipstick and clear gloss.

"I'll be right there," I called when another knock came. It took me three attempts to apply the lipstick and dab a little gloss on top. *What have I gotten myself into?* No, I hadn't gotten myself into anything. Someone dragged me into this mess, probably believing I wouldn't have the constitution to fight back. Well, I was stronger than people thought.

I practiced a couple of bright smiles in the mirror, and, once satisfied, I opened the door to see Quinn on the other side, dressed in blue slacks and a striped blue and white shirt with a navy sports coat. I met his gaze, noting he didn't come across as I'd painted him a moment ago.

He smiled and then focused on my face as if he discerned something off about me—probably sensing my ambivalence. "'Evening. You okay?"

Of course, even with my most gallant attempt at hiding my emotions, Quinn would see through me. It was his job, after all, and denying my inner turmoil wouldn't be the most intelligent approach. I decided to use it instead. No one would blame me for being upset by the fact my ex was arrested, especially when his crime had to do with another friend of ours.

I smiled at him. "'Evening. Yes, I'm fine. Just had yet another shock today."

"If you don't feel like going out this evening, we could stay in." Ah, he hadn't said we could do this another time, which surprised me, and it must have shown because he said, though not convincingly, "Unless you'd rather just take a rain check."

I gave my head a small shake. "No. I'm ready. It'll probably be better for me to go out. Staying in and brooding over what I never saw or didn't suspect isn't ideal." All truths.

"Okay, then." His eyes roamed up and down my body, and then his tight expression eased with his grin. "You look amazing."

"Thank you—so do you."

"Thanks. I put a little effort into it." He stepped aside, and I joined him on the stoop.

"Oh. My. God." An exclamation came from our left. Ellen stood a few feet from us. "I knew it! You were so damn jealous of my connection with Kevin that you and your stupid boy-friend here framed him."

Quinn took my arm and tried to guide me away from my cousin. "Ellen, I would advise you to think before you speak. I'm not here on an official capacity." His gaze held a warning. "That can change."

Ellen folded her arms and glowered at us. "I'm not breaking any laws. And I have the right to speak to a family member of mine any time I damn well please."

I moved out of Quinn's grasp. As much as Ellen and I were always at odds, I didn't want her to be caught up in this tangled web. Family was family. "Quinn," I said softly. "Could you give us a minute, please?"

After a quick assessment of the situation, he said a terse, "I'll be in the truck."

"Thanks."

I held up my finger and waited until Quinn was out of ear-shot. "Listen, Ellen."

"What are you going to do, get rid of me too? Well, I'm not defenseless," Ellen spat, though she did take a step backward.

No one on God's green earth irked me the way she did. It was a fight to restrain myself from shaking her. "Are you nuts? I'm not going to do anything to you."

"Uh-huh. Just so you know, I've called Uncle Calvin."

My mouth popped open. What was wrong with her?

"He knows what's been going on while he's away. You may be able to pull the wool over a lot of people's eyes around here, but not mine. And Kevin must've discovered what you've been up to. He got beat up in jail! Did you know that? Of course, you did because you went to see him. To gloat!"

Ellen's lost her ever loving mind!

She opened her mouth to continue, and I'd had enough and growled in frustration. "Shut up."

She flinched and took another step away from me.

"I don't want to fight with you. Please, for once in your life, just listen."

To my utter astonishment, she bit the inside of her lip. I couldn't believe how scared she acted. *Of me!*

"I didn't have anything to do with Kevin's arrest. And my God, how could you even think for one second I had anything to do with Carol's death? Sheesh, we're cousins for God's sake." I lowered my tone. "I hate this. I mean *hate* it." I drew out the word hate. "I'm not going to lie and say you and Kevin didn't bother me. It was awful of y'all." I motioned to her townhouse. "Uncouth and just plain mean."

She lifted her chin defiantly.

I closed my eyes and slowly shook my head. This girl! She believed I was some crazy killer, and still she defied me. I looked her square in the face. "It doesn't matter now. My relationship with Kevin was and is over. Make him hubby number four and have lots of babies together, for all I care."

"Then why did you go see him?" She sounded suspicious.

"Because I needed to see for myself if he had anything to do with Carol's death."

"And?" She sounded a little calmer.

"I don't want to believe he's guilty either. I want to know who is and put them behind bars."

She opened her mouth and then closed it again. "Calvin knows about this?"

"He's aware I'm investigating," I said ambiguously.

"Can I help?"

Glad to no longer be fighting with her, my shoulders relaxed an infinitesimal amount. "You can stop going around accusing me of murder, for one. Then anything Kevin's lawyer finds, let me know about it." It would be good to know what defense the lawyer planned on using and if he had anyone doing any digging on Kevin's behalf.

"I can do that." She dropped her arms. "Is Uncle Calvin going to get involved? I'd feel better if he did."

"He's out on an assignment at the moment. He'll be in touch when he's able." Boy, I hoped he would be able soon.

"Yeah, that's what he said." She nodded toward Quinn's truck idling away in the parking lot. "What about him?"

"It's just dinner."

A cunning smile played on her lips. "You're working him?"

I gave her the sternest warning glare I could muster. "It's just dinner."

She held up her hands in what I took as defeat and started backing toward her house. "Be careful. Kevin believes we have a murderer in our midst, who has power to wield. Now that I think about it, who has more power than our chief of police? Wasn't he there when your car ended up a blood bath? He's always had it in for Kevin."

"Who told you about my car?"

She shrugged. "People talk."

She nodded her head toward the truck. "My money is on him, the jerk."

And a moment ago she'd thought I was responsible.

Chapter
Thirty-One

Quinn and I didn't speak much on the ride to the restaurant. We were seated in the back of the dining room, sipping on a glass of red wine and pushing around a beautiful starter of fried calamari on our plates and breaking the ice with small talk.

"You spend a lot of time fishing these days?" I sipped from the glass. I wanted to show my interest in his boating story he'd just been telling me about. Ellen's words regarding her suspicions came rushing back.

He swallowed a sip of water. "As often as I can. Since buying the new bass boat, I'd feel like I wasted my money if I just let it sit in the garage all the time."

I nodded to show I was listening when, truthfully, I'd only been half listening because I noticed Judge Timms seated in the corner with a woman I didn't recognize.

"What about you? Any new hobbies?"

"Not really. I'm still in the book club and—"

To my surprise, Judge Timms walked over to our table. "Chief," he nodded to Quinn and then to me, "Lyla."

"Hello, Judge Timms." I forced a smile. The man made me feel extremely uncomfortable, but I had to deal with it for now. I needed access to his house.

"Judge." Quinn didn't look happy to see him.

I watched them intently over the rim of my glass.

The man had the look of someone marinated in alcohol for days. His forehead and temples appeared damp, and his eyes were glassy and bloodshot. Not that people would grudge him his mourning process. The heavyset woman he'd been dining with sidled up next to him and took his arm. The woman was a good fifteen years or so older than Quinn and me, I estimated.

"'Evening," she greeted Quinn and me. "David, maybe we should call it a night."

"My sister." The judge patted her arm and then pulled at his double chin. "She's come to look after me." He made a face as if he hadn't been so keen on the idea.

She smiled, and now I could see the resemblance. Same round face and eye shape. "I hoped getting him out of the house might improve his spirits."

"It has, Marigold."

He winked at me then and reached out and touched my shoulder, feeling the material between his thumb and index finger. "Thought you'd come by and see me. We have unfinished business."

I shifted uncomfortably in my chair.

His sister met my gaze and frowned. "You'll have to forgive my brother. He isn't himself tonight."

"I'm fine." Judge Timms grinned. "Lyla and I are friends now, aren't we, Lyla?"

Quinn rose. "Judge, is there something we can do for you?"

"Come on, David. Let's leave these two youngsters to enjoy their evening." His sister tugged at his waist, where her hand rested.

"Okay. Yeah, let's go have our dessert." His gaze was on me the entire time he spoke, and I fought a grimace.

Quinn's stance did nothing to deter the judge as he stepped around and put his hand on the back of my chair. He leaned down and held his face close to mine. I could smell the amount of garlic he'd consumed, mingled with alcohol, as he whispered loud enough for everyone to hear, "Don't go barking up the wrong tree now."

I flinched, and he gave me a hard pat on the back. A little too forcefully because I was shoved into the table, rattling the plates and silverware. The candle on the table flickered and nearly toppled over. Thankfully Quinn saved us from disaster by securing it.

"Oops." The judge put his finger to his lips.

"I'm sure you want to get back to your dessert," Quinn said between clenched teeth, and gripped Judge Timms's upper arm.

The uncomfortable silence stretched for a few more minutes as the men squared off in a silent battle.

Judge Timms jerked his arm out of Quinn's hold and adjusted his tie. The tension in the room eased when the siblings went back to their respective tables.

Quinn's cheeks flushed with anger, and he was clearly rattled. He took a large swig of wine.

I decided to take advantage and whispered, "What do you owe Judge Timms, Quinn?"

He coughed and placed his glass on the table, saying nothing.

"I overheard you the day I came to your office. And later Judge Timms let it slip that you owed him. I'm not an idiot."

Quinn glanced over his shoulder, where Judge Timms conspicuously watched our table. He snorted. "Love to stir up drama, don't you?" Quinn's gaze hardened. "You're older and infinitely more beautiful, yet you're just as stubborn and direct as you were in your late teens."

"Answer the question."

"So you can twist it around and make more trouble?"

"I'm not the one who conveniently lost a valuable piece of evidence. It should've been made available to Brad."

"Brad, now is it?" he said in mock falsetto. "You haven't changed a bit."

"Did you think I would change? That when I grew older, the ingrained part of my personality would vanish?" I wiped my mouth with the black cloth napkin and leaned back in my chair.

"Not vanish; perhaps soften." He sounded bemused.

"Soften I have. In those days, I would have made a scene. Shouting to everyone about you colluding with Judge Timms."

White brackets appeared around his mouth.

I picked up my glass and sipped as he studied me, unmoving. "I never would have even kept our date before. Yet here I sit being civil."

Our entrees arrived, and I leaned back to allow the server to place the cedar-smoked salmon with sautéed spinach and a rice pilaf before me. Quinn had the filet mignon and a loaded baked potato, which took up half the plate.

"Thank you. It looks delicious," Quinn and I said in unison, and we both smiled a little. Even when our world crashed down around us, Southerners were nothing if not polite.

"There isn't any collusion."

"There's something." I sampled my salmon, which was indeed delicious.

"It has nothing to do with Carol's murder. I'll tell you about it when we're not out in public. Okay?" Quinn glanced around.

Admitting he would be willing to confide in me later made me feel a little better. "Okay."

Quinn cut into his medium-rare steak and took a bite.

"And losing evidence isn't okay." I scooped up some rice.

His fork paused midway to his mouth. "It isn't lost, and I'm not sure it's even evidence. But, I'll find it and make sure Brad has what he needs to leave my town for good." His lips had curled when he said Brad's name.

"And what if the cases are related? What if Kevin is innocent?"

"I wondered how long it would take you to jump to his defense. Even after everything that idiot has put you through, you still believe whatever he says. The man has a record of violence, Lyla. Did you know that?"

"A juvie record doesn't count, Quinn." I took a bite of the spinach.

"I'm not referring to his juvie record."

I froze and met his ice-blue gaze.

"You don't have the full story. Have you spoken to Kevin's lawyer yet? I know you went to see Kevin."

I shook my head, unable to speak with a full mouth.

"Well, I'll save you the trouble." He wiped his own mouth. "Allow me to enlighten you further. Carol filed a complaint against him two weeks before she passed away."

I started to choke and took a sip from the glass. "What type of complaint?"

"He showed up at her home drunk. He threatened her and demanded she sign the agreement regarding the inheritance he'd had drawn up. Judge Timms overheard the commotion. He called us."

I mulled the information over. I felt frustrated Kevin hadn't told me everything. He had admitted to arguing with her, and I'd seen the pictures where he grabbed her, which was inexcusable. "Carol didn't file charges—Judge Timms did?"

"No. Carol did. She said he'd become enraged when he found out she'd been left the bulk of the estate. And when she tried to talk to get him to calm down, he went berserk."

Had Kevin lied to my face? I warned him to withhold nothing. Now I sat here with figurative egg all over my face. I was so angry I could scream.

"She agreed to split the inheritance, though. Why would he—"

"He wanted it all. What about the photos, Lyla? The ones the judge had his private eye take. I know he gave you a copy. And you said yourself, Kevin watched you from his window when those texts came through. Have you so quickly forgotten about the blood in your car? It could've been him."

I shook my head. "The smell of death isn't one you easily forget."

He flinched. "You're right." He sighed. "I'm sorry. That wasn't fair. But you have to admit your eyewitness account proves Carol was in distress while in his company. You'll be contacted by the DA to testify to that fact." He placed his fork down. "I don't want you to get yourself in any trouble because of some notion you're obliged to help him."

"I honestly can't say it was him for sure. And I won't lie under oath, Quinn." My tone betrayed how insulted I felt. I wouldn't argue the fact Kevin claimed he hadn't been with her that morning. Surely someone had checked his alibi. "And we'll never know if it was Kevin who terrorized me at the precinct, because your security camera just happened to be malfunctioning. Convenient, don't you think?"

The muscle in his jaw clenched.

"Are you sharing information with Brad—I mean Special Agent Jones?"

He fought a sneer and, surprising me, sounded jealous. "We are sharing what is necessary. The GBI is only interested in solving their Jane Doe crime. They aren't interested in the welfare of our community, which is my top priority."

With a slightly shaky hand, I sipped my wine. Quinn seemed to notice. There wasn't any helping that. "You're doing your job, and he's doing his."

He made a face that told me how he felt about that topic. Same ole Quinn. "None of which is your job."

"I beg your pardon. Judge Timms hired me."

He leaned back and crossed his arms. "It's staggering how determined you are to continue to intertwine yourself in the inner workings of law enforcement even after being physically threatened. Are you a glutton for punishment? Why don't you find something else to do with your life? It's clearly having a negative effect on you." He nodded to my hand as I placed my glass back on the table.

"Why do you care? It's my life," I whisper-railed.

He looked at me, seemingly stunned. "Because I care about you. I always have."

"We haven't spoken in years. You were engaged."

"And it didn't work out, now did it?" He shifted in his chair and leaned forward. "Since spending time with you again, even under these circumstances, I can't get you out of my head." He ran his hand over the back of his neck.

I took a sip of wine, glancing away. This was so not the time to be having this discussion.

He reached across the table and took my hand just as I released my glass. "Babe, this is a scary business. You are so fixated on this Jane Doe thing it's crazy. It's over. We have the right man in custody, and yet you're still harping on this." He held my gaze. His look pleaded. "Work with me here. Step away from this."

For the life of me, I didn't understand how he could be so obtuse. "What if you're wrong. Can you even fathom the possibility?"

"I don't think I am. But either way it doesn't concern you."

"You forget I've been hired to investigate this case."

He gave me a pitying look.

I stared at him for a few long moments. He expected me to lash out, and I wouldn't. I folded my arms defiantly.

"Look," he said, tossing his napkin on his plate, "I don't want to argue with you about this. There's no point. I had a conversation with your uncle this afternoon and stressed my concerns."

I met his guileless blue gaze.

"He agreed with me that there's no reason you should be involved in this since we've arrested someone. He said Judge Timms would be satisfied with the job my office is doing."

Calvin wasn't aware that Judge Timms wanted a murder charge.

I clenched my fists in my lap. My face heated, and my ears grew hot from my uncle's betrayal. I wouldn't show my worse side to this man. This dinner had been a major eye-opener.

I kept my tone low and matter-of-fact. "I'll deal with my uncle. And while you're sitting over there with an air of masculine superiority, you should know Brad doesn't believe I'm too fragile. He took me to the crime scene. He believes I can be of use in his case."

Quinn sat up straight as a board, and I could almost feel ambivalence wafting off him. "What? Your interest in men is based on whether they share their crime scenes with you or not?"

I studied him, considering how long to let him stew. "You'll never understand. This was a mistake."

"Lyla"—his tone rose, and he cast a glance around—"let's discuss this someplace else."

"You know what? I don't think I want to discuss this, period." I rose. "Excuse me." I turned to leave.

His hand reached out and snatched my wrist. "Lyla."

"Excuse me." I jerked my arm away. "I'm going to the ladies' room."

While I handled the necessities, I heard the main bathroom door open and close. I sat on the closed toilet with the intent to check my messages. I couldn't believe this night. The stall door rattled, and I paused. "Just a minute." Feeling ridiculous for hiding out, I shoved my phone back into my bag. The door closed again.

I emerged from the stall, finding the low-lit restroom empty. I was so angry with Quinn, Uncle Calvin, and the whole damn situation. I flipped on the water and began scrubbing my hands, grumbling, "High-handed men."

Was it too much to ask for equality? I snatched a couple of paper towels and went to check my reflection in the mirror. I froze. The paper towels slipped from my fingers as I read the message written in red lipstick on the mirror.

One little Jane Doe left all alone; She hanged herself and then there were none.

My heart was beating like a jackhammer. Adrenaline shot through me. I spun around the bathroom and checked under the only other stall. Alone. I was alone.

The door opened and I screamed.

Chapter
Thirty-Two

S itting in a booth next to the ladies' room, I sipped on a glass
of ice water. I'd disturbed most of the diners. Quinn rushed
inside, weapon in hand. He stood a few feet from us, now con-
versing with Officer Taylor.

My thoughts were in a tumult. Quinn's theory about not
receiving anything after Kevin's arrest was way off base. It was
inexplicable, but a rhyme had been written on the bathroom
mirror in the same fashion as *And Then There Were None*. And if
whoever was behind this followed the pattern of the book, it
would be the last rhyme. My last warning. My hands shook in
my lap. I scanned the room, wondering if the responsible party
would stick around to see the result of their handiwork.

Who would know I was having dinner with Quinn? *Ellen!*
Could my own cousin be involved? Ellen knew Quinn and I
were having dinner. She could've followed us here. Then there
was Judge Timms. He'd also been here with his sister and told
me not to bark up the wrong tree. Although, in his condition, I
doubted he'd be able to write anything legible. But maybe his
appearance at our table, "intoxicated," had been a ruse to clear
him, and he'd sent his sister in to do it.

"Hey, honey," Mrs. Ross slid next to me in the booth and wrapped her arm around my shaking shoulders.

"Mrs. R-Ross?" I stammered.

"I was having dinner with my niece, right over there." She motioned behind us. "I saw you go into the restroom. I about had a heart attack when you screamed."

Condensation slid down the side of my water glass.

"At first I thought that Quinn Daniels had slipped into the ladies' room"—she lowered her tone—"to, um, . . . you know."

"Wait! What?" My head whipped up. He'd not left the table when we were together.

Her eyes were wide, and she appeared flustered. "Well, I've seen programs where men want to engage in sex stuff in the ladies' room."

"No, not that. When did you see Quinn near the restrooms?"

"I don't know. Not long before you started screaming."

I glanced over my shoulder, where Quinn had his back to me.

"Mrs. Ross, I have to ask you again. What did the note Chelsea gave you say when you first looked at it?"

The older woman glanced down at her hands. "Something like, 'before there wasn't anyone.'" Someone called Mrs. Ross. I'd hardly registered it before she gave me a swift kiss on the cheek and slid out of the booth to leave.

I struggled with my warring instincts. I wanted to run. I wanted to fight, to confront Quinn and make him explain everything. And all along I knew the one common denominator in this entire situation was me. My head spun. Carol's murder and two Jane Doe cases, and Quinn didn't want me anywhere near any of it. Yet the evil had found me. Kept coming for me.

I took a surreptitious look around and pulled my cell from my purse. With trembling fingers, I typed out what I hoped was a coherent text to our GBI officer. If anyone should be here, he should.

My phone rang, and I put in an earbud inconspicuously into my ear and let my hair drop around it. "Hey."

"Where are you?" Brad asked tersely. He'd obviously read my text explaining my predicament.

"Trail Head Grill in the Sweet Mountain Square," I told him in a soft, low tone.

"I'm in the car now. Take a breath and summarize it for me."

I explained what had transpired from the time Quinn had showed up till now. I included everything I could think of in my current rattled state. Answered his questions about people I knew who were here at the time. And what Quinn and I had discussed.

"These cases *are* related, and someone's worried I'm getting close to the truth. How far away are you?" I hated the desperation in my tone, but this wasn't about me. It was about Carol and Jane Doe. Brad had a doggedness this case needed.

"I'm close. I was already on my way back to see you."

"Oh."

"Lyla, the scarf is an identical match to the majorette scarf you mentioned."

The room spun a little, and I steadied myself with a hand on the wooden tabletop. "How'd you discover that?"

"I had the forensic team go back through all the evidence. A piece with the crest managed to slip behind the lining of the suitcase. I'm not sure how it was mis—"

Quinn touched my shoulder, and I jumped. "Sorry," he whispered.

Keeping my back to him, I pulled the bud from my ear and allowed it to drop back into my open purse and turned to face him.

"We're going to be conducting interviews for a while. I want to make sure we aren't missing something." He kneeled in front of me and placed a hand on my knee, and I fought the urge to slap it off. I managed it. "I'm not going to let anything happen to you. I honestly believed we had our man, and still do. But if it turns out I'm wrong, I'll hunt the bastard down." He meant every word. Or at least I believed he did. Now, I was beginning to second-guess my assumptions.

"You need to help me out here. Keep a lower profile until we close this case." He earnestly searched my eyes.

"Meaning?"

"Meaning, you've been running around town asking questions and"—he took a breath—"painting a giant bull's-eye on your back." He rubbed the back of his neck. "Kevin could be getting desperate and having someone plant new evidence."

I opened my mouth, and he cut me off. "I'm not saying I have tunnel vision where he's concerned. I'm just worried about you. All this," he said, gently squeezing my knee, a personal gesture I wasn't comfortable with, "and still, you won't let this go. You've created a reputation, and not a positive one. Kevin could use that to his advantage."

Jerking my leg away in one fast motion, I wrestled with my emotions. "Are you actually saying I brought this on myself? Is that what I'm hearing, Quinn Daniels?"

"No, hell no. Is that what you think of me?"

I dug the picture from my purse and thrust it into his hand. "Did Amelia bring that on herself? Because that was taped to the bottom of her cake plate when she went to retrieve it from Judge Timms's house after the reception."

He stared down at the image. "Why didn't I know about this?"

I gaped. "Because you weren't hearing me before."

"I'm listening now." His head turned toward the door that had swung open with a loud creak.

Brad Jones filled the space. He had one of those imposing presences that made everyone turn and take notice. For some reason, all the men in my life were that way.

Chapter Thirty-Three

Brad and Quinn were locked in a jurisdictional debate. Both were on the phone, vying for control over the cases. The tension was palpable. The whispers and stares of the other patrons got to me. I waited until both men were out of sight, and I slipped out of the booth, threaded through the crowds, and escaped out the door into the night.

I wandered aimlessly around the square. The food establishments and bars were bright with light, and folks with cocktails were mingling outside.

Music from the bar across the street kept slipping through the crack of the front door every time someone entered or exited. I bumped into a couple of people and rushed out a stuttering apology.

"Lyla." I heard my name and turned to spy Melanie getting out of her car, and I could have cried with relief. I waited for a couple of cars to pass before crossing the street to catch her.

"Oh, Mel, thank God." I hugged my friend.

"Mel, Lyla!" Val came rushing over. "Lyla, what in the world?"

"It happened again," I whispered in a low voice. "I got another message. A warning." I was getting fed up with feeling frightened.

Val shot me a sideways glance. "What sort of message. A text?"

"A rhyme on the mirror in the ladies room at the Trail Head Grill." Mouths gaped, and I explained what happened.

"Kevin's in jail!" Melanie's eyes were round as saucers.

"Quinn thinks he may have an accomplice."

Val chewed on the side of her index finger. "I hate to say this, but Ellen has been acting odd lately."

I let out a nervous laugh, glancing around and feeling jumpy. "Wait. What are y'all doing here?"

Val pointed to the front of the restaurant across the street. "I was having dinner with Greg. Remember? We planned it. He got the call from Quinn."

"Oh, right." I rubbed the space between my brows, hoping to ease the ache.

"I was picking up takeout." Mel pointed to the bag in the front seat of her car. "And—"

"You thought you'd wait around and tail Quinn driving me home?"

She nodded, looking sheepish. "I couldn't sit by and do nothing!"

Val pointed to the crowd outside the Trail Head Grill, where several officers were scanning the perimeter. "We better get off the street."

"We can slip into the crowd at the bar. The first place Quinn will check is our houses, Mel."

"Good idea." Melanie nodded.

"Y'all go ahead. Greg will be looking for me, and if I'm MIA too, they'll know we snuck off together." Val kept scanning the area. "I'll go back and give y'all a chance to get a head start."

"Okay. But stay safe." I squeezed her hand.

"I'll be careful, I swear." Val disappeared in the throngs of people before we could protest.

Mel and I meandered through the crowd as a local band made a gallant attempt at playing a popular U2 song.

"Want a drink?" Mel asked at my ear, and I nodded emphatically. "You okay to scope out a table? I'm worried about leaving you alone."

"Don't be. I'm fine." And somehow being here, away from the threats and Quinn, I felt not fine, but more like me. "Go." I gave her a little shove.

As she edged up to the bar, I scouted the place and staked out two tables. A woman at the back table, near the signed autographs of country legends and actors, was searching through her purse. When she pulled out a tube of Chapstick, I focused on the table closer to the restrooms. Bingo. Three women were hopping off the high chairs, and I made a beeline to secure the table.

I hopped up on the chair facing the front door. Having my back to the wall felt appropriate. I hated to be so paranoid. No wonder poor Carol had been labeled. If she'd been dealing with threats, God only knows how she'd managed to remain sane.

My cell buzzed in my bag. Uncle Calvin.

"Where in God's name have you been?" I barked without preamble. "You take time to call Quinn, but not me?"

"I'm in Guatemala. It's a long story. Now, calm down and tell me what happened." He sounded out of breath.

"The job in Atlanta took you to Guatemala?" I seethed.

"No. I finished it up two days ago. I'm helping out a fellow SEAL, a buddy I served with. I can't go into it further. Don't ask." His tone told me he meant business. "Now, what's going on?"

While I relayed the entire ordeal to my uncle, my phone buzzed multiple times. Quinn was trying to get in touch with me, and I didn't want to see him. When I finished, Uncle Calvin said, "And where is Chief Daniels now? And the GBI officer?"

"Still at the Trail Head Grill, I think. I can't believe you told Quinn you'd rein me in." I couldn't hide the hurt in my tone.

"He said Judge Timms asked to drop the case and you wouldn't."

"Quinn is such a liar." Though he knew me well. Even if Judge Timms had dropped it, I wouldn't have until I knew all the facts.

"It sounds as if you've rattled some cages, and that worries me."

Mel came to the table and passed me a drink with mint leaves. I took a sip and nearly coughed—high octane. Bless her heart.

"I don't know who to trust." I took a drink. "All I know is I'm on to something. The rhymes, the picture, and the scarves were a match." I wiped the sweat from my forehead.

"You don't sound so good."

"I'm fine. A lot freaked out, but fine." I finished the drink. "Kevin said Carol left evidence. After the notes and evidence she left for me, I'm inclined to believe there's truth to his words."

Melanie eyed me with interest. She mouthed, "What?"

I held up a finger and took another sip. The line began to crackle. As if a switch flipped, I had an idea of what Carol had done with the potential evidence. I recalled the recordings of her session with Daddy.

"If I were to write a novel, one that my club, the Jane Does, might read and discuss, I'd have my protagonist, um, Maggie, hide evidence about a murder in plain sight. Like in a framed print!"

I worried, since she continued to follow the style of Agatha Christie's novel for hiding evidence, that Carol had something to do with the killing of her Jane. She knew too many facts. I swallowed. And her death hadn't silenced her. She'd planned for it.

"Lyla! Lyla, are you there?"

Lots of crackling on the line.

"Yes, I'm sorry. I just got an idea."

"Can't I talk you into going to stay at your parents' place and waiting on this until I return?"

I turned away from a group passing our table en route to the restrooms. "And bring this danger to their doorstep? Not a chance."

He gave out a low growl of frustration and then let a string of curses fly. He was so loud that Melanie's eyes flared, hearing his rant. Now, with the latest brazen threat so out in the open for all to see, this felt more personal.

"If I can't persuade you not to act on something stupid," Uncle Calvin said, "there's a revolver locked in the safe in my office. The combination is your mother's birthday."

"Mother's birthday—that's weird."

"Pay attention. You'd rather have the gun and not use it than need it and not have it. This could be life and death here."

"I hear you."

"I'm flying back on Sunday. I'll try to leave earlier if I can. I'm going to have a talk with this GBI fellow and see where his head is. You trust him?"

"Yes."

"All right. Be careful."

"You have my word." I disconnected the call.

Melanie scooted closer to me, her brows pinched in the middle. "What are you planning? I can see the wheels turning."

"We need to go home. I'll fill you in on the way." I kept my tone low. "And I need to get out of this square without being seen."

Mel stared at me for a few heartbeats and nodded. When she slid from the chair, I looped my arm through hers, not wanting us to get separated, and we rushed to her Corolla.

I stayed low in the seat as we rounded the square. I spotted Quinn and several other officers milling around. The corners of Melanie's mouth turned down in concern when Quinn noticed her car. "Explain. You better not be planning something stupid."

I gave her a condensed version of my thoughts regarding Carol and the novel, and instructed her to take me to the office and park in the back.

Melanie kept slowly shaking her head as I opened the safe. "You know I love you, and I'm all for you being a private detective—I mean I was right there with you—but this scares me. I can't lose you too." She wrapped her arms around herself. "Your uncle is on a rampage, and we might take that as a warning sign. That GBI officer is all *Men in Black* and dangerous looking, and he's confirmed we're on to something. Whoever is behind this proved tonight he could get to you wherever you are. Now trusting Quinn is up in the air because he potentially concealed evidence, and now you're in hiding."

"When you put it that way, it sounds like a conspiracy theory. And normally I would say I agree with you. I won't lie: I'm terrified, but I'm pissed off too. I want to finish this once and for all. I'm tired of playing defense."

When I turned around with the firearm in a holster, her eyes nearly bugged out of her head. Her hands flew to her face. "And you're carrying a gun! Sweet Jesus!"

"I won't let another one of us die." I slid it in my bag.

"Okay. Okay. I get that. Do you even know how to operate that thing?"

I turned, and my bag faced her.

"Ah, don't point that bag at me!"

"Don't worry, and yes, I know how to operate it. Daddy taught me how to shoot when I was young." I locked up, engaging the security system.

"This is too scary. But I get what you're saying." Melanie made the sign of a cross over her body, and we dashed to the car. "I'm not sure how I feel about this. Why not back off and let the police run with it? Rest your brain. Maybe we're missing something because fear is clouding our judgment."

I clicked my seat belt into place. I'd expected Melanie to have reservations and to be worried about me, but to maintain her supportive nature. "I need you to trust me to know what I'm doing."

She gave me a skeptical glare before pulling out into the traffic.

"I'm figuring it out. What happened to your nail-the-bastard attitude?" I asked.

"It doesn't seem so simple now. What if we're wrong, and Kevin is guilty? The hunky ones always seem to have skeletons in the closet." She shivered.

"You act like we stumbled on another body."

"The rhyme, Lyla! It's the last line."

"I know that."

"Just think about it for a second. The Kevin thing. We read all about the Bundy case. And there are loads of others written about men manipulating women to help them get free. Female accomplices on the outside trying to make them look innocent." Her eyes were big, and her brows nearly disappeared in her hairline. "Think about it—the Wicked Witch of the West, Ellen. She'd do anything for Kevin. She's cray-cray!"

"I hear you. I've had the same thoughts. And in order to solve this, to discover what happened to Carol, we need to find out the identity of the Jane Doe and who killed her. I don't care who I have to expose. It's the best course of action."

"You're right." Mel puffed out her cheeks. "That makes sense. Sorry I freaked out."

"You're allowed. This is a nightmare." I straightened in the seat. "I really believe Carol knew the Jane's identity and might have left evidence behind. I have a good idea where she hid it."

Her head whipped in my direction until someone honked behind us. "Okay. Okay. You're thinking along the lines of the novel."

I nodded.

The car slowly rolled forward.

"And where is this evidence? Not the bottle thing where the killer left his confession on an island of dead people?"

"Whatever she left, I think she left it at her house."

"Oh no, no, no. You're not going to Judge Timms's house by yourself. Forget Quinn. Tell Mr. GBI. He'll meet us there."

I pondered that for a minute. "Judge Timms wouldn't allow him to search his house. At least I don't think he would. No." I shook my head. "I can't risk it."

"Well, now we're talking about it, what if everyone is completely off base here?"

"Meaning?"

"Meaning," she said, her cheeks flushed, "I'm thinking now that maybe hubby did it. That's one of the reasons I came out to tail y'all tonight. My brother called me after you left to go on the date with Quinn. According to him, the judge and Quinn used to bet at the track together, and my brother says he and Judge Timms lost a lot of money. They nearly came to blows, according to my brother."

"Why would they come to blows over a lost bet?"

Melanie shrugged. "I don't know the specifics, but Chris said the race was a sure thing. So, I'm guessing maybe it was fixed or something, and they were double-crossed."

"Fixed?" I made a face.

"Maybe that's what Quinn owes Judge Timms for. And both of them have the juice to derail the investigation. Hell, I don't know. It's just an assumption. And if the judge is hard up for cash, that might be why he's so hell bent on keeping Carol's inheritance for himself."

I'd had my serious suspicions about the judge. Which is why I was packing tonight. I needed to know more. Secrets were hard to keep in this little town. *Case in point,* I thought when my phone rang and I saw it was my father. "Hi, Daddy."

"I take it because you answered the phone you're all right."

"Yes, sir. I'm out with Melanie." I hit the mute button when Melanie took a left on Cloverdale instead of a right. "Where are you going? You're supposed to be driving us home."

"I told you, if you're going to go to the potential killer's house, you aren't going alone."

It was one thing if I put myself in danger; it was a completely different thing if I took a friend along. "No."

"Yes."

"No way."

She glared at me. "Yes way! The Jane Does started this together. We're finishing it together." Her stubborn expression left no room for further negotiation.

"Okay, but you'll wait in the car."

"Lyla!" my daddy said. I jumped and took him off "Mute."

"Sorry, Daddy."

"Quinn called. He said you disappeared during your dinner with him, and wanted to know if I'd seen you." Quinn hadn't told daddy about the threat.

My stomach flip-flopped. "Quinn and I had a disagreement. I decided to skip out after we finished dinner and to have a drink with Melanie before going home."

Melanie's knuckles were as white on the steering wheel as her face was.

"Thanks for checking up on me. I'm fine. Love you."

"Love you too. Call Quinn. He sounded worried."

I bet he did. "I will."

"Oh, and Lyla? I want you to know you can come to me. We may not always see eye to eye on certain matters, but I'm here for you."

I squeezed the phone. "Thank you, Daddy."

"Quinn called my dad." I slipped the phone back into my purse. "Hey, I've been thinking. Judge Timms might be asleep, and his sister could decide not to let me in."

"We can hope." Melanie rolled up to the house next door.

Smart move, I thought.

"I'll keep it running," my friend said.

"You're sure?"

She took a deep breath and closed her eyes while nodding. "He might clam up if the two of us go in there. Since he hired you, it would make more sense for you to go in alone."

I put my hand on the door handle. "I won't be long."

She patted the steering wheel. "You text me. Anything. A single letter or number if that's all you can manage—and the second you feel threatened. I mean it. I'll ram this car right through his front door."

"It won't come to that." I hopped out of the car, hoping it was the truth.

Chapter
Thirty-Four

To my surprise, the door opened on the first knock, and Judge Timms stood on the other side. "Lyla, is everything all right? Come in." He stepped aside with a little stagger.

"I hope I'm not disturbing you or your sister." I glanced around to see if his sister was near.

"She decided to stay at a hotel tonight." He closed the door behind me, and nerves kicked up in my stomach.

I'd assumed Marigold would be staying with him. If I'd known he would be alone, I never would have come inside by myself.

"We had a tiff. She's always mothered me too much for my taste." He smiled at me, his eyes even more bloodshot than they were earlier, and I attempted to return the smile. "Tonight must have been a horrible shock. Are you okay?" He reached out and touched my arm, and I fought not to flinch. By the way he didn't react, I figured I must have succeeded.

I nodded. "Yes. I think so."

"Quinn should do a better job of watching out for you. I was surprised to see the two of you together. I didn't know you were back together."

"Oh, no, we aren't. It isn't anything like that."

He smiled and put his hand on my lower back and guided me ahead. "Come into the living room and have a drink with me."

"I wanted to ask you something." I perched on the edge of the studded Italian leather sofa while he made two scotches.

"Hmm?"

I took the glass he extended to me, and he sat a little closer than I was comfortable with. And being at the end of the sofa, there wasn't any place left to go. It was time to be calculating and ruthless. "I wondered, after what happened tonight, if I could take a look at Carol's computer? Maybe go through her files?"

He leaned back and slurped from his glass. "The police went through everything and didn't find anything." He picked up the remote from beside him, and a second later the room filled with classical music. He moved his hand as if conducting the orchestra.

"I'm sure I won't find anything. I just need to have a look, especially after the arrest. I can't believe I didn't see what was right in front of me. It angers me, you know?"

He studied me for a few long seconds over the rim of his glass. "I can understand that. You think you know a person, and then you find out your whole life was a lie. Go ahead. She has a little office down that hall and to the left." He closed his eyes. "My Carol . . . Why?"

I wasted no time excusing myself from the room and hustling down the hall. My smart watch pinged with an *All okay?* from Melanie. I sent back a thumbs-up emoji and opened the door. It creaked ominously. I reached inside and felt along the wall for a switch. The room, bathed in soft light, still had a faint hint of Carol's perfume. The small writing desk sat catty-corner to the bay window with a bench seat, where I recalled her saying she loved to read and have her morning coffee. The morning sun came through at just the right angle and made this room perfect.

There was a little empty frame on the desk that had to be where the picture Amelia found had come from. Anyone could have slipped back here and taken it. My heart ached, and a swell of anger welled within me. "Okay, Carol, show me where you hid it," I murmured to myself. I went to her desk, where she had old yearbooks open, with sticky notes attached to several pages. I scanned the images. A couple of her and Val in majorette outfits made me smile. Then she had old photographs lying loose on the desk. I found a picture of Melanie and me at the alumnae bonfire when we were about twenty. Carol had searched where I was searching now.

I had my arm around Mel's shoulders, and we both looked wasted. The next picture was at the same bonfire. I was sitting on Carol's lap, with one arm thrown out, and she and I had our mouths wide, singing or maybe laughing. I didn't even remember that picture. Come to think of it, I didn't have a single photo from that night. The night that charted the course for the Jane Doe's death and Carol's—a tremor shot through me—*and potentially mine.*

Tears began to stream down my cheeks. I swiped them away and started opening drawers and checking underneath them. I checked every framed print in the office and behind paintings. Five minutes later, I stood deflated and discouraged. I'd hoped whatever she'd hidden would be in her office. I couldn't very well scour the entire house. Time wouldn't afford that. I slipped from the room and down the hall, checking every framed print as I passed. The judge was snoring loudly, the cup of scotch at his feet. I had some time unless a maid let herself in late. It was a chance I'd have to take.

As quiet as a mouse, I began to work my way around the living room. Then I went into the kitchen and checked there. I got the stepladder out of the little broom closet and checked the two large paintings in the entryway. Nothing.

Could I have been entirely off base here? Of course I could. What I'd surmised as clues could've been the ramblings of a mentally ill woman. Judge Timms's mouth was wide open; his head lulled to the side. Still he snored as loud as a freight train.

Taking advantage of his slumber, I considered going upstairs and checking the master bedroom. Then it felt as if Carol herself whispered into my ear. I turned and saw a framed "Ten Little Soldiers" poem on a table in the corner, behind a floral vase. My heart rate sped up, and I picked up the frame and slid off the back. A sticky note!

It read, *Be like Maggie. Before there are none.*

Be like Maggie . . . be like Maggie. I chewed on the inside of my cheek. Then it hit me. Carol's tape recording: *"Maggie would be really creative. Perhaps in a bath—"*

The bathroom!

I went to work, checking all the bathrooms on the second floor to no avail. Back on the main floor, I scurried down the hall on tiptoes and into the hall bathroom. I secured the lock on the door and started searching. The cabinet under the sink held nothing but toiletries. Next, I checked the mounted mirror and behind the toilet. Carol had an antique washboard under the small window. I checked inside the bowl and behind the mirror. I blew out a breath and turned slowly in the small bathroom. *"Be like Maggie."* Melanie had been waiting for twenty minutes, and I had to get going. I tapped the speaker on my watch and dictated, "Coming out now."

Good!!! came the instant reply.

I studied the antique piece once more, checking around for any special hiding places. A crack around the edge of the basin caught my eye. I searched through my carryall for something I could use and settled on a nail file. Carefully I pried up the edge, and the corner of a bubble mailer stuck out. The pounding in my chest became so loud, I could hardly focus. I pulled the mailer through the opening and allowed the basin to settle flush. Inside were pictures and a flash drive. I slipped the drive into my purse. There were five prints, ones from a home printer. My breath came in pants as I studied the images of remains. Carol's Jane Doe remains. The scarf was wrapped around the victim's neck, and not in a fashionable way. She'd been strangled and shoved inside a suitcase. The room spun, and anxiety began to build.

What was she doing with these pictures? Had she been involved, as I feared? She had sounded obsessed with serial killers in the recordings.

When I turned to the next picture, I recoiled. I took a couple of deep breaths. Steeling myself, I glanced back. The remains appeared to be progressively deteriorating. I had no idea who this woman was. With shaky hands, I looked at the final image, one that showed significant decomposition. Maggots covered the flesh on the skull.

My stomach revolted, and I stumbled forward, just making it to the sink in time. The soap dish hit the floor with a loud crack as I continued to lose the contents of my stomach.

The doorknob jiggled. "Lyla, are you all right in there? You sound ill."

Thinking quickly, I stuffed the pictures into my carryall and hefted it over my shoulder. I flushed the toilet and furiously rinsed out the sink, stopping to retrieve the fallen dish and soap. "Yes. Bad fish, I guess. Sorry."

"No, don't apologize."

I washed my hands and rinsed out my mouth before opening the door. Judge Timms studied me intently for a moment. Luckily, I could blame my sweaty brow and flushed face on the bad fish. I wiped my brow. "Forgive me, Judge—"

"It's David. Don't apologize. I'll call the manager at the Trail Head Grill first thing in the morning. We can't have the chef serving subpar cuisine. It's inexcusable." He put his hand on my back, oddly more sober than I'd seen him in days. "If you're too ill to drive, you can stay the night in one of my guest rooms."

I stumbled, and the judge wrapped a meaty arm around my waist. The close contact made my skin crawl. If Carol felt the need to hide this from her husband, there had to be a good reason.

"That's so kind of you, but really, I should be getting home."

He kept a sweaty hand on my side. "You might be better off here. I'd hate for you to be ill on the drive home. I could even have my doctor come by and take a look at you in the morning. Make sure you don't need fluids."

He was way too worried about my health for my taste. "That's so kind, but I should be getting home."

His phone rang, and I could see he was struggling whether to allow the close contact to end or answer the phone. Relief flooded me when he stepped aside to glance at his cell. He looked up. "Perhaps you'd consider having dinner with me some night. Since you and Quinn aren't exclusive."

How could he even ask that? Carol's body was barely cold, and she was my friend. Appalled, I forced my lips to turn up as

I edged toward the front door. With my hand over my abdomen. "Perhaps ask me when the idea of food is more appealing."

His eyes lit up. "Of course." His phone buzzed again, and he placed it to his ear, "Judge Timms."

Using his distraction to my advantage, I lifted my hand and swung open the front door.

"What evidence?" Judge Timms bellowed, and I paused on the steps and turned to face him. Before I could inquire, the judge stepped over to me. "They're amending the indictment to include manslaughter. They think the killer has an accomplice, and that's who was threatening you tonight, Lyla. Looks like we we're finally getting somewhere. Manslaughter is better. We're on the right track. I'll see that bastard fry if it's the last thing I do."

My fingers went to my parted lips.

"You should really consider staying over tonight."

I took a step back and forced my lips into a small smile. "Thank you kindly for the offer, but my mother would have a fit."

He ran his hand over his head. "Yeah, I guess she would. At least call and let me know you got home okay."

"Yeah, sure. You try and get some rest."

The second the door closed, I hustled down the driveway and all but leaped into Melanie's car.

"I was so worried. You can't ever do that to me again. You got it?" Melanie's face was white as a ghost, and her eyes were glassy as she pointed her shaking finger in my face.

I slammed the door. "I didn't find anything." I lied. "Now go."

Chapter
Thirty-Five

My phone was ringing off the hook when I got home and barricaded myself inside. It was close to ten but felt a whole lot later. After finding the pictures, I feared to involve Melanie further. She was right: we'd started this together, but my God, after seeing the detailed decomposition in stages, it cast a whole new light on the type of killer we were dealing with.

Quinn was fuming when I finally answered his call. He'd been leaving me voicemails all evening. "Where did you go? I turned around for one second, and you vanished. You understand how dangerous that is with some lunatic on the outside working with Kevin. We have no idea who we're dealing with here."

I had a good idea. "You thought I was crazy, Quinn. That I brought this whole thing on myself for obsessing."

"I'm sorry I doubted you regarding the threats. And you'll be happy to know I'm working alongside the special agent as we now believe there is a potential connection between the two cases."

No shit, Sherlock. And I have the pictures to prove it. But hearing the edge in his voice, I decided I'd pass them on to Brad instead.

"I just had to get out of there. Besides, you were attacking me." I took my loop earrings out and put them in my jewelry box.

"I wasn't attacking you. I care about you. You're a bullheaded woman." He sounded as if he were speaking through clenched teeth.

"Gee, you're really winning me over now, you sweet talker."

"Please. Please."

"I don't want to argue with you. I'm home, and I'm safe. Don't worry." I was worried enough for both of us.

"Who else knew about your book club's pick?"

His question caused me to falter.

"Lyla, first the note Carol left you referenced the book the club was reading, now whoever is threatening you—"

"And Amelia," I added.

"And Amelia—also began to follow suit."

"That's what I've been trying to tell you! And your 'bull-headed comment'? Pot meet kettle," I said, flabbergasted.

"Okay. You're right. Just please, who else knew?"

I puffed out my cheeks. "Well the library posts each month's book club pick on the message forum online and in the library."

"How long has that been going on?"

"Since the beginning. We use it to draw new members. Oh, and Sweet Reads on the square also puts the Jane Doe Book Club pick of the month in a small display at the front of the bookstore."

"So anyone and everyone who is interested in what your club is reading can easily find out?" Quinn blew out a breath.

"Yeah."

"And a club full of women isn't exactly known for their secrecy. Patsy spread the news of the note to half the mothers in

Sweet Mountain. My office has been receiving calls of concern from her Mommy and Me class."

I rubbed my forehead. *Oh Patsy.*

A number flashed up on the screen.

"Listen, I've got another call. Let's take tonight as a warning sign that we should never be involved on a personal level. If you need me to come down to the police station to make another statement or to answer more questions, call me. And thanks for dinner."

I answered the call from Sweet Mountain Correctional. "Hello."

"This is a collect call from Kevin, an inmate at Sweet Mountain Correctional Facility. Press one to accept the charges."

I did.

"Lyla, have you heard?"

"Yes. Just now, actually." I unzipped my boots and sat on my bed, pulling them off. "I've had sort of a rough night myself. Someone left me a warning on the bathroom mirror at the Trail Head Grill."

"What? What kind of warning?" Kevin sounded so exhausted.

"A 'stop meddling or you'll end up dead' message. In the form of a rhyme." I pulled the scarf off my neck and shivered before gingerly placing it on my carryall beside me.

"My God. A nursery rhyme like the Agatha Chrissy book?"

Goose bumps traveled across my flesh. "Christie."

"Huh? Hey, wait! If you got a warning, that proves it isn't me! It's good news."

I glanced heavenward and closed my eyes. "Yes, I'm so glad I have a stalker who might prove you're innocent." I didn't want him to think I suspected him. No wonder we never worked out. The first thing that entered his mind was his own safety.

"I'm sorry. That's not what I meant. You have no idea how horrible this place is. I won't make it in here long."

A loud ruckus sounded in the background. I couldn't imagine being inside. Just the visitation had me on edge.

"It's okay. What do you know about Agatha Christie?"

"Not much." He sounded hesitant. "Just that someone is leaving threats like some book she wrote. Don't jump to conclusions! Ellen told me."

Ellen isn't a reader!

"Kevin, did Carol file charges against you?"

"I told you we were at odds. She was going to drop the charges. She didn't want her stupid husband to suspect she told me anything, so she filed the complaint one night when Judge Timms came home and caught me there. I was worried about her and ran out. It was stupid. I should have gotten her out. Instead, I angered the beast. That's what she called him, you know, 'the beast.' I'm innocent, Lyla! I swear on my life."

"Well, not to pull you down further, but they think you have an accomplice out here. Someone angry enough to come after me." I walked into the bathroom and dropped my dress into the hamper. "Or maybe whoever threatened me is trying to, as you say, make you appear innocent. You did know about the rhyme." Opening the glass shower door, I turned on the shower to let the water warm up.

"Appear innocent? I didn't do it! I did not do it! My God. Did you find anything? Evidence or pictures or whatever?"

I froze. First, he'd known about the book club pick. Now he was claiming the evidence Carol left was in the form of pictures. Was Quinn right after all?

"You say she left pictures? Did she say where she left them?"

"I don't know. I think she might have said . . . um . . . pictures."

"Of what?"

He blew out a breath. "I don't know. But if you find them, you'll turn them over to my attorney and no one else. Right? That asshole Quinn won't do right by me, and you know it." Bitterness traveled through the line.

The phone started making a clicking noise, and the automated voice came over right before the line went dead.

Feeling filthy after the night's events, I took a long, hot shower, scrubbing my skin multiple times and shampooing twice. I dried my hair and threw on some PJs, dead tired when I finally crawled into my king-sized bed and opened my laptop. I plugged in the flash drive.

I should call Brad right now and have him come over and get these. But I didn't. I stared at my cell for a few long moments. Dozens and dozens of pictures flashed over the screen. I recoiled from the images and had to steel myself to go back to them every time. If I had to detach to examine these images, then that was what I was going to do.

The pictures were taken of the same corpse over several years' time. The first pictures were in the fall, with the Jane Doe crammed into the paisley suitcase. The image was reminiscent of how I'd found Carol. To take these pictures, the person would have to unzip the suitcase every time for a new shot. I swallowed the bile that made its way up my throat.

There were some shots in the spring and some in the summer. None in the winter. She'd indeed been a Caucasian woman, just as the article had suggested. Her clothing had been blue but was now threads and rags.

"Who are you?" I asked the deceased woman, who might've been in her early twenties before her murder—the ligature marks and bruising of the eyes proof of a crime. Though there wasn't much blood pictured. There hadn't been with Carol either. She must've been killed somewhere else, crammed into the suitcase, and then dumped there.

I was about to close the computer when I had a thought. The article asked if anyone recognized the jewelry the woman had on her person. So caught up with the scarf, I'd completely forgotten to see if I could find other images of the necklace. I clicked through the pictures, hunting for a closer shot. There! I zoomed in on the woman's V-neck shirt. A silver or perhaps white gold necklace was around her neck. I needed to get a better look and zoomed just as close as I could without making the image too grainy.

I gasped. Hopping off my bed, I dug through my jewelry box, tearing everything out until finally I found what I was looking for. Hurrying back to the bed, I held my necklace next to the screen. Oh. My. God. The Jane Doe had on the exact necklace with an angel pendant with a single blue topaz stone in the middle. What were the chances it belonged to the dead Jane Doe? Mother had said Grandmother had them custom-made for Ellen and me. My necklace dropped from my fingers. *What was the Jane Doe doing with Ellen's necklace?*

Chapter Thirty-Six

Val called at midnight. It was late for her to call, but I wasn't sleeping.

"Hey." I yawned and sat up higher in the bed, pausing the episode of *Friends* I been watching. My go-to when I needed to zone out and remain lighthearted.

"Hey. How are you doing? When I called to check in on David, he said you were sick from the fish you had for dinner."

"It wasn't the fish. My nerves were wrecked."

"I can imagine. You poor thing. I've been stewing ever since I left. I wish I'd been waiting in the restroom. I'd have given that person a 'come-to-Jesus' meeting, and I mean in the real sense of the word: Bitch, meet your maker!"

"Wow, Val, take a breath, my friend. While I appreciate you caring and all, I don't want you to end up behind bars because of some psycho, or worse, dead. I can't bear to lose another friend."

"I'm just sick and tired of people rocking our nice, calm little boat. And I miss Carol."

"I know, hon, and I'm sorry. I miss her too."

We settled into silence, and I heard *Friends* in the background. "Watching Netflix reruns too?" I smiled and clicked the "Play" button to unfreeze the frame.

"Yeah. It's my choice for sleepless nights."

I snuggled into the down pillow. "Mine too. How was the judge when you talked to him?"

"Drunk. I called Marigold to go over and look after him. They fight all the time. Like kids. Carol used to be the peacemaker in the family." She sighed. "I guess they'll have to fend for themselves now."

"Guess so." I fast-forwarded to where she was. I didn't like to hear conflicting scenes.

"I spoke with Ellen," Val casually said, but I caught an edge to her tone.

I didn't respond, just waited.

"Ellen said you two have sort of made amends. I think it's good."

"We called a truce for now. Real-life problems supersede family drama."

A cat howling outside caused me to jump.

"Makes sense. I forgot to mention I went to see Kevin with Ellen the other day."

"Oh?" How could she forget that?

"Yeah, he claims innocence, and, on the one hand, I almost believed him until he started speaking in a kind of code to Ellen. And he wasn't happy she brought me along. I just went for moral support, but hey, if he doesn't want me there, then fine. Once he's convicted, he'll have to put people on a list for visitors anyway." *Was that true? Huh.*

"He called me tonight from jail." I pulled the down comforter up higher on my chest. "He keeps asking for my help. But

Quinn told me Carol filed a complaint against him. He claims it was for show. I don't know anymore."

"Some nerve!"

I swallowed. "Did you happen to mention to Ellen about the note Carol left? The reference to the book, in particular."

"She already knew. She heard it from a friend of a friend that got the information from Patsy."

My head ached as Quinn's words rang in my ears. No wonder he believed we were all gossiping females.

"Don't let Kevin play on your sympathetic nature or your past relationship. The man's a murderer. Plain and simple. I don't care if he meant to hurt Carol or not. The result is she's dead. Now someone is trying to cast doubt by using our club and that stupid rhyme!" Val was getting worked up.

"I know you loved Carol. I'm sorry you're hurting."

"I am hurting. People think I'm stone. That I don't have feelings. I do. They're just different from the rest of y'all's." She sighed. "I know about the pictures, Lyla."

"How? Did Carol tell you about them? Where she'd hid them?" I felt relieved to be able to share my discovery with someone. I'd planned on keeping the evidence quiet until I turned them over to Brad. I'd call him in the morning.

She went quiet for a second, "No." She seemed to be choosing her words carefully. "David told me he gave them to you. And his investigator took documented images of Kevin abusing Carol."

Oh. Those pictures. "I just took possession of the pictures the day he was arrested. I asked Kevin, and he admitted to the arguments and losing his temper, but he swears he wasn't the one I saw in the car with her."

She scoffed. "You saw him in the camo hat that day, for God's sake. You found the same hat in your trash. Add that to the images where he's threatening Carol while wearing it, and we have a slam dunk."

"It seems like a slam dunk."

"Look. I get it. He's attractive and is good at sweet-talking vulnerable women. I don't blame you or Ellen. But we're talking about murder here."

I sat up. "He claims there's evidence to exonerate him." But if he was counting on what I found, he'd be out of luck. They were more damning than anything else. He was the one that told me they existed. I could see Val's point. It just didn't feel right.

"And you believed him? Ha! So, where is it? This evidence?"

"I don't know." It wasn't a complete lie. What I found wouldn't help his case.

"Exactly. The point is that whatever Kevin told you is bullshit. He wants you to stand by him at the trial. Don't let him manipulate you. Let's make a pact. Here and now. Whatever you find out about any of this, you'll tell me. And I'll do the same for you. We'll keep each other strong. For Carol."

"Okay." I agreed, even though I was already breaking the pact. With all the gossip flying around town, I needed to safeguard what I'd found. Val knew her mind better than anyone I'd ever met. The expression *"Not always right but never in doubt"* came to mind when I thought of my friend. She didn't let her ignorance of any subject cloud her strong opinions. She'd already convicted Kevin. Maybe he was guilty. Maybe he wasn't. After tonight, and what I'd found and the way Judge Timms had behaved, my thoughts were in such a tumult I could scarcely find my way to a coherent one.

"Okay." She went silent, then sighed. "'Night."

"'Night."

* * *

The next morning, I sat in the office, gathering together all the evidence I had in my possession. I'd called Brad and left an urgent message. I was ready to deliver what I'd found. My mind felt sharper after a few hours of sleep. I needed to delve into the nitty-gritty of the case. I thought of Ellen and our complicated relationship. How could the Jane Doe get her necklace? Had she given it to her? Pawned it? Had I been wrong, and the necklaces weren't custom-made? Could she stoop so low as to be a killer's accomplice?

First things first. The necklace. Only one way to find out if Ellen still had hers. I blew out a breath and called her.

"Lyla."

"Ellen. Can I ask you a question?"

"Will it help Kevin?" She sounded tense.

"It could. You remember the necklace Grandmother gave us when we were younger? The one she had special made?"

"I don't understand what this has to do with anything."

I heard voices in the background. "Do you have company?"

"No . . . um, it's the TV." It didn't sound like the TV. "What about the angel necklace?"

"I just wondered if you still have yours."

"I don't know . . . Oh, wait! It was stolen. I had it at the alumnae bonfire. Yeah, that's right. I took it off and put it in my purse. My purse was stolen."

"What about your majorette scarf?"

"I have no idea what happened to that ugly ole thing. What does this have to do with Kevin?"

"Maybe nothing. Thanks for answering my questions."

"You're a terrible PI." The call dropped. The truce must have ended without my knowledge. Could the Jane Doe have bought the necklace at a pawn shop? Or had she stolen it from Ellen?

Feeling way out of my depth, I needed more answers. I picked up my cell and dialed Brad's number. "Jones here."

"Brad, this is Lyla."

"Oh, hey, I was just about to call you back. You disappeared last night without a word."

Was I detecting a bit of irritation or suspicion in his tone? I was getting way too paranoid.

"I know—I had to get out of there. But I'm reaching out now, and we need to talk in person and soon. I found something at the Timms's residence I believe you need to see."

"You didn't search without permission . . ."

"No! I asked Judge Timms if I could look through Carol's things. Well, I found something the police missed. Something big." I took a breath. "I found pictures of your Jane Doe. And Brad, these pictures aren't just the skeletal remains. They were taken in progression as the body decomposed for years."

"Where are these pictures now?"

"I have them. They're on a flash drive."

"Okay. I'm in Atlanta, attempting to gain a court order from a judge to allow me to be the lead on the case in Sweet Mountain."

"Quinn said you were already working the case together."

He snorted, and I felt ill. "I'll call you the second I'm back in town. Do not, and I repeat, do not share what you've found with the local police or anyone else. And go somewhere you'll be safe."

Of all the things he could've said, that last part was the most frightening.

Chapter
Thirty-Seven

With shaky hands, I locked up the office and checked both ways, waiting to cross the street. A hand gripped my arm, I screamed and nearly leaped out of my skin, scaring an elderly couple as they were walking past. "I'm so sorry," I managed to get out, thankful I hadn't given the couple heart attacks.

I turned to see Melanie with giant eyes and her hand over her mouth. "Are you okay? I didn't mean to scare you. I called your name."

I shook my head. "No, I'm not okay. Things are spiraling way out of control, Mel. I'm in way over my head."

Melanie took my arm and guided me across the street, toward my car. "What's happened? I mean, you said you didn't find anything. Did you tell me the truth?"

I ran my hand through my frizzing hair. I'd not even taken the time to flat-iron it this morning or dress appropriately. I'd thrown on a pair of yoga pants, a sweatshirt, and running shoes. "I found something. Something a-awful, Mel," I stuttered. "Kevin called me last night, still swearing he's innocent, but he knew about the rhyme. And the Jane Doe had Ellen's necklace,"

I rambled on, so fast I had a hard time keeping up with myself. "This killer among us isn't what we thought. He's . . . he's meticulous. He enjoyed watching his Jane Doe decompose." Which was why I didn't buy my cousin's involvement. She was neither meticulous nor clever.

"Hold on. Slow down. I can hardly understand you." Mel gripped my shoulders. "Lyla. You don't look so good. You're wild-eyed."

I thought of Carol and how she was perceived, and no freaking wonder! This case would make anyone go a little mad. I tried to sound calmer. "You were right last night to be concerned. Did I tell you that Carol filed a complaint against Kevin a couple of weeks back because he threatened her?"

"Yes." Mel said slowly, drawing out the word.

I felt jittery, like I couldn't stand still.

"And now they've upped the charges to manslaughter. Because they discovered new evidence."

I nodded.

She leaned closer to me as some pedestrians walked to their cars. "Let's try and keep our voices down."

I chewed on the inside of my cheek and vehemently shook my head, my hair flying about my face. If I told Melanie about the pictures, would I be putting her in harm's way? "I haven't a clue what to think. The special agent is trying to get a court order to take over the case."

"Right?"

"The weird thing about that is Quinn told me last night he was working with Brad." I raised my brows and lifted my shoulders. "Then a minute ago, Brad instructed me not to trust the Sweet Mountain Police. And not to share—" I stopped talking before I said too much.

Mel's eyes narrowed. "Why do I get the feeling you're hiding something from me?"

"Because I am. And you have to trust me on the reasons why I can't share. I'm going home and locking myself inside until Brad contacts me. Then I'm turning everything over to him and stepping away from this."

Mel hugged me tightly. "You're trembling."

"I'm in way over my head, Mel. People in this town are bat-shit." *Including me!*

"Okay, listen to me, Lyla Jane Moody," Melanie said sternly, taking me by the arms. "You go straight home. I'm going back inside and wrapping things up. I'd leave now, but there's no one to finish for the day. I'll close up the second I can and come over. Don't open the door to anyone you don't know. We'll eat junk food and drink wine and wait for that special agent to get there."

I didn't say what weighed heavily on me, though. What if someone got to me before Brad did? It could be anyone.

"You can do this. Say it."

"I . . . I can do this."

I steeled my nerves after I started the engine. Rubbing my forehead and my tingling face, I drove home, following the speed limit and keeping a close eye on my rearview mirror. Brad must've had a reason to want me to hide out until he got back, and that scared the pants off me. My phone rang through my speaker, and I shrieked. I didn't recognize the number and let it roll to voicemail.

After barricading myself inside the house, I went on autopi-lot. I took out Calvin's gun, set it on the bar, then pulled my hair up in a ponytail and checked my watch. How long would it take for Brad to get back here? And when he did and I turned every-thing over, would that be the end for me? I decided I wouldn't speak to Kevin again. Not until Brad took over the investigation and had a chance to interview him. And if he didn't get the court order, I planned on taking a long trip to someplace tropical. Far, far away from Sweet Mountain and the killer. I was beginning to doubt my judgment, and it made me feel unstable. Yes, that was the plan. I could still research from the beach. I'd be safe and could still affect the case for Carol and the Jane Does.

I went to the kitchen to get a glass of wine. I didn't care what time it was. When I rounded the bar, I froze. Something wasn't right here. My canisters weren't in the right place. Sugar was spilled all over the counter. I turned slowly. The cushions on my couch were thrown onto the floor. The dining chairs were all turned over. The bookshelf empty. My books were in a heap in front of it.

My heart was in my throat as I grabbed the gun with shaky hands. My breathing felt erratic as I slowly went up the stairs and down the hallway with my gun ready. I peeked inside my bathroom, thankful to find no one there. The hallway was littered with my clothing and dresser drawers. Slowly, ever so slowly, I pushed the door to my bedroom open with the barrel of the gun. I gasped.

My mattress had been shredded with a knife. Feathers from my pillows had drifted all over the room. I fell to my knees, trembling as I took in the wall behind my bed. The same picture of the Jane Doe Book Club was secured to the wall by a knife in my face. A tiny hangman's noose hung from the knife. Written underneath in a red marker was *Naughty little Jane. Turn over the pictures. One little Jane Doe left all alone; she went and hanged herself and then there were none.*

"Oh no, no, no!" Who knew about the pictures other than Brad . . . Kevin did. How did someone get inside my house?

With shaky hands, I took a picture and sent it to Brad.

I scrambled to my feet, tossed the envelope and flash drive in my shoulder bag, and ran out the front door to my car. I was going to FedEx the pictures to Brad. That's when Ellen came flying out her front door with mascara running down her cheeks along with big giant tears.

She tried to open my car door, but I was vehemently shaking my head as I started the engine. "Lyla! Open the door!" Ellen's voice shook. "My mother's been in an accident, and they've air-lifted her to Grady."

I froze, putting the car back into park.

She openly sobbed.

"Oh my God." My hand went to my heart. If they'd felt the need to airlift Aunt Elizabeth to the best trauma center in the state, her injuries must be horrific.

"Will you drive me?" Ellen broke down, and seeing her in such a state, I managed to snap out of my panic.

"Did you see what happened to my house?"

Her face was a picture of shock. "What? "What's wrong with you? They're not sure if she's going to m-make it." She went around to the passenger side and I let her in. I could handle this. Then I'd leave. I embraced my cousin, who sobbed on my shoulder, thanking me for my help.

Chapter Thirty-Eight

With the directions to Grady Memorial punched into the GPS, we were on our way. "What happened?"

Ellen continued to wipe her eyes, but her sobs had ceased. "A car accident. All I know is it's bad. Can we not talk for a bit. I'm just . . . I'm . . ."

I reached over and patted her arm. "Of course."

We rode for a long while in silence. Then Ellen's phone kept going off. She didn't share who was calling and texting her like crazy. Then it occurred to me she'd not mentioned telling my mother about the accident.

"Did you call Mother?"

Ellen glanced out the window, still in shock, I guessed, and shook her head.

"It's okay. I'll call her. She needs to be there." I hit the button on the steering column. "Call mother, ho—" Before I could finish, Ellen disconnected my phone on the screen.

When I opened my mouth to argue, she pulled a gun from her bag and held it on me. I couldn't help the long blink. Her mother hadn't been in an accident. It was all a ruse to get me to come with her—something I wouldn't ever have done otherwise. I'd ultimately tipped my hand when I inquired about the necklace. Only someone in our family would've been able to identify it. Ellen and I had always been at odds. Sure, she was the queen of mean, but never in a million years would I have believed she was capable of murder.

"You need to reach into your bag and hand over those pictures." She jabbed the muzzle into my side.

I slid my hand into the bag I kept pressed against the driver's side door. It had been a subconscious action. I usually tossed my bag in the passenger's seat. I pulled the bubble mailer from it and slid my phone inside. With my finger, I pushed the Bluetooth connection off so that it wouldn't connect to the car. Then I hit the call button. It would contact the last person I'd dialed—Brad.

I passed it over to Ellen, who didn't even look inside.

There was a manic look in her eyes. "Take I-85."

Oh, sweet Lord. I did as she bade me.

"Why, Ellen? I don't understand why? Are you doing this for Kevin?"

"Yes. Now drop your watch into your purse and toss it out the window." She was smarter than she looked. I slipped the watch into my bag and tossed my lovely Kate Spade bag out the window.

"You don't have to do this. It isn't too late. I can turn around, and we'll forget this ever happened." I cast a glance at my fidgeting cousin, her eyes dark from smeared mascara. I considered driving off the side of the road and wrecking the car to try to get free, but the way her hand shook on that trigger, I feared I'd be a goner.

"I do have to! I love him. I'd do anything for him. I've always loved him, unlike you, who used him and threw him away when you were done. He's too kind-hearted for his own good. Believes that this will all work itself out in the end. That you'll do whatever it takes to free him." She shook her head. "He doesn't know you at all. The only thing you did was call me and ask about the necklace."

"So it wasn't stolen then?" If I could get her to make some sort of confession on record while Brad was on the phone, it'd give them time to trace us. I just prayed he was on the line.

She stared at me like I was a fool. "Of course it was stolen. Just like I told you. Get off at the next exit."

My heart hammered away in my chest. I knew exactly where we were going. I slowed down to the speed limit of thirty-five miles an hour and followed the winding road around the little vacant Baptist church, praying that Brad would soon follow.

"You really are a horrible PI. I don't know why Uncle Calvin keeps you on."

"Technically, I'm just a receptionist with hopes of becoming an actual partner in the firm," I said in a shaky voice. "I'm learning."

She snorted. "Everything was right in front of you, and you never saw it. Now you'll see!" She shook the gun too close to my face. "I had to do something. I couldn't just let Kevin rot away in a cell forever."

"Right." I nodded with my eyes wide. "I get it. You love him. We do crazy things for love. But I'm your freaking cousin!"

We rounded another bend, overcrowded with a cluster of tall pine trees covered with poison ivy. She pointed to the left side of the woodsy area. "You never liked me. Pull into the tree line. And slowly get out of the car."

It was so overgrown out here that unless you were hunting our signal, no one would ever find me. The keys rattled as I turned off the engine. I got out of the vehicle. My mind filled with pleas, escape plans, and doubt. What was I missing? Surely my cousin wouldn't kill me. "What did I miss, Ellen?"

"Walk," she barked, with the mailer in her hand. She hadn't seemed to notice the phone inside. She glanced around at her feet.

Ellen wasn't an outdoorsy kind of gal. She didn't run or hike. There I had the advantage. If I timed it correctly, I could easily get the jump on her and make a run for it.

"The suitcase was your big clue. But that went right over your head." She stumbled over a log and went down, taking me down with her and I heard a distinct crack as her knee hit the log. "Ouch!"

I started to scramble to my feet, but she shouted with the gun against my shoulder, "I'll shoot you, Lyla! Just stay there. Give me a second."

Blood welled from her pant leg and she kicked at a dirty mason jar covered in leaves and dirt inside the log. There was something inside it! Mel had been right! *A message in a bottle— or in this case, a mason jar!* My heart thundered in my ears. I grabbed it, turned my back to Ellen, and twisted open the lid.

"What is that? What are you doing?" Ellen rose to her feet, hobbling a little. "You better not be getting any wild ideas. What's that? A note?"

Too late to try and hide it. "Yes."

"What's it say? Drop that jar!"

I gave my cousin a look of disdain as I dropped it at her feet.

"Why did you kill Carol? Because of the inheritance? I heard Kevin wanted it all."

Ellen pushed me deeper into the woods. She gaped when she got closer to me. "Kevin should be inheriting all the money, not Carol." Doubt shone in her eyes, and I heard ambivalence in her tone.

"Because of the Jane Doe, then?"

She shook her head as if pushing the notion from her mind. "I didn't kill Carol or that stupid Jane Doe. You're so blind."

"Then enlighten me." I stumbled over a tire wedged in the dirt.

She leaned closer to me, and I was ready to knock her on her ass, when she whispered, "Read that note. It might be important."

I gaped. She was insane!

She nudged me with the barrel of the gun, and I jumped, staring at the pages. In Carol's hand was a written confession of sorts.

The Jane Doe has a name. She had parents. She had a sister . . .

Oh my God! I kept reading.

Ellen read over my shoulder, pressing the gun to my side, "Sweet Jesus! Listen to me," she said urgently, her eyes darting rapidly around. "The gun isn't loaded. Play along and we might get out of here alive."

Play along with what? Had my cousin snapped because of Kevin? A shotgun being cocked echoed in the woods, and Ellen grabbed my arm. Panting, I scanned the area, and my heart nearly stopped when I spied a person dressed in camouflage step from the cover of the overgrowth.

"One little Jane Doe left all alone; she went and hanged herself and then there were none."

"Val?" I hardly recognized her. She had a hangman's noose wrapped around her arm. My mind spun, and I recalled the person in the car at the Fast Trip. It had been her! "Why?" I croaked, my eyes filling with tears.

"Toss the mailer over here, Ellen, and kick that gun away."

Ellen complied. "I-I did what you asked. I'm here to trade my cousin and the evidence for Kevin's freedom."

Did she believe Val could free Kevin? Ellen paled and seemed to become disconcerted. I was no longer shaking; I was downright furious.

Val poked her lip out. "Poor Ellen, so in love she can't see straight."

"You'll call the authorities now, right? Hand over the evidence that proves his innocence." Ellen squealed as a bug swarmed at her face.

Val let out a giant belly laugh. "Kevin can rot, for all I care."

If Ellen had ever taken the time to read a mystery or true crime novel or, hell, watch the news, she'd have known not to bargain with killers. I had no disillusionments regarding my predicament. Val's presence made everything apparent.

I stared at the stranger standing before me, and pieces of the puzzle started to fall into place. She'd dropped me hints. Little crumbs along the way she wanted me to piece together. Her anger toward Carol, not for dying, as I initially thought, but for attempting to betray her. She'd manipulated everyone and everything around her to control what I found out and when. Until the pictures. "You! It was you all this time."

"Do I detect some hostility or maybe jealousy that my intelligence far supersedes yours, Miss PI?" She took her cap off, shook her hair out, and gave a little smile, trying to appear modest, as if she'd done something amazing. She failed. The woman was proud of her actions, and I felt ill.

Gone was the person I thought I knew. It was as if she'd shed her humanity like a second skin, and what remained was sheer arrogance, hubris, and gall.

"I don't find you all that clever. I find you monstrous." Her life had been a skein of lies.

She laughed. "I'm cleverer than any killer in any true crime novel we've ever read. You were living in a true crime story and never knew it. And after Chelsea told me about the rhyme Carol left with her, I couldn't resist playing along. She'd promised to hand the scarf and rhyme over to me, and would have, if her stupid mother-in-law hadn't swiped it." Val puffed out her chest as she watched me process the fact she'd known about the note before I did.

"You're a monster," I grated through clenched teeth.

She grinned, pointed the shotgun at me, and I hit the dirt. A shot echoed over my head. Ellen screamed.

"Not so brave now, are we? That's the problem with all y'all rich girls. Talk a big game, but when it comes down to it, you ain't got nothin'." She pointed the barrel of the shotgun right at me, and I quaked in my shoes. "Get up."

I did.

"Girls like me, we do what we must to survive. Silence who-ever we have to."

Ellen started backing away, "This has nothing to do with me. I did my part. I'm not one of the Jane Does. You said, you were going to kill the Jane Does."

"Shut up and start walking."

I grabbed Ellen's hand and pulled her along. Blood pumped in my ears so loudly I could hardly hear anything else. Ellen kept sobbing and stumbling over her feet. The briars were scratching our legs and arms as we waded through, very aware of the crazy woman at our back with a loaded shotgun. If I didn't do something soon, Ellen and I and the rest of the Jane Does were dead. Fury replaced fear within me.

I kept my tone even. "Carol was smarter than you give her credit for."

Silence for a few beats.

"What's that supposed to mean?" I detected the hint of concern in Val's tone.

"Well, she left one note—how do you know she didn't leave another. One exposing you for the friend-killing monster that you are."

"Ha!" Val mocked, though she didn't sound as convincing as she had before.

A minute later, Val came around in front of us, red faced. "You're such a fool, Lyla. I didn't kill Carol. She was my one true friend."

"Why should I believe anything you say? You told Ellen you were going to kill the Jane Does. Your friends," I bit out and instantly wished I could retract the words.

Her eyes narrowed. "I wouldn't have considered it if stupid Carol hadn't sent the e-mail out. I even tried to stop the chain reaction. But the club decided to get involved in something y'all knew nothing about."

Ellen started crying again loudly. Val kicked at her, and she went down hard on one knee. "No more talk!" I helped Ellen to her feet, and Val shoved me forward.

Ellen started blubbering again and shaking all over. Her anxiety was infectious. "Please let me go. I won't tell a soul, I swear. I gave you Lyla."

"Shut up." Val kicked Ellen's injured leg, and she grunted in pain, lifting her hand to grip Val's camo sweatshirt. Val batted her hand away as if she were a mere insect.

My eyes darted left as I made eye contact with Ellen. She waited a single beat before she made a dash to the left, toward the direction of the car, screaming and pumping her arms. Val hit me in the head with the butt of the gun and I went down. I lay still with my eyes closed. The pain was excruciating. Val gave chase to Ellen, and I wasted no time scrambling to my feet and running in the opposite direction, deeper into the woods.

A shot echoed above my head. I dove to the ground as the birds took flight, leaving the safety of the trees. Filled with adrenaline, I army-crawled behind an ancient oak, hearing Val screaming my name and thanking God she'd decided to hit me instead of shooting me.

"Lyla! Come on out now."

My heart hammered so loudly I feared she'd hear it.

"Lyla. Where are you? I have your cousin. I'll kill her. You know I will."

From my vantage point I couldn't tell if she had Ellen or not. I couldn't chance it. If I kept quiet and hid, I had no doubt Val would execute my cousin. And I would not let anyone else die at Val's hand. "Let Ellen go and we can work this out. Carol did leave a note. She told us everything. Don't add to it by hurting someone else."

"Stop trying to be clever. You're not. You don't know anything."

"The Jane Doe is your biological sister! *You* set the fire that killed your parents!" I yelled from the dense cover of overgrown brush, peering through to see if I could spy my cousin.

Val's steps slowed. "Stupid Carol." She sounded annoyed. "Whatever. I can change my plans."

What did that mean?

"You hated your sister so much you actually killed her? You're a monster, Val. And you made Carol live with the murder all these years and then killed her?"

Val snorted. "No one on the planet could push my buttons like Loretta. And I saved her ass too. Without me setting fire to the house, she'd have continued to live in that hell hole till our horrible parents killed us both."

I heard her steps, coming closer. Only one set of steps. Ellen wasn't with her or at least she wasn't walking with her. I prayed Ellen had made it to safety and called for help.

"Loretta had some nerve showing up at the alumnae bonfire. I'd sent her money before when she threatened to out me. It was never enough. So that night, I'd had it. Carol and I were out in the parking lot, doing tequila shots in my car. Loretta had been stealing what she could from those too drunk to notice. That's how she got Ellen's necklace." Val sounded disgusted.

"Still, how could you kill your own flesh and blood?" I darted to another tree. I had to keep her talking. I'd know where she was if I did.

"I didn't have a choice! She threatened to tell everyone all about how I had a personality disorder and killed our parents. We scuffled. Carol tried to help me, and she got knocked down and hit her head. Loretta started screeching murderer at the top of her lungs. I had the scarf around my neck."

"Surely, there was another way!"

"What would you know about it? Living your stupid charmed life. I warned her. Told her to shut her stupid mouth. I gave her chances, even after I wrapped the scarf around her neck."

"So it was an accident," I said as calmly as I could manage.

I could hear Val moving through the brush. "Carol had her suitcase in the trunk of her car. She'd been planning on spending the night at my house. It was a feat to get Loretta into the suitcase without anyone seeing. But I managed." She spoke as casually as if we were discussing a sale on sandals. "I lived a few miles from here before the adoption and knew there were a lot of rural areas where a person could disappear. It seems I'm not the only one. When I sobered up the next day, I drove her up here. Carol was so wasted that I convinced her it never happened. Time passed, and no one came forward to report anyone missing. That helped."

"That's why she battled with paranoia and anxiety?" Poor Carol.

"Yes. And it was all okay until that damn dumping grounds article, and she started seeing your father. He wanted her to question everything. To get to the root of her fears." That sounded like Daddy.

"But it wasn't Carol's fault. She wrote about how much she loved you and had tried to save the rest of us from you."

Val coughed. "I did love her."

Getting too close. I moved again. *Oh!* "Carol never feared for her own life. She wrote you were the one she was going to run away with. That y'all would start a new life."

Val huffed. "Carol wanted to go away. To hide me from danger since we both thought for sure you knew it was me in the car. It was a stroke of luck when you found the camo cap and also that the judge had Carol followed. Pinning her death on Kevin was easy from there. David was blinded by rage, and Greg—well, he was easy enough to manipulate. I knew about the camera being out at the police station." She laughed. "You screamed like a little girl when you found the possum. And seriously, I knew you were having dinner with Quinn. Slipping in and writing on the mirror was nothing. You never suspected a thing. Texting you with a burner phone should have been enough to scare you off, but oh no, you wouldn't relent."

"Let me help you." I shoved the paper back in my waistband and, as quietly as I could manage, went deeper into the dense forest.

"Ha! That's what Carol said. I believed her until that night when she came into my house without calling. I had just loaded the new pictures to the flash drive. She stole it, and I thought for sure she'd turn me in. But she didn't."

"So you killed her!" I shouted, then changed locations.

"No! I pleaded with Carol to return them. I coaxed her to the house to explain. I came clean and told her everything. How I kept revisiting the body of my sister. Documenting her decomposition. She couldn't under the reason I came back and had to see the body, again and again. And I couldn't explain my need to see Loretta but promised I would stop. My promise did nother to appease her. She said she couldn't keep it to herself any longer. I convinced her we should take a trip. Relax and consider starting over in a new place. Her marriage with David was over, and everything she saw around here just reminded her of what we'd done."

What *Val* had done—Carol wasn't complicit in the murder, if you asked me.

"I would have gone through with it too. But at the last minute, while we were on our way to the airport, she freaked out and decided we should turn ourselves in. Some nonsense about freeing ourselves by telling the truth, something she learned from your father. I pulled over into a back road, and we fought. She had an attack."

I spied Val's boots several yards away. Too close. "That must have been awful for you." *Weapon. I have to find a weapon.* As quietly as I could manage, I moved behind a couple of pines, my fingers digging into the bark.

"Yes. She clutched her chest and fell to her knees. She needed her pills, but they were in her purse. I told her she could have them if she swore to forget this again. I begged her to swear." I could see Val shaking her head. "She did, but she complied far too easily. I wouldn't let her have them. I meant it to teach her a lesson. She died before I could get my point across. I was so angry at her. She did this!"

A shot rang out and I jumped. Blood thrummed in my ears. She thought she'd found me.

"All she had to do was trust me. I would have taken care of everything. She would have never gone down for it."

Sirens blared and a helicopter whirled above the trees.

"Hear that? You might as well throw your weapon down, Val. You're going to prison for what you've done."

"Oh, Lyla, neither one of us is leaving these woods. Too bad we couldn't take all the Jane Does with us." She sang, "Two little Jane Does running in the woods; one got shot and then there was one. One little Jane Doe left all alone; she went and hanged herself and then there were none."

My breath came in pants. "Not funny, Val!"

"I think it is. Too bad Melanie didn't come with you. We could have added another dead Jane Doe."

I moved again.

"Stupid Melanie. She went and ranted on Facebook about losing her luggage. When I went by to see the townhouse with Ellen before they signed the lease, I saw her dumb suitcase being delivered. I took it before I left. I planned on throwing it out. I get so sick of Melanie thinking the world revolves around her."

Melanie did not believe the world revolved around her.

"But when Carol and I got into it, I was glad I still had it. I thought, 'Fine.' Carol wanted drama. Wouldn't let the Jane Doe die. So, I stuffed her in Mel's suitcase just like her precious Jane Doe. Loretta deserved to rot for all eternity without her identity."

"You delivered it the day you visited Ellen and Kevin?"

"Yes. I meant to put it at Melanie's door. The idea of Mel's face was priceless." She smirked. "But Ellen came out before I could. I dumped it at your stoop instead. I had no idea it'd stir up your old issues and you'd become like a bitch with a bone."

I scoped out the area for a weapon and found a big fallen branch. I used my foot and hand to crack a piece off and readied myself. I heard her footsteps. She wasn't a light walker.

"Put your weapon down and come out with your hands up," I heard over the megaphone.

Val cackled. She actually cackled.

"Two little Jane Does . . ." she sang, and I shivered as she racked in another load, "walking in the woods."

Anger consumed me like never before. Not only had she hidden her true nature from us, she'd try to terrorize me and the others in our club, when we began to discover the truth. She would have killed us all. That's why she'd threatened Amelia at the funeral reception. Her entire life had been a farce. Val lived among us and pretended to be one of us when, in actuality, she embodied pure evil. What was that saying? *"Hell is empty because the devils are here."* I gripped the thick branch and listened carefully.

"It could've been so different between Carol and me. Now . . . well . . . now it's too late."

I heard crunching to my left, and I slowed my breathing and tossed a rock farther left. She came toward the sound, crowing loudly, "And then there was one."

The second I caught sight of her camo shirt, I stepped out and swung with all my might. Down she went like a ton of bricks. "One devil down."

Chapter
Thirty-Nine

"Hello," I called and walked into Mother and Daddy's grandiose home and searched through the house. Daddy lifted a hand as he read today's paper. There was an article printed about his work with Valerie Heinz. He'd asked my permission before he'd taken her on as a patient. She'd made a deal with the DA and confessed to everything. She'd exhibited psychotic behavior and the defense requested a psych evaluation, and she'd been admitted to the maximum-security psychiatric hospital. She'd asked for my father. She wanted the same doctor Carol Timms had worked with. Twisted. Truly sick, if you asked me.

She'd been completely unconscious when Brad and the team swarmed the woods that day. I'd handed over Carol's confession, and since Val had shoved the bubble mailer containing the pictures and my cell phone into the waistband of her pants, her entire confession had been recorded by a nifty app Brad had on his phone. I would be downloading said app for my future investigations.

I'd also heard several authors were interested in writing a novel about Val. Not that I was surprised. In her TV interview she'd bragged about her crimes. Gloated how she'd manipulated local police. The lack of empathy she showed as she detailed burning her parents alive astounded. When she discussed her present-day crimes, she did, however, show a little regret that her best friend hadn't trusted her. Though she managed to turn that around to be Carol's fault in the end of the interview. If you asked me, I suspected the use of the manipulated nursery rhyme is what drew the writers.

Officer Taylor later confessed to letting Val into the evidence room. She'd told him how hot it would be to make out in there. *So stupid.* He claims he didn't see her take the scarf from one of the lockers.

The arrest blindsided Judge Timms, and it took him hearing it from Val's lips to believe it. Kevin was released, and he moved out of Ellen's townhouse two days later. The inheritance is being split between Judge Timms and Kevin. After all the press, the judge decided it was fair after all.

Quinn and I had dinner after everything settled down. He claimed it was important for him to clear the air and that it bothered him to think he was dirty. Turns out Judge Timms *helped* him get the job as chief of police for an occasional favor here and there. Quinn swore up and down it never crossed any lines. I decided it wasn't any of my business. But it was a confession I wouldn't soon forget.

Ellen received probation and community service for her part in things. Aunt Elizabeth was so distraught she booked a spa getaway to calm her nerves. Mother hadn't been surprised. I could tell she wished she'd warned me to steer clear of Val, and almost used the tragedy to connect with me. Perhaps even open up about her past. I held out hope we'd get there in time.

Mother was in the backyard, instructing her gardener where to plant the spring annuals. Uncle Calvin was on the back deck, drinking a cup of coffee with Gran. Our family had grown closer since the horrific ordeal. I slipped through the doorway and joined them, sliding onto the swing next to Gran.

She wrapped her bony arm around me. "How's your honey?" I asked.

She shook her head. "He's history. I was too much for him"—she wagged her brows—"you know, in the boudoir department."

Uncle Calvin choked on the sip he took. "I guess I'll be going. Let you gals talk." He rose, and Gran and I both laughed. "See you in the morning, Lyla. We have a busy day ahead of us."

I smiled. "I'll be there bright and early."

While Calvin said farewell to mother, my phone chirped.

I smiled at the text that read, *Dinner next Friday at six?*

Sounds good, I texted back.

Brad Jones and I had worked closely together on another Jane Doe case with Uncle Calvin's blessing.

Jane Does meeting at my house tonight came the text from Mel. *You're on wine duty.*

I texted back, *No problem. See you at seven.*

"Who's that?" Gran wanted to know as I slid the phone back into my pocket.

"Mel. Reminding me about the book club meeting tonight."

Gran nodded. "I hear you've attracted some new members."

"We have. It's all the publicity surrounding Val's case. Everyone is interested in the crazy woman who belonged to the Jane

Does. We're having to become more stringent with who we allow to join." I nodded. "It's good, though." I'd decided to embrace life to the fullest. I could work my cases and still have a positive outlook.

"Maybe I should join?" Gran blinked at me.

"Maybe." I kissed her on the cheek.

Acknowledgments

I t's impossible to measure and adequately express my gratitude for all those who had a hand in bringing this book to publication. I'm incredibly grateful to my agent, Dawn Dowdle, for helping me find a home for this series at Crooked Lane Books.

Thanks to the entire Crooked Lane Team: my fabulous editor, Jenny Chen, for her superb editorial advice that exponentially improved this book, the illustrator, who blew me away with the gorgeous cover, and the copyeditors who made the book shine.

Thanks to my super supportive husband, kids, extended family, and friends who make up my personal cheering section. And a special thanks to my best friend, Julie Bromley, for her endless support, beta reading, and suggestions that make my books better. And lastly, to all my readers, thank you for reading.